ТHERINE SHAW is a professional mathematician and
ɪdemic living in France. *Fatal Inheritance* is her fifth
stery novel.

FATAL INHERITANCE

CATHERINE SHAW

Allison & Busby Limited
12 Fitzroy Mews
London W1T 6DW
www.allisonandbusby.com

First published in Great Britain by Allison & Busby in 2013.
This paperback edition published by Allison & Busby in 2013.

A CIP catalogue record for this book is available from
the British Library.

10 9 8 7 6 5 4 3 2 1

ISBN 978-0-7490-1485-8

Typeset in 11/16 pt Sabon by
Allison & Busby Ltd.

The paper used for this Allison & Busby publication
has been produced from trees that have been legally sourced
from well-managed and credibly certified forests.

Printed and bound by
CPI Group (UK) Ltd, Croydon, CR0 4YY

To the daughter whose cello fills my soul with music

VANESSA WEATHERBURN'S CASE DIARY

Winter 1900

CHAPTER ONE

*In which Vanessa listens to a concert of chamber music
and learns of a suicide*

The music spilt forth, welled up, flooded over, and ran down and away in twinkling rivulets that thinned as they disappeared into unfathomable distance.

The piano rose up in a roar, then subsided as the deep voice of the cello became audible, and swelled to ride the crest of the piano's wave. The violin entered then, its pure and steady tones bringing to mind a small but sturdy boat, handled by competent sailors, forging a path through wild seas under a mad Northern sky filled with streaks of swaying light and gleaming stars.

I listened to the trio for more than a quarter of an hour, allowing free rein to the images which the music evoked naturally in my mind, before beginning, imperceptibly at first, then more clearly, to wonder if they were really the images that the composer would have intended. The cockle boat, tossed up and down by the violent waves, always at risk but never quite succumbing, had provoked my admiration; now it began to cause a certain irritation. Listen to this theme, now – why so tame? I thought. Should the violin not be soaring ever higher and more powerful, dominating the underlying clamour of the other instruments, representing the very power of nature, like a gigantic ocean bird, wings outstretched, gliding unaffected over the turmoil below? Or a powerful ship, the captain stern at the helm, cleaving the water in spite of the troubled waves and crashes beneath?

The prick of irritation jerked me back to conscious thought, and I turned my eyes to the offending violinist, then glanced down at the programme to see his name.

John Milrose sat on the edge of his chair, his dark hair parted at the side and combed smoothly over his broad, clear forehead. His fingers flew over the ebony fingerboard, and his bow swept the strings with large and generous gestures; his tone was pure and melodic, he paid careful attention to his partners, there was no cheap showmanship in his playing, his love of the music was patent and sincere. In fact, he played altogether beautifully, and really, I exhorted myself, there was nothing one could reproach him with.

Except . . . that little cockle boat!

The piano took the theme again. The young woman playing had white hands which lifted high into the air like flying birds after each sweeping chord; her face was lowered, her cheeks flushed, and sometimes I thought she closed her eyes. Rose, my little pupil Rose – a blooming young woman now – sat near her, playing her cello with total abandon; she almost never glanced at the music on the stand low in front of her, but watched now the pianist, now the violinist, and melted her entrances into theirs, or paused with a waiting as alive as breathing, till they had reached the very point of diminishment to allow a new voice to rise up in all its ripeness. The sound of her instrument, thick as honey, strong as mead, overshadowed the violin in intensity, though never fully covering its fluting higher notes.

The trio came to an end, and the three players stood up and bowed. They were dressed in deep mourning, and the small stage had been decorously draped in crêpe. I fingered my programme. It was black-edged and folded over; the front held only a box enclosed in a small wreath of black leaves, containing the words:

IN MEMORIAM

The remainder of the information about the concert lay within the flap.

A concert by the Cavendish Trio
dedicated to the memory of Sebastian Cavendish

John Milrose, violin

Claire Merrivale, piano
Rose Evergreene, violoncello

Piano Trio in D major ('Ghost')	Ludwig van Beethoven, 1770–1827
Piano Trio No. 2 in E-flat major	Franz Schubert, 1797–1828

Inside my programme lay the small note that I had received along with it in my mail earlier in the week, the note which had brought me to London without a moment's hesitation, and for which I was seated presently in this small theatre, with its dim lights and lugubrious atmosphere of mourning.

> *Dear Vanessa,*
>   *It has been at least three years since we last saw each other. I know the fault is entirely mine. I have been so busy, and I am really very remiss! I hope you forgive me enough to attend the concert shown in the enclosed programme. It would give me immense pleasure to see you again, and also – I wish to speak to you about a very strange matter.*
>   *Very sincerely,*
>   *Your former pupil,*
>   *Rose Evergreene*

I slipped the note back into the programme and closed it as applause began and grew all around me. I joined in, but my gloved hands made almost no noise; I wondered for a moment whether it was worth removing the gloves, and then decided not to, for the sound of the applause in general was muted and respectful as befitted a mourning ceremony. The clapping went on for exactly the seemly amount of time; the three musicians, having left the stage, returned, bowed once again politely, and left again in single file. They were deadly serious; the face of the young pianist was ravaged.

The audience began to rise and gather up fans, programmes, handkerchiefs, reticules and other personal items. The large double doors at the back of the hall opened up, leading into the foyer. I joined the line forming in front of this door and, after some minutes of advancing very slowly up the aisle between the seats, reached it and emerged into the large space, dazzling with lights, gilt mouldings and a shining copper counter on which glasses and bottles had been placed, surrounded with piles of snowy but black-edged napkins.

A hall led away from this foyer, curving around the concert hall itself from the outside. I followed it, and passing through a baize door at the end, found myself in the rooms behind the stage set aside for the use of the artists. A murmur of voices led me to the area where the three musicians were still engaged in packing away their instruments and their scores. A man's voice was speaking; the youthful violinist.

'You're kind to say that, but I know it isn't true. I can't be part of the Cavendish trio. It was just for this evening; for this one time. I can't replace Sebastian and you know it.'

'Oh, John, can we not always play together?' asked

the pianist, who was holding his arm, looking straight up into his face. 'It isn't a question of replacing Sebastian. Of course no one can replace him, ever. But you *understand* about him – you were his friend! That's why I couldn't bear the idea of anyone but you playing with us tonight.'

Rose said nothing; her back was turned to the other two, and she was kneeling down in front of the large, open cello case, fitting her instrument carefully into its velveteen bed. This done, she took a silken square and dusted the traces of rosin carefully from the burnished wooden surface, passing under all the strings. She then used the square to tuck in the instrument as tenderly as a child, after which she closed and latched the lid. The round shape of her shoulders as she concentrated made me suspect that she wished to stay out of the discussion. I thought that perhaps she did not wish for John Milrose to continue as part of the trio.

'Well, we'll see, Claire,' Mr Milrose was saying. The baize door behind me swung again, and two or three more people entered to greet the artists; an elderly couple, a dark-haired young lady, then a moment after, two young men. One of them wore the red, rubbed mark of a violinist under the left side of his chin. Mr Milrose and Miss Merrivale separated immediately and turned to greet the newcomers. Rose stood up and came forward also. Her face lit up with a wonderful smile as she saw me.

'Vanessa!' she cried eagerly. 'I am so glad that you came. It has been much too long! Let me introduce you to Claire and John.' She kissed me warmly, and taking me by the hand, drew me over to where John was now talking to the people who had entered behind me. Claire was standing near him, listening, but her attention had wandered to Rose, and she took a quick step towards us as we approached.

'This is Vanessa Weatherburn,' Rose told her, in a tone which clearly indicated that she had already spoken of me to Claire, and that Claire was expecting, for some reason, to meet me. I shook her hand and spoke admiringly of her playing. But still holding my right hand in hers, she brushed off my praise with a quick sweep of her left, and said,

'Rose tells me I can talk to you – I *must* talk to someone, I don't know what to do – I can't bear it any longer!'

'Just ten more minutes,' said Rose quickly, 'we must be polite. Let's just wait until everyone's gone.'

A few more people had entered. Claire saw them, and drew herself together sharply.

'There's his mother,' she said, and crossed over, as though pulled by a string, reluctant but compelled, to a somewhat elderly lady who was speaking to John Milrose. I drew nearer to observe, and noticed how the woman's banal words seemed charged with meaning, because of the quiet intensity and poise with which she spoke them. Her hair, a greying ash-blonde, was dressed with the kind of simplicity that bespeaks taste in ample quantities, compensating, perhaps, a certain lack of wealth. Like the three members of the trio, she was wearing deep mourning; the cut of her gown was just fashionable enough to hint at an awareness of fashion without the slightest ostentation. The shoulders puffed too gently to be qualified as leg-of-mutton sleeves, underlining the slender waist without unduly attracting the eye. The skirt was close fitting, deeply gored at the back but devoid of ruffles and ribbons, and the collar rose high on the neck. A row of jet buttons gleamed down the front of the bodice. The woman who wore this dress was a woman of quality.

Her voice was quite extraordinary; it was of an exceptionally rich timbre, as though it came more directly from the chest cavity than from the throat, and her speech was very slow, each syllable enunciated carefully and yet without any sign of particular effort. She radiated a strong personality in which Claire Merrivale seemed caught like a little silver fish in a net. She looked up at the older woman, her voice trembled, she seemed unable to find words.

'That's Mrs Cavendish,' Rose explained in my ear, 'Sebastian's mother.' She tapped the *In Memoriam* on the front of the programme that still dangled from my fingers. 'We'll tell you everything in a minute.' She went to join Claire, and half-consciously laying a comforting hand on the other girl's arm, she undertook to answer the lady's remarks herself, with more aplomb than her friend. I watched intently, guessing that this little scene and everything concerning the defunct Sebastian

Cavendish would soon become the focal point of my attention.

Claire and Rose were much of a size, and Mrs Cavendish dominated them by a good five inches; however Claire appeared slight and weightless in front of her, whereas Rose stood firm and strong. I found it odd how, although the lady spoke with only the kindest words, her remarkable tallness and the sheer force of her character produced a desire to oppose some resistance to it, even though there was not the slightest conflict in her speech or attitude. But perhaps this impression did not emanate from the lady only, but also from Claire's display of weakness; she seemed on the point of breaking down. Perceiving this, Mrs Cavendish bent down a little towards her, taking her hand, and I heard her say,

'Try not to yield to despair, my dear. You must take courage from your art.'

She then kissed her affectionately, turned away, and departed upon the arm of an extremely elegant gentleman with side-whiskers and a gold-topped cane, who had been waiting silently at some little distance. The room having emptied considerably, Rose addressed a vigorous goodbye, tantamount to a dismissal, to John Milrose who was still standing amongst a few remaining friends. He smiled at the girls, took up his violin case and left with his group, and we found ourselves entirely alone in the green room.

'There,' said Rose. 'Now, Claire, you can tell Vanessa everything.'

There was a short silence, during which Claire struggled with tears.

'Well, I had better begin,' said Rose, although even she seemed to have some difficulty finding the words to tell me what had happened. 'You see, Vanessa,' she explained finally, 'the violinist of our trio, Sebastian Cavendish – Claire was engaged to him – he – well, he died a month ago. Tonight's concert was already planned; we turned it into a memorial concert for him . . . we had to find another violinist . . . John Milrose was one of Sebastian's closest friends . . . No, why am I talking about him? The problem is . . .'

Her voice tailed off, and I perceived that although more stable and less emotional than her friend, she was also deeply troubled. A cold fear seized me. What dreadful thing could have so disturbed her?

'How did he die?' I asked gently, leaning forward to look in her face.

'He committed suicide,' said Rose with what was clearly a conscious effort to steady her voice. 'He left a note for Claire. That is what she wants to ask you about. Claire – Claire? Come, you must explain things to Vanessa. And show her the note.'

Claire was already fumbling with the clasp of a little black brocade bag she held in her hands. The note she took out was written on a sheet of small, thick letter-paper of admirable quality. The ink had penetrated deeply into the soft fibres. The gentleman's handwriting was large and dashing. The short note filled the entire page, which had been rendered soft and grey by Claire's incessant handling of it.

Darling Claire,
How can I say this to you? I've found out something about myself – I can't go on with it any more. I'm sorry. I'm so sorry. Cursed inheritance – it's too dangerous to take such risks. Please try to understand.

Comforting words usually fall easily from my lips in the face of distress, but this event seemed so utterly dreadful, so totally beyond comfort of any kind, that I remained silent, staring at the letter. I admired Mrs Cavendish for having been able to find kind words for this young girl, when her own bereavement was so sudden and so awful. Rose echoed my thoughts.

'You saw Sebastian's mother, who was here earlier. Did you notice what she's like? So upright, so tall, so strong somehow; well, Sebastian was like her in some ways. He had that strength, that vitality – except that he was almost too emotional. And the way he played . . .'

'Like a god,' finished Claire. 'I never heard a violinist like him. Even though he was still young, he had everything – technique beyond most violinists' wildest dreams, infinite imagination and the power to express it. When he played, people in the audience were always in tears. *I* used to cry. It was almost beyond human.' Her words came out in a rush, as though once she had overcome the initial difficulty of talking about him, she couldn't stop. 'He used to play the Paganini Caprices as though they were a sort of joke. I've never heard anyone play so fast . . . Did you know that people used to say that the devil stood behind Paganini when he performed, helping him? Sebastian was like that. You couldn't believe he was just an ordinary person; when you saw him play, sometimes it was as though he was possessed.'

'Sometimes,' interjected Rose hastily. 'When he played madly difficult pieces. But he wasn't like that for chamber music. There was nothing diabolical about him then. He played as though the trio was a single instrument. We worked so hard; we were reaching for something very rare, and I think . . . we were approaching it.' She stopped. I said nothing, feeling humble in the face of a disaster, wondering why they had asked to talk to me.

'But what can I possibly do?' I asked.

'I want to understand why he killed himself,' said Claire, in a small, stern voice. 'Nothing foreshadowed it – nothing! The week before, he was exactly as always – and he was *happy*. Happy and vital and intense and full of projects. Oh, Mrs Weatherburn, I've lost my sleep from wondering and wondering and wondering, why, why, why? What do his words mean? What did he find out? What was that *something* that made him not want to live any more? What dreadful thing can it have been? Why did he kill himself? Why? Why? Why?'

Her words startled me. I had read his message differently, as though he had written 'I've found out something about myself: that I can't go on.' As though he had discovered that he had not the strength to live up to what was required of him. But Claire was understanding something else – that he had found out some particular mysterious *thing*, some actual thing that had driven him to despair. I saw at once that she might, indeed, be right, if it were true that a few days before his suicide, he had not a care in the world. If a man is not depressive or miserable; if he has no visible cause to be deeply despairing or disappointed, and is perceived by those closest to him as happy, vital, intense; then there must indeed be some essential outside *something* to drive him to sudden suicide.

'You believe that he found out something specific? Some dreadful thing that he could not endure?' I asked.

'He must have! What else could it mean?' she exclaimed, clutching her little bag convulsively with her fingers.

'I agree with Claire,' said Rose. 'I have thought about it also, again and again. We have talked it over and discussed everything we can remember about Sebastian, especially about the days and weeks before he died. If you are willing to investigate this for Claire, we will tell you everything we know. The only trouble is that we don't see how what we know could help you, because Sebastian was absolutely fine until the last time we saw him. And he wasn't the type of person who could easily have hidden something that was disturbing him deeply. He was very extroverted, very emotional. And it would have been especially difficult for him to hide anything from Claire, I think.'

'I could easily tell if something was amiss with him,' she agreed, rubbing her eyes although they contained no tears; she had reached a stage of grief beyond such expression. 'The last time I saw him was five days before . . . it happened. It was the day after Christmas. We hadn't spent Christmas Day together, because he had to be with his mother. But we met the next day, the 26th. We rehearsed the *Geistertrio* together—' she glanced at Rose, who nodded in confirmation, 'and then when we stopped, Rose left, but I stayed and Sebastian and I played Brahms. It was utterly beautiful. And he kissed me goodbye . . .'

'It isn't easy to recall everything exactly,' said Rose, 'and yet it is. Because there isn't anything special to say about that day. We've been through it again and again, and it was just as usual. That doesn't mean dull or routine. Sebastian was like a wire when you see the electricity go crackling down it, with sparks.' (I noted with pleasure that some of the scientific lessons I had provided during Rose's tender childhood appeared to have left some trace.) 'I wish we could describe him to you better. Imagine his mother – a bit larger than life, you know – but young, handsome, and happy. Yes, he was happy, not contented or cheerful, but with a happiness that was like – like bated breath, for life was so unexpected, and the things it brings so fearfully wonderful. Oh, Vanessa, you don't have to believe just us! If you're willing to do this, you should talk to his friends, his teachers. Then you'll see what he was like. No one, but *no one* could believe that he had killed himself.'

I steeled myself to ask a terrible question.

'How did he . . . ?'

'He drank a cup of poison. The police told me; they say he took something that he found in the house, and put it in a cup of coffee that he left next to his bed. Something must have happened on his trip – something dreadful, unspeakable, to provoke such a gesture!'

'He went on a trip?' I asked.

'Yes – he left in the evening, after the last time we saw him, that we just told you about,' she replied. 'He took a night train to Zürich, where he had been invited to play the E minor Mendelssohn Concerto with the Tonhalle Orchester. It was a great honour – they've built a new concert hall and it's said to be the best in the world. He was going to talk to them about the three of us coming, to play the Beethoven Triple Concerto . . .' She stopped speaking, and swallowed.

'Have you tried to find out anything about what he did in Zürich, and whom he saw there?' I asked.

'No,' replied Rose in a small voice. 'We're not detectives. We didn't actually *do* anything. We didn't know what to do. We just tried to think.'

'And you are sure there was nothing strange about his behaviour before he left? He didn't seem to have any special plans?'

'No-o,' Claire put in. 'But there was something

strange afterwards. His concert was on December 28th, and I'm sure he meant to come home the day after. At least, I had understood that, although I can't remember that he specifically said so, but I'm sure he would have told me if he actually meant to spend time away. But he didn't. Then when I didn't hear from him, I did wonder what he was doing, but of course I wasn't in the least bit worried. I just thought that he must have met some interesting people, and stayed on.'

'Because he did not return home, in fact?'

'It seems that he didn't, until he was found dead.'

'And when was that?'

'In the morning of January 1st, by the charwoman who comes in by the day. Mrs Cavendish was at home in bed, but she had come in late from a New Year's celebration and had seen nothing of him.'

'We had an idea,' intervened Rose. 'We thought that maybe he discovered that he was ill with some horrible illness which would kill him. We thought he might have felt ill and gone to see a doctor. Not that he ever seemed at all ill, but we couldn't think of anything else. So after the inquest, we asked the doctor who . . . who . . .' She glanced awkwardly at her friend.

'. . . performed the post-mortem?' I helped her.

'But he said there was nothing,' she replied quickly, 'no illness of any kind. Nothing was wrong with him.'

'Still, some doctor somewhere could have made a terrible mistake, couldn't he?' said Claire. 'And told him he was dying? Or something like that. I just want to understand . . . I *must* understand what happened, and whose fault it was. I must . . . I can't sleep . . .'

She stood up and wandered half-blindly across the room and out of the door which led directly onto the stage. After a moment, a turbulent storm of music flowed into the room.

'Chopin's twenty-fourth prelude,' murmured Rose. 'It was the piece he most loved to hear her play.'

'If I understand rightly,' I said, 'the police are not actually undertaking any investigation.'

'No, they're not. For them, it's just an ordinary suicide, nobody's fault, and there is nothing to investigate. As long as they can make sure he did it, they're not interested in his private reasons. But we are! Oh, please say you'll try to find out what happened. Please! It's – I can't tell you what it's done – it was so sudden, it shattered our lives. Claire's worse than mine, but it isn't just that they loved each other; it was the music, too. We were all together in that; we were doing something like – like one person. We put our whole lives into it; we were discovering new ways to interpret, new ways to express the music, something really, truly different. How could he have smashed it all and abandoned us? What could have been more important to him than music, that was his very soul?'

The sound of the piano continued to flow in from the stage, its voice so gripping that it absorbed and held all my attention. I found it hard to continue to speak, hard to organise my thoughts.

'I will do it,' I said. 'I can only try, you understand that. I have no idea what I may or may not find out. Whatever I find, I will tell you about it frankly, Rose – but only you. What you do with what I tell you is up to you.'

I glanced towards the stage, from which the last notes of Chopin's prelude resonated despairingly.

'I understand,' she whispered, clasping my hand in hers. 'Thank you, Vanessa.'

CHAPTER TWO

In which Vanessa visits the charming town of Basel
and meets an orchestra conductor

Old, crooked houses leant together along the Rheinsprung as though for support, like a group of elegant dowagers. Crowned with ancient tiles dusted with chill powdery snow, painted in unexpected pinks, blues and greens, frozen flowerpots ready at the windows, awaiting the advent of spring, the houses spoke of centuries devoted to order, duty and gentility. I moved along the row admiringly, my eyes hesitating between the delightfulness of the pretty row of house-fronts and the glorious beauty of the Rhine shimmering in front of me. On I went past Münsterplatz and down the Rittergasse, then right on the broad St Alban-Graben to the Steinenberg, where the Stadtcasino concert hall rose impressively in front of my eyes.

This was my first experience of Switzerland, and it had lasted all in all barely an hour until this point. Arriving from Paris and then Mulhouse, the train never really left France, but deposited one upon the very boundary between the two countries; only upon crossing some corridors on foot and displaying suitable papers to uniformed guards was one permitted to actually enter the country. And from the Basel train station to the centre of the old town was but a short ride, although one so remarkably charming, as the cab wound its way among narrow cobbled streets, as to fill the mind with enduring impressions. I sat happily, thinking how many of the most extraordinary experiences of my life had come to me through my detecting efforts, and how very lucky I was to have stumbled into the profession, almost by sheer accident.

The cab deposited me at a small pension, the name of which had been given to me by my dear friend Mrs Burke-Jones as being highly reputable and filled with travelling English ladies. I was not completely sure that this was the kind of company I most desired, but on the other hand, my German was so very rudimentary – and the language that I heard spoken all about me, in any case, so very unlike even my elementary notions of German! – that I thought it must surely be useful to be able to communicate in English. So I booked a room, spent the entire night crossing the Continent, and arrived at midday, ready to offer myself the gift of an afternoon and evening devoted to exploration, before presenting myself at the rendezvous so kindly granted me by Maestro Friedrich Hegar in Basel, where he was conducting a special concert.

I had written to him immediately after the conversation with Rose and Claire, for it seemed as clear to me as to them that whatever had driven Sebastian Cavendish to sudden suicide, it was something that he had learnt within the course of his five days' absence, and I could think of nothing more urgent or more useful than to retrace every step that he took during that short period of time. It was so recent that the project struck me as eminently possible, and I determined to begin in Zürich, whither he had travelled to give his concert with the Tonhalle Orchester.

I hesitated over leaving at once, but my husband advised me that it would be more prudent to write to the conductor, explaining the situation and requesting an interview at his convenience. Arthur said that orchestra conductors are busy and often widely-travelled men, and he turned out to be quite right, for the Maestro informed me that he would be out of the country for a few days, and then he would be spending a short time in Basel for a series of concerts with the Chorale there, before returning to Zürich. If I could not wait until his return home, he offered to receive me in Basel for a short meeting, and gave me a most precise day and hour during which I might come to the concert hall;

it was very nearly the only free time that he would have. I accepted immediately by telegraph, made my preparations, deposited my things at the pension and went for a roundabout walk: and thus I found myself wandering along the banks of the Rhine in the wintry sunshine, somewhat early, somewhat timid, but very much charmed by my surroundings.

Upon the stroke of four o'clock I entered the building, and soon found the main concert hall. The orchestra members were putting away their instruments and leaving; the conductor, who must be none other than Herr Hegar, was gathering up his music. I approached him with a little trepidation, hoping that he had not entirely forgotten about our meeting.

He turned as he heard me coming up to the stage from the seats, and I saw a head of white hair brushed artistically back, giving a peculiar effect of being rigidly windblown, a pair of sharp, commanding blue eyes, and a general air of being used to authority and to public observation. Then he came forward, his hand outstretched, and shook mine. His score under his arm, he invited me to join him in the room set aside for his use before and after concerts, and I followed him there under the curious glances of the musicians. It was a simple, pleasant little room furnished with a wardrobe and a mirror – important accessories for the conductor, certainly – a desk and lamp, and two or three armchairs. He settled down in one of them – it seemed almost too small in character, although not in size, for such a personality – and ushering me into another, leant forward to speak.

'So you have come about Sebastian Cavendish,' he said. 'Terrible, terrible, that he should be dead. I can hardly believe it. He was so young, so vigorous, so extraordinarily talented – a true artist, such as one meets but few over a lifetime of music. Only weeks ago he was playing here in Switzerland – only weeks ago. And now he is dead. I am horrified. I would wish to express my greatest sympathy and condolences to his family. If I may be so blunt, how did he die?'

His English was elegant, carefully pronounced yet strongly accented with the rhythmic singsong and peculiar vowels that characterised the incomprehensible Swiss German I heard spoken all about me in the streets. It made me want to smile, but the very thought of the dreadful nature of the response I must give to his question effaced that desire at once.

'He committed suicide by drinking poison,' I replied, unwilling or unable to be flowery on the matter.

His expression changed; he looked stern.

'Really,' he said. 'I had thought it must be some accident. I am sorry to hear what you tell me. Some tragedy of love, perhaps. But it is not clear to me why you wished to meet with me upon the subject. I was hardly acquainted with young Mr Cavendish, though I would gladly have hoped to become more so in the coming years.'

'We, his friends and family,' I began, smoothly adopting a polite fiction that I often used to avoid presenting myself as a detective, 'believe that he had no reason to wish to do away with himself before he left on his trip to Zürich. All are of one mind that he was happy, excited, hopeful and full of plans and projects, as well as being engaged to a charming young lady who was also a brilliant pianist and a member of his trio, the Cavendish Trio. In fact, it seems that he meant to broach the subject of a possible return to Zürich with the trio, in view of a performance of the Beethoven Triple Concerto.'

'Ah yes. He did speak of that,' replied the conductor with a wave of his hand. 'We had a discussion at the party that followed the concert, about his possible return. I expressed my preference that he should return as a soloist, to play something in contrast with the splendidly romantic Mendelssohn; something that would electrify rather than move. Paganini, perhaps. The Beethoven Triple Concerto is extremely difficult to organise; three soloists, three payments, and then generally more than the usual three rehearsals to put everything together. As an established trio, of course, they would have been able to prepare it in detail beforehand. On the other hand, the names of the other two members were unknown to me, although I cannot imagine that Cavendish would have participated in a mediocre trio. Still, I would have wished for further guarantees, and in addition, both the pianist and the cellist are women, which seemed to me to be a poor arrangement.'

'Oh,' I said. 'And why would that be?'

'We Swiss are lovers of tradition!' he responded firmly.

'Our women are not expected to attack the professions, as so many do in your advanced English society. We do not wish for such forwardness here. Women are content to stay at home in their kitchens, and they do not rush about getting up on stages to show themselves in public, or clamour loudly for the vote. Not even to mention the peculiar appearance of a young man travelling with *two* young women. It would not have done here, not at all, I assure you.'

I wondered inwardly whether to laugh or cry over the description of England as an advanced place for women, then decided that it is always best to count one's blessings. I could not guess whether Swiss women were truly as he described them, or whether this was a man's description, offered under the optimistic assumption that women were as he wished them to be. It is not that I am not acquainted with a certain number of Englishmen who would be likely enough to hold the same discourse (except, of course, that they would be obliged, additionally, to fulminate against the modest progress we women have achieved in attaining to the professions, and against the multiple demonstrations women have unsuccessfully staged in order to obtain university degrees, the right to vote, and other carefully protected male prerogatives). The question is both infinite and close to my heart, so I considered it wisest to nod my head sagely and appear as kitchen-oriented and profession-free as possible.

'I see,' I said humbly but encouragingly.

'However, I did assure young Cavendish that he

would be invited again for next year's opening season,' continued Herr Hegar, 'without yet specifying what concerto would be played. He had a very bright future in front of him and seemed very enterprising, full of energy, and happiness also. I assure you that I cannot have the slightest notion of why he should have committed suicide.'

'Neither do we,' I answered slowly. 'It seems to all the members of his family that when he left, he was as you describe him. Therefore, we have determined to follow his traces and attempt to discover everything he did while he was away, to see if we can recapture what led to the tragedy. I ought to explain to you that he left a note to his fiancée, telling her that he had "found out something" and "could not go on". We are all quite certain that whatever it was, he must have found it out during the course of his trip to Switzerland, for he left in good spirits and died immediately upon his return. That is why I am trying to go to the places where he went, do the things that he did and speak to the people that he met: in order to discover the cause of his sudden despair. Perhaps the most I can ask of you is to tell me how much you saw of him while he was in this country, and if you know where he stayed, or of any other people he was in contact with while he was here?'

He hesitated, then shook his head.

'I cannot be of much help to you, I am afraid,' he began. 'I do not know exactly when he arrived, but he was certainly here on December 27th, the day before the

34

concert, for we had a three-hour rehearsal in the evening of that day. Cavendish did not stay for the three hours, of course. He waited while we went through the overture to Fidelio, then we rehearsed Mendelssohn, and he left while we worked through the second half of the program, Schubert's unfinished symphony. The first rehearsal was only moderately successful in that his playing was so free that it was not easy to comprehend his style and predict his rubato. For the next morning's rehearsal, I summoned him an hour early to discuss the score in detail, and he explained his interpretation to me with a high level of technical mastery and also poetic expression. The rehearsal went much better. The concert was on the evening of that day. After the concert, there was a soirée during which Mr Cavendish appeared at the top of his form; that was when we had the conversation about his possible return for next year's season. This is all that I saw of him. I cannot tell you anything further.'

'But that is already a great deal,' I said. 'He played on the 28th of December. The . . . the death occurred during the night of December 31st; he was supposed to join some friends celebrating the arrival of the New Year. What did he do in between? Did he stay on in Zürich?'

'I have no idea what he did or where he may have gone after the evening of the 28th,' said Herr Maestro Hegar, beginning to look slightly impatient.

'I quite understand, and you have already given me some most important information,' I said hastily. 'Perhaps I may ask you if he received many people backstage after the concert, and who organised the soirée?'

'The soirée was organised and hosted by one of our most faithful sponsors,' he replied, a faint smile hovering over his lips. 'Her name is Frau Adelina Bochsler, and she is a great lover and supporter of music and musicians. She would certainly have gone to greet the evening's soloist after his concert and can tell you more than I about what occurred there. As it happens, she is also the person to ask about who was invited to the soirée. As always in her home, it was a formal and carefully organised affair, so I should not be surprised if she could provide you with a list of guests. I will write you a letter of recommendation to her, so that you may present yourself at her home in Zürich.' He seemed relieved at the idea of handing me over to the care of someone else, and, moving over to a small writing table, he wrote, folded and sealed a letter which he gave me, together with a note containing the lady's name and address.

'You may present yourself directly at her home and leave a card,' he said, 'upon which you should write that you are sent by me. If she is in, she will receive you, and otherwise she will certainly send for you at her earliest convenience. I am certain that she will be willing to render this service to the cause of Music. I would be happy to accompany you to visit dear Frau Bochsler, if I could, but I will not be returning to Zürich for several days. Basel is a lovely place,' he added, looking around him, then out of the window, with a smile. 'I lived here as a child and still have excellent friends here, who sometimes even come to visit me in Zürich for the concerts. This city is filled with old associations that, by some mysterious contrast, serve to refresh and renew me. It is good for the soul. But I expect that when I return to Zürich, you will probably no longer be there.'

It was clearly a dismissal, but I estimated myself successful with all that I had obtained, and bid the Maestro goodbye with the greatest respect. I felt optimistic about my next step, hoping for much rich conversation from a music-loving and party-arranging lady.

CHAPTER THREE

In which Vanessa visits Zürich and hears all about a charming party which took place there

Frau Adelina Bochsler was very friendly, very helpful, and very, very voluble. She was horrified by the so gifted young virtuoso's dreadful death. She had seen in him a great future. She was always, but always, looking out for young geniuses such as he. She had hoped for a long and fruitful collaboration. She had heard him in London, and it was her idea that he should come to Zürich. She had persuaded Herr Maestro Hegar, who had hesitated to take risks on yet unknown youth, but the young man's gold medal at a famous competition had helped convince him. Sebastian was so young, so strong, so handsome, so appealing. Those who had never met him could not even understand, was it not, dear Frau Vetherburn? She had been lucky to meet him even once. As for myself, how lucky I had been, and how sad my bereavement! I nodded until I felt like a Chinese mandarin.

I asked if dear Sebastian had stayed on in Zürich after his concert. No, Frau Bochsler did not believe that he had. In fact, she had asked him, for if he had been staying longer, she would have gladly taken him on an outing in her carriage to see the sights. But he was leaving the very next morning. Where was he going? Why, she didn't know. She supposed he was returning home. But had he said so? She didn't remember, but she did remember that he was quite – how could she say? He seemed eager to go. It was as though something important was awaiting him next. But she hadn't seen anything out of the ordinary in this. Surely the life of such a handsome young man must be filled with exciting events.

So he had seemed nervous? No, nervous would be the wrong word. Not nervous, but tense, excited, wound up. He was to leave quite early in the morning. The trip to London was a very long one. Such musicians were in great demand; they must resolve themselves to a great deal of travel.

Had poor Sebastian spoken to her of his trio, or his fiancée? Why yes, he had. He had told her of his hopes to come with his trio to play the Beethoven Triple Concerto with the Tonhalle Orchester. But Frau Bochsler had felt a twinge of dismay, as she did not know whether it would be right to encourage him in this idea. She was not at all certain that Herr Hegar would agree, and of course it was Herr Hegar who took all such decisions. She did not say so, but she seemed very much to prefer the idea of Sebastian coming all by himself, to be petted and taken under her wing. The idea of his arriving flanked by two radiant young ladies did not seem to appeal to her much. She sighed, and agreed that of course his fiancée must be utterly devastated.

Could she tell me anything she had noticed about Sebastian's mood over the course of the evening? You see, I told her, we were convinced that at some point between his leaving for Zürich and his death, he had learnt something which had a profound and terrible effect on him. We were trying to trace his every movement and gesture during that lapse of time in order to pinpoint the moment at which this had happened. She understood perfectly. But she could not see how anything of the kind could have happened at her soirée. Well, obviously, there had been many people there. Thirty-five or forty people. Dear Sebastian was not previously acquainted with any of them, as far as she knew. She had kept him near her for the whole first part of the evening, introducing him to the cream of music-loving Zürich society; magistrates, doctors, men of law, men of government, and their elegant, artistic wives. He had not encountered any familiar faces that she knew of, except for Herr Hegar's, of course. At least there had been no sign that he had done so. His mood was excellent, and he was such a lovely young man, so full of charm, such easy manners. Of course he spoke mainly English, but he had some German, and these two languages sufficed for him to enter into many a more or less broken conversation. No, he was not in the least bit shy; quite the contrary. And he seemed to enjoy making friends. What a personality; he was truly the star of the evening, truly, truly. To think he was dead, it was dreadful. Frau Bochsler took out a handkerchief and wiped her eyes.

Yet he seemed somehow tense when he spoke of hurrying home. Why would that be? She didn't know, hadn't thought about it. Probably he simply missed his fiancée. Perhaps, indeed. But, I asked, could it possibly be that he had had a particular conversation at the soirée which had disturbed him? She could hardly imagine it, yet – her eyes sparkled with excitement – it was not impossible; no, she supposed that it was not impossible. Did she think that Sebastian had spoken with more or less everyone at the soirée? Yes, he had probably exchanged at least a few words with nearly everyone. Had she noticed him in particular conversation with anyone? Well, on and off she saw him talking and laughing with several people. What did they talk about in general? Well, music was the subject of the evening. Sebastian's talent, his superb interpretation of Mendelssohn, his gold medal, his budding career, his future. He spoke of it all with such grace; he was modest and at the same time eager and hopeful and so gifted it was quite impossible to believe that he was gone. Frau Bochsler wiped her eyes again.

How could we possibly find out if he had had any particularly striking conversation that evening? Well, she was eager to help. What could she do? She herself had participated in the most fascinating moment when Mr Cavendish had actually taken out his violin to show it to some of the assembled guests. It was a most extraordinary violin, but I would know all about it, of course. (More nodding.) A lion's head was carved at the end of the fingerboard, at the place where there is usually a scroll; a lion's head with a strangely long, extended tongue. The young soloist had explained that the violin was made by a certain Jacob Stainer of Austria. I perked up my ears at the mention of an actual name, only to learn further that Jacob Stainer had lived and died in the 17th century. Frau Bochsler believed that the name meant no more to her guests than it did to herself – namely, nothing whatsoever – although some of them had appeared to pretend to know all about him. Mr Cavendish had smilingly explained that the sound of the violin was not as powerful as certain others that had been made in Italy, but that it was so extraordinary an instrument in tone and quality that he would not wish to change it; he felt it belonged to him by destiny. She remembered that he had said that the violin had been inherited from his grandfather. Was it not remarkable that grandfather and grandson should both be violinists? But perhaps it was quite a normal thing. Frau Bochsler herself loved embroidery, and she had shared this taste with her grandmother. Her mother had not seemed to enjoy it so much, she recalled. Frau Bochsler's mother had been given to making lace, and she had taught her daughter to make lace, but little Adelina had preferred to embroider poppies and cornflowers and violets, like her grandmother. She had made these napkins herself, she recalled, extracting some from a drawer to show me. I admired the ability of a child to form such perfect stitches, and wondered fleetingly if my own little Cecily would be able to hold still long enough to master such an art. But this was a digression. I drew Frau Bochsler firmly back to the matter at hand. Yes, yes, she said, her eyes still on the napkins, but Sebastian had not wanted anyone to say that he inherited his gift from his grandfather just as he had inherited the violin. The joke had been made, but he had said it was impossible, out of the question. Frau Bochsler did not see why it should be out of the question. Such things could be inherited, certainly. She continued to finger the napkins. But Sebastian had said it was impossible. Then he had laughed. He was a young man of infinite vitality; the guests had been won over by his charm.

All this was relevant enough, but although it appeared that the guests were learning many an interesting fact from Sebastian, I could hardly imagine what he might have learnt from any of them during the course of such banal conversations. Yet it was tantalising. The violin must have been of tremendous importance to him – I could well imagine a flamboyant personality on the cusp of a grand career appreciating the effect produced on his public by the unusual sight of a lion's head at the tip of his instrument. The fact that he associated the violin with his 'destiny' was also intriguing, indicative of something fundamental in his life. Yet, what on earth could he have possibly learnt that night about his own violin? And what fact about a violin could possibly provoke a suicide? Even discovering that it was a fake or a fraud would surely not produce so dramatic an effect. My imagination was failing me.

I drew Frau Bochsler back to the subject of Sebastian's suicide. She could not imagine any relation whatsoever between this terrible event and anything that had transpired during the soirée. It seemed to her, alas, much more probable that poor Sebastian had made some dreadful discovery in London. Could it not be – she leant towards me, dropping her voice to a whisper – that he had found out something *about his fiancée*? Such things had been known to shatter the happiness of young men.

I told her that the fiancée was more distraught by the mystery of it all than anyone else, and described the note that Sebastian had left for her. Frau Bochsler sighed deeply upon hearing about it, and the distaste for having doubts shed upon the absolute success of her party was slightly overshadowed by the glowing account I gave of the mystery of it all, and the realisation that she might possibly yet play a role in its elucidation. I asked again if she could be sure that there had been no other significant moments for Sebastian during the evening, and if she had noticed his mood when he finally left. Well, it was as she had told me; he left somewhat early as he had an early train to Paris on the following morning, and he was definitely tense when he told her this, as he shook her hand. Perhaps there had been something to cause that. It was possible, after all, although she had certainly thought nothing of it at the time.

Could I, perhaps, arrange to meet some of the other guests and ask them the question?

It would be a little socially awkward. Yet, she thought it could be done. Without saying so directly, she intimated that certain people might be quite interested to hear details about the terrible tragedy that had passed so close to them. She could arrange something. She had the list of guests, of course. Her soirées were highly prestigious, highly desirable. Everyone who was anyone in Zürich wished to be invited. She must keep lists and be careful to exclude undesirables. Anything might happen if one were not strict; people who were not received because of a social scandal could attach themselves to other people and, on the grounds of visiting them, could worm their way in. Frau Bochsler had had to yield on such matters many a time when she was younger and less experienced, and more than once she'd had a soirée ruined by the presence of an obnoxious or unwanted guest. She knew better now. She had precise lists and they were given to the servants. Yes, we could consult her list. It would be awkward but not impossible to visit her guests and explain the situation. There were not as many visits to make as it might seem, since many of the guests had come as couples or families. She found it very hard to believe that I would discover anything of significance, however. As the hostess, she had spent the larger part of the evening near Sebastian and heard whatever people had to say to him. Music was much discussed; the young man's studies, his professor, his musical preferences, his concert experiences, his future plans, and his instrument. She could not remember any other topics; she had heard nothing that struck her as the slightest bit unusual. Of course, there were necessarily many things that she had not heard. And I, who knew Sebastian personally, might perhaps pick up some allusion, some reference that others had not noticed, although she could not even imagine what it might be. She really could not believe it possible that the fatal knowledge acquired by the poor young man before his death could have been learnt at her soirée. No, truly she could not. For if it had been, why would he not have committed suicide that very night, at the Pension Limmat, where she herself had organised his lodging. What a horror that would have been; a horror and a scandal! All the more so because she knew the lady who ran the Pension Limmat quite well. It was a very proper place, and Frau Dossenbach would not have liked a suicide there. She, Frau Bochsler, would never have lived it down. It was indeed fortunate that it had not occurred thus. The mere idea made her feel faint. Well, in any case, she quite saw how important it was for the family to try to understand why he had felt that he had to die. A true tragedy. Although Frau Bochsler had many engagements, she was free the next morning, and, if I wished, we might begin our round of calls then.

In the meantime, she recommended me to the Pension Limmat. It was right on the Limmatquai, a short and pleasant walk over the bridge from the Tonhalle. If I did not yet have a room somewhere, I should certainly go there. It was short notice, but she would write a letter of recommendation to Frau Dossenbach, which I could show her directly I presented myself there. It was not extremely far, and very easy to find; I need only walk straight down the Kirchgasse to the river and then turn along the quay. I could go there by foot if my bag was not too heavy.

I thanked her, took the missive which she sealed with a large ring, and left, feeling a slight relief, in spite of all her kindness, at leaving the plush and pillowy surroundings of her parlour behind and emerging into the crisp, sunny air.

I was in a hurry to reach the pension, but my eyes and my feet had other desires, for the daintiness of the streets, the fresh colours of the houses, the old beams and the bright flowers at every window constantly distracted my attention so that I found myself pausing on my way, staring about me in delight. When I reached the river, instead of turning left along it, I walked onto the Quaibrücke and spent an enchanted moment hanging over the edge. A solid mass of black ducks, many dozens of them, was wedged into the corner formed by the river and the old bridge, reposing or simply socialising, and amongst them, two enormous white swans were etched out against the black background. I forgot momentarily where I was in the contemplation of this astonishing spectacle of Nature, then suddenly remembered Sebastian. Had he also paused on this bridge, on his way to the Tonhalle which lay just a short distance from the other end? He must have, surely. It was so beautiful, and he had loved beauty.

Sebastian was still a mystery to me. His feet had probably trod the very same bridge; his smile had lit up the very same parlour in which I had just now been offered some overly sugary tea, his music had blended with that of my darling Rose whom I had known since her childhood. But human beings are mysterious enough to one another even face-to-face. And those who had known Sebastian best had not understood why he had done what he had done. How could I hope to penetrate his secret?

What was most important to Sebastian? His violin and his music, on the one hand, and on the other hand the people he loved: his mother, presumably, and Claire. Was there anything else? For the time being, I should proceed on the assumption that there was not; otherwise, surely Claire would have known. So, the terrible thing that he had found out must have concerned these things, or been triggered by one of them. The violin – the music – the mother – Claire. In asking Frau Bochsler's guests to recall their conversations with Sebastian, I would concentrate on these four points. Something, somewhere, had triggered a terrible realisation in him. Surely it could not be impossible to find out what it was.

If only I had met him. It was so hard, feeling my way blindly, trying to understand the innermost thoughts of a young man I had never met. If only I had seen him but once. But I shook my head briskly, and scolded myself. I must stop thinking this way: as though I had missed my chance. Frau Bochsler had met him and Herr Hegar had met him, and they understood as little as I. Having met him was not the point. Trying to understand the secrets of his mind was not the point. The point was simply factual, I reassured myself. Sebastian had been to Frau Bochsler's; I had been to Frau Bochsler's. He had walked to the Pension Limmat; I was walking the same way. He had met some people whom I would meet tomorrow. *Somewhere* along that path that he had trod, and that I would tread after him: *somewhere*, his secret must be hidden. If, after having followed it, it still seemed to me that everyone I spoke to said nothing more than platitudes and banalities – my greatest fear at that very moment – why then, somewhere, I would have missed the single pebble that was actually a pearl. I might do so. Yet that did not mean that the pearl was not there. Its existence was a matter of plain fact: of that much I was certain.

I left the bridge and wandered on up the street in the direction of the pension. Doubt was not an option.

CHAPTER FOUR

*In which Vanessa meets a retired violinist
and asks him a number of questions*

I sat in a comfortable armchair in front of a small table decorously laid with small pastries. It was already the fifth of my morning calls in the company of Frau Bochsler, and each host had offered us something to eat. I was beginning to feel foolish, frustrated and exhausted. It had been obvious to me in the first five minutes of each call that no information was to be had, and yet we had been obliged to spend another ten minutes each time in polite conversation, most of which took place between Frau Bochsler and the host or hostess, and escaped me entirely, held as it was in singsong Swiss German.

My enquiries had begun on the previous evening when I interviewed Frau Dossenbach, the proprietress of the low-ceilinged, medieval Pension Limmat, but from her I had learnt nothing but the barest of facts. Frau Dossenbach's English was rudimentary: she appeared to possess an exactly equal and minimal knowledge of English, French, Italian and high German; precisely those words and phrases necessary to attend to the immediate wants of her numerous foreign guests, such as 'Do you wish for hot water now?' and 'The evening meal is at seven o'clock precisely'. My attempt to pose a few modest questions about Sebastian Cavendish had met with blank incomprehension until I was rescued by a gentleman passing through the hall. He took the trouble to interpret my questions and Frau Dossenbach's answers, but as might be expected from one so entirely devoted to the necessities of her daily work, she had only facts of this nature to tell (and some reluctance, due no doubt to the natural discretion of one in her profession, to mention even those). I could learn absolutely nothing about Sebastian's state of mind, and gleaned only the simple confirmation of the fact that he had departed early on the morning of the 29th of December, whether to Paris, London or elsewhere she could not say.

Giving up on this source of information, I turned to thank the gentleman who had helped me, but he had already disappeared up the narrow, crooked staircase that led to the chambers above. I was left to my imaginings as I went up to my room and proceeded to freshen myself with a pitcher of hot water carried in by an obliging maid not two minutes later. In entirely incomprehensible words proffered in the local dialect, but using the most unmistakeable gestures, she was able to communicate to me the fact that dinner would be served when I should hear the sound of a bell or gong belowstairs, and leaving me with this welcome piece of information, she removed herself and I removed my shoes and reclined upon the bed.

I felt anxious and troubled, and was worried that I would have difficulty finding sleep in such unfamiliar surroundings. However, after consuming the extremely heavy meal of a bowl of cabbage-and-rice soup followed by breaded veal, together with potatoes cut to tiny ribbons and fried to a crisp golden brown, I felt overcome by exhaustion, and dragged myself up the stairs to my room again, feeling as laden as though I were carrying a weighty suitcase. I went to bed at once, in order to be at Frau Bochsler's at as early an hour as was reasonable to begin our round of visits.

Some two hours after we had started forth, bored to tears by endless repetition of banalities, I began to wonder if Frau Bochsler was not becoming as impatient and sceptical of the whole procedure as myself, and was on the very point of calling it all off from sheer enervation, when her carriage stopped in front of an elegant town house, and she rang at the doorbell, saying,

'Now you shall meet a very dear friend.'

The door was opened by a sempiternal aproned maid, who ushered us into a sempiternal velvet-upholstered parlour. After a young lady, an elderly lady, a middle-aged couple and an elderly couple, it was now a single gentleman who entered the room: a gentleman of a certain age, small, wiry and friendly.

'I am so pleased to meet you,' he said in excellent English, once Frau Bochsler had explained something of the nature of our call. 'My name is Leopold Ratner. Please, do sit down and by all means let us discuss this strange story.' For the fifth time that morning, we sat down and the maid was sent for something to offer the unexpected guests.

'I was greatly interested in Sebastian Cavendish, and terribly shocked to hear of his sudden death,' Herr Ratner told me with sincere feeling. 'You see, I follow the careers of as many of the rising young violinists of Europe as I reasonably can. Luckily for me, my dear Tonhalle is one of the very best of all the European orchestras, so that some of the most extraordinary players come to perform right here where I live. I attended Cavendish's phenomenal concert in December, and afterwards, of course, the charming evening party at Frau Bochsler's home.'

I noticed then that half-hidden underneath his grey beard, Herr Ratner had an old, well-rubbed mark on the left side of his neck.

'You are a violinist also?' I asked.

'I was one, not so long ago,' he replied with a smile. 'I was an orchestral musician for several decades. When I was young, I had some talent and I thought I might go far, but such a career is not given to many. Ah, then, when I was still young and energetic and filled with dreams of ambition, I travelled far and wide to hear the greatest violinists of my day, and that is how I came to hear Josef

Krieger – or Joseph Krieger, as he called himself after moving to England – and to be inspired to become his pupil. You wish to know what I discussed with young Cavendish during the evening: we talked about my teacher, Joseph Krieger. Alas, what I learnt above all from Krieger was that I would never be a great violinist. He used to shout at me during the lessons, which I believe he gave only because he was in need of money at certain times; his career knew some dramatic ups and downs because of the terrible disputes he had with some of his patrons and protectors. He was, to be straightforward about it, a cruel and violent man. I remember one time when an eminent professor from the Royal Academy of Music had come to visit. He arrived early and I was still having a lesson, on the Saint-Saëns concerto. Start from the beginning, my teacher told me. Eagerly I lifted my violin to my chin, fired up to give my best on this splendid work in front of the stranger. After the first two notes of the superb initial theme, Herr Krieger stopped me with a cry of "Too high!" Undaunted, I began again, only to be stopped after the same two notes by "Too low!" He continued in this manner for a full quarter of an hour. I never played more than those first two notes, after which he declared my lesson over and turned to talk with his colleague as though I no longer existed. I cannot even remember my thoughts as I packed my instrument and left his house, so black were they. He destroyed my ambitions, and if he had lived longer, he would probably have succeeded in destroying my love of playing and even my love of music.'

'How horrid he sounds,' said Frau Bochsler consolingly. 'Why ever did you stay on?'

'You don't know how things were then,' he said. 'They have perhaps changed a little nowadays, although I am not so certain about it. For the young and aspiring musician, his teacher was like a god. One did not shop for a teacher as for a pair of shoes. One selected a teacher, and humbly requested that he deign give lessons, and accepted that his rebukes were merely the thorns along the path to greatness. I did not realise the harm that Joseph Krieger was doing me until long after his death. I was too used to habits of respect.'

I thought of Rose's tone, on divers occasions when I had heard her speak of her cello teacher, and recognised the same phenomenon of infinite and unquestioning respect. Yet in Rose's experience, that respect and admiration went hand in hand with an attachment as deep as love, that contained no trace of pain or humiliation. Perhaps she was one of the lucky ones, and there were still students who suffered as poor Herr Ratner had done at a time when young whippersnappers were not expected to protest ill-treatment at the hands of their masters, but to profit from it, and improve.

'However,' the elderly violinist was continuing, 'he died when I had been with him for less than two years, and I found myself suddenly obliged to make my own way as best I could. In that same year, Sir Charles Hallé formed a new symphony orchestra in Manchester, and to my great good fortune, I was able to become a member. Thus I had the infinite joy of making the splendid music in a group that I did not feel able to make by myself. Then, ten years later, when the Tonhalle Orchester was formed here in Zürich, I chose to join it, and thus to return to my native country. I retired only a few years ago, and since then, it continues to be my greatest pleasure to attend the concerts.'

Something in his tone and manner indicated that he was not merely indulging in a flow of memory, but that all this had some connection with Sebastian Cavendish. I encouraged him to continue with a nod and a murmur.

'Now, Joseph Krieger possessed a very remarkable violin,' he went on. 'I had occasion to see and even to hold and play his violin very frequently, over the two years I spent attempting to learn something from him, while he fulminated against my playing and told me that my accent in music compared to the composer's intentions was no better than my Swiss compared to his own pure and elegant High German. However, all of that is past and finished, and Joseph Krieger has been dead for nearly half a century. I meant to speak of his violin, because when young Cavendish showed us his instrument that evening at Frau Bochsler's, I felt absolutely certain that I recognised it. It was not just the astonishing lion's head, although this caused me to identify the violin at once as a Jacob Stainer. Stainer made more than one violin of that type, although they are rare, but here there was something more: I felt quite certain, seeing and running my hands over the violin, that it was none other than the very instrument that had belonged to my former teacher.

A certain stain and discoloration on the back, certain worn marks, and then, the very sound of the instrument itself, as I had heard it during Cavendish's concert – fiery and infinitely subtle – I was quite certain that this was the same instrument!'

'Did you tell Sebastian about it?'

'Not at once. I have always felt a nearly insurmountable repugnance at mentioning the name of Joseph Krieger, such was the burden of resentment that remained within me even after his death. I cannot speak of it without bitterness even today; even now that the ice has been broken, you cannot but sense something of my feelings. Cavendish was far too young to have ever known Krieger, of course, and I thought it quite possible that he had bought the violin from a dealer, or that it had been lent to him by an anonymous foundation, and that I might be able to indulge my curiosity about the instrument without mentioning the name of Krieger at all. But before I had time to put the question, I heard him telling others that Joseph Krieger was his own grandfather, and that the violin was a family heirloom.'

'Quite,' I assented. 'Sebastian certainly knew that his grandfather was a famous virtuoso, although I do not know whether he knew much about his character. But the violin was certainly a treasured inheritance.'

'I should say not just the violin, but the extraordinary, flamboyant talent as well! As soon as I heard it, I realised how much his playing resembled his grandfather's in style. Yet the boy must have been born a good quarter of a century after his grandfather's death, and cannot have had any more idea of his playing than what reputation and family tradition may have communicated to him. Is it not strange that something as intangible as the manner of playing the violin can be inherited in just the same way as a material object like the violin? Yet the evidence of it was there before me!'

'It is extraordinary,' I agreed. 'And so, once you knew that he was Joseph Krieger's grandson, did you tell him anything about his grandfather?'

'What do you think?' he smiled sadly. 'Politeness dictated that I tell him only the facts; that his grandfather was my teacher, and that he was one of the greatest of violinists. Nothing more.'

'Did you tell him what you just told us about his playing being in the same style as his grandfather's?'

'Yes, that I certainly did.'

'And what did he answer?'

'He laughed it off and denied the possibility; said he did not believe such a thing could be inherited, and at any rate in his case he knew it to be impossible.'

'What could he have meant by that?'

'I have no idea. I suppose he was merely enjoying feeling original.'

'Did you tell him anything else about his grandfather?'

'Nothing; certainly not a word of all I have just told you. Indeed, I have never spoken of those feelings to a living soul until this very moment. It is strange, but when I realised that this blithe young man with the ready smile was Krieger's grandson, I felt a wave of pleasure; it seemed to me as though a chance had been offered me, to undo the twisted knot that Krieger had left in my heart. I intended to continue to see the young man, to be his friend, and to follow the development of his career, without ever telling him why. It would have been a kind of redemption! And then – I heard about his sudden death. I cannot tell you the effect the news had on me. I had just begun to feel that my hidden shame was finally to be dissolved in friendship, that my anger against the grandfather could finally dissolve in the form of kindness to the grandson. And then the process was suddenly cut short! I will not deny that at first I was literally in despair. But after some days, I came to realise that something had changed within me after all. It was as though the brief contact with the young man's vibrant personality had somehow broken the hold that Krieger has exercised over me through all these years. His playing and his personality provoked in me the old feelings of passion for the violin that I had lost long ago, without the despair and frustration caused by my teacher's attitude. In that short evening, he gave back to me what his grandfather took from me. And although I spoke of this to no one, I realise now, with you, that I am able to speak of it after all, and that this signifies that indeed, everything has changed.'

He sighed and paused for a moment, then continued.

'It is indiscreet of me, but may I ask you how Cavendish died?'

The sadness in his eyes communicated itself directly to

my soul as Claire's mourning had not. Love is essentially intimate, and although I could sympathise, I could not really share her sorrow at her loss. But music is for everyone, and although I am no more than a mildly appreciative member of the audience at the best of times, Herr Ratner had suddenly made me feel that a musician like Sebastian could bring people a sense of the power, the marvel, the sap of new life. I acutely regretted never having seen him, and never having heard him play. For the first time, I felt more than merely handicapped in my research by my ignorance of what he was: I felt a sharp pang of regret at not having known him. I wanted to comfort this old man, or at least explain to him simply and exactly how and why Sebastian had died, but I didn't know! And the little I could say was anything but comforting. Sadly I was obliged to explain to him that Sebastian, his newly discovered fountain of life, had committed suicide for a reason that no one understood. I told him frankly that my quest in Zürich was to find out if that reason had anything to do with Sebastian's visit. I told him about the words 'I've found out something about myself'. I asked him if he, who had been acquainted with the grandfather that Sebastian himself had never known, believed that the connection with Joseph Krieger could have anything whatsoever to do with Sebastian's suicide.

'I cannot imagine how it could,' replied the old gentleman in a subdued tone. 'He knew of his grandfather already. What could he possibly have "found out" from our brief discussion?'

'Perhaps he knew very little of his grandfather. Are

you sure you told him nothing at all that might have been new to him?'

'I told him that I had known his grandfather long ago and heard him play often, in the years just before his death. I mentioned being his student, frequenting his home over that space of two years. I cannot remember mentioning anything else in particular. Not one word, I repeat, of the things I have just told you. I spoke of Joseph Krieger only with admiration and respect.'

'Since Sebastian's name is not Krieger,' I observed, 'I presume that his mother must have been Mr Krieger's daughter. Did you know her? She must have been quite a child when you were still taking lessons.'

'Ah yes. I remember knowing that Professor Krieger had a wife and children, though I never met them that I can recall. I may have glimpsed his wife once or twice, but I have no clear memories. She must have been very self-effacing. I cannot imagine being able to live with a man like Joseph Krieger otherwise. I do not recall his children learning to play music, for example, as many musicians oblige their children to do. In fact, now that you mention it, I believe he had only daughters, because I recall his once telling me that it was a pity he had no son, as I would have been just good enough to serve as his practising tutor. That was the way he spoke in general. And mind you, many girls did learn to play musical instruments or sing even in those days. But that would not have been the way of a man like Professor Krieger. Women learnt music for the betterment of their lives and the lives of those around them, not as a profession, and Joseph Krieger was only interested in music as a life-dominating profession, and, even then, only in those who might have the capacity to reach the heights of genius. I do not believe his children were trained at all. It is all the more striking a miracle that the gift should survive intact into the next generation, is it not?'

Herr Ratner did not seem to recall anything further about his conversation with Sebastian Cavendish; it really seemed unlikely that he had said anything that could have produced such a tremendous shock as to drive a man to suicide. We were both somewhat disappointed by the paucity of the information we were able to provide to each other. But try as I might, I simply could not imagine why hearing any mention of the grandfather who had died so long before his birth should suddenly appear important to Sebastian now. Nevertheless, I noted down Herr Ratner's address, ostensibly in order to write to him if any deeper understanding of Sebastian's sad fate should be obtained, but also simply as a source of information about the past if such should be needed. And upon that we said goodbye, and I left to continue the round of calls with Frau Bochsler; without, however, discovering anything further of interest.

'Whatever poor Mr Cavendish learnt, it was not said at my soirée,' she pronounced finally, with a mixture of relief and disappointed curiosity, at the close of the wearisome and monotonous day. Wearisome and monotonous for me, at least. She, to be sure, had many more reasons to enjoy it than I; the people we had visited were her friends, and she had the benefit of a common language to communicate with them; and, being quite generously built, she had presumably suffered less from the ceaseless intake of pastries than had I.

'It is a pity that dear Dr Bernstein is not in Zürich at the moment,' she said later, as we sat in her parlour, taking stock of the day. 'He has been a dear friend of mine for decades, and of Herr Ratner's as well. You would like him. He is so highly educated, so cosmopolitan, our dear doctor, and I did notice him speaking for some time with that poor young man. He seemed quite excited, but that is not surprising, such a lover of music as our Dr Bernstein is. You would have appreciated his intellect and knowledge. As a matter of fact, he wrote a book . . . I have it here somewhere. Ah yes, I remember, here it is. I have never read it, but I am sure that it is most interesting.' She took from the mantelpiece a bound volume whose dustless state was obviously due to careful work on the part of the housemaids rather than to any effort at reading the contents by anyone whatsoever, given that the pages were still uncut. I read the title: *Automatische Schreibung: Diagnose und Bedeutung.*

'Diagnosis and meaning of automatic writing. What is that?'

'Yes, our dear doctor is greatly fascinated by the phenomenon, and has been for as long as I have known him. Don't you know about it? The patient writes down all kinds of nonsense in a state of unawareness, like a medium in a trance. Such things used to be all the rage and people were convinced that spirits were speaking through the writers, but Dr Bernstein insists that true understanding of the phenomenon is still lacking, though it has nothing at all to do with spirits from the other world. I know that he speaks of a patient of his own somewhere in the book. Take it, if you like. Perhaps you will enjoy it. You speak some German, as I heard. Do you also read?'

'Haltingly, but with a dictionary I can manage,' I said, thanking her and taking the book. Automatic writing! Either the doctor was a charlatan or – or he was not, and there was something interesting behind a phenomenon that my husband Arthur had taught me to consider essentially as a swindle. I felt intrigued, and determined to spell my way through at least part of the book before coming to a conclusion of my own.

'Well, if the subject interests you, you may have a chance to meet Dr Bernstein in person, and then you can ask him the questions you wished. He moved from Zürich to Basel some years ago, but he travels quite regularly to London, to attend the meetings of the Society for Psychical Research there.'

'Really!' I exclaimed. During a previous case, I had already had some dealings with members of the SLR, in a manner that had deeply affected my natural scepticism. 'Thank you so much for telling me about this. I shall certainly look for him at their next meeting.'

CHAPTER FIVE

*In which Vanessa returns home to Cambridge
and discovers the existence of a theory of heredity*

Sitting in the winter sunshine in my little Cambridge garden, I took Cecily's small face between my hands and stared at it closely. Heredity! What was it? What secret lay behind Sebastian's 'cursed inheritance'? Was it material, or did he refer to the incorporeal conveyance of traits and features between the generations? Cecily wriggled and gave me a kiss, and all the mystery of motherhood, of the miraculous transmission of flesh to flesh and blood to blood lay revealed before me: her brown eyes, her soft hair, her little upturned nose, my features inexplicably reflected in the enigma of her face, radiant with love and the joy of being reunited.

The magical moment passed and the mystery sank

into opaqueness once again; the children grasped my hands and pulled me into a dance of wild Indians about an improvised totem pole, and the capacity for rational thought melted away from my mind, leaving behind a mass of confused images and associations. The scales, which had fallen momentarily from my eyes and showed me the reflection of my own face in my child's, returned and I perceived it no longer; Cedric's resemblance to Arthur was pronounced (and he even looked a little like me – another mystery, as Arthur and I do not resemble each other in the least), but Cecily was once again nothing other than a little elf who had strayed into our garden by mistake.

As a matter of fact, as I watched her dancing about, I was reminded, not for the first time, of my own dearest sister, Dora. I used to think this was nothing but pure foolishness, since Dora and I are identical twins, and therefore I could hardly imagine a likeness to her and none to myself. But over time the impression persisted, and I came to understand that as Cecily's character was closer to Dora's (far sweeter, gentler and more thoughtful than I seemed to recall myself as ever having been!), I came to believe that the ephemeral similarities I sometimes fleetingly perceived arose as much from expressions and from movements as from the plastic features.

How often it is said that children have inherited their looks from Papa, their character from Grandmamma, and even their very troubles, which are imputed to Uncle James or Auntie Joan! But what can such a thing mean?

How can a character, how can even a face be inherited in the same way that a material object, such as a violin, is inherited? How is it that we humans so freely confuse these two types of inheritance, even using the same word, although one is simple and the other complex and beyond all comprehension? That the face of a child can reflect both mother and father, and even back to the previous generations, is a phenomenon so familiar that we no longer question it. Although we do not understand it, we accept it and it seems natural to us; yet surely there must be some physical mechanism by which our physical attributes pass through our bodies to the child we create together.

I could not help mulling over the question, to the point of making theories whose expression would have been a perfect example of scandalous impropriety. It was a delicate subject to broach at dinner (for Arthur hates unseemliness), but I did so with tact, and encountered unexpected enthusiasm!

'Why,' he answered with the characteristic pleasure that exposure to new scientific ideas invariably gives him, 'there is more known about the mystery of inheritance than you might think! In fact, I heard a very fascinating lecture on the subject some time ago, by a visiting German professor engaged in some research that I'm sure you would find very interesting. He told a story you would like, although I cannot quite remember the details, about someone having reached an extraordinary level of understanding of the subject and then having died and all his work having disappeared. Now, why would that have been? I'm sorry, I can't recall; it's the kind of thing you would remember better than me. What struck me in the lecture, the reason why I went, was the role of mathematics in the whole theory; probability, to be exact. For example, if a certain physical feature appears in the parents, then certain physical features may appear in the children with greater or lesser probabilities, which can be mathematically calculated, and certain other physical characteristics may be totally precluded in the children of a given couple. Theoretically, at least. Professor Correns' studies concerned plants, which have a simpler constitution than human beings. But he strongly expressed the belief that humans, animals and plants function analogously.'

'But plants do not have children,' I said. 'What is the means of transmission?'

'Ah, but they do! When you take a pea (I believe he spoke of peas) from a pea plant and plant it to obtain a new pea plant, that is considered to be a child, and, according to Professor Correns, it is not so different from . . .'

He paused and blushed, but I finished his sentence with a smile.

'Than the planting done by us humans. So, the pea-plant plays the role of the father and the earth that of the mother?'

'No, I believe there is a matter of two pea plants . . . Now you are getting me all interested! I can't think how I managed not to seize the physical aspects of the theory, so interested was I by the mathematical.'

'That doesn't surprise me in the least. It is too bad, however,' I remarked.

'Well, it should be an easy affair to manage to encounter Professor Correns at some social event around Cambridge, if you would enjoy that. If it would compensate for my foolish distraction, I will be happy to speak to my friends in the department of biology and see if such an event cannot be arranged, or, if it is already arranged, if we cannot be allowed to join.'

'I should love that!' I exclaimed, with sudden impatience. Could it be that a light would suddenly be shone directly, and for me personally, upon one of the greatest mysteries of life? Could it be that scientists understood the secrets of heredity, if only for peas? It was, to be sure, a mystery that had never occupied my spirit particularly until that very day. But now that it appeared as one of the most important elements in a puzzle that concerned me, it suddenly seemed to me to be one of the essential secrets of nature, and I could not resist the desire to learn as soon as possible whatever there was to be known on the subject. I felt as impatient to meet fusty old Professor Correns as a young girl waiting for a midnight tryst with her first lover.

Professor Correns was being much celebrated in Cambridge, and as it happened, I was destined to meet him quite by chance on that very same afternoon, for as I was returning home along Silver Street carrying a few purchases of haberdashery, a carriage drew up in front of the Darwin house and a woman emerged with a very small girl, followed by two top-hatted gentlemen. One of them was familiar to me as one of Mr George Darwin's brothers; I knew he was also a professor at the university, but could not remember of what subject. The other was a tall, dashing fellow, obviously a foreigner, with striking blonde hair and beard worn in a longer style than is usual hereabouts.

As these gentlemen approached the gate, the Darwin children appeared *en masse* from the stable where they often play, and greeted the newcomers effusively. The youngest one, William, spotted me as he was displaying his prowess to impress the visitors by climbing atop the high wall that separates the Darwin property from the road, and running eagerly back and forth along the top. Though I no longer live next door to them, the children still treat me cordially as a neighbour.

'Mrs Weatherburn!' Willliam cried out with great enthusiasm, as an additional means of drawing attention to himself. 'Here's Uncle Francis and Aunt Ellen with a German for tea! Do come!'

I glanced through the gate, not certain whether an invitation proffered by a six-year-old was to be taken at face value, and encountered the welcoming smile of Mr Darwin's lovely American wife, who had emerged from the house in her relaxed fashion, without a wrap, to take charge of her unruly brood, two more of whom had now joined their brother atop the wall.

'Please, do join us if you can,' she said. 'Professor Correns must not be kept isolated amongst dons! He ought to meet as many as possible of the ladies of Cambridge as well, don't you think? Such a different style of conversation!'

My heart leapt at the mention of his name; this was really a stroke of luck, for the satisfaction of my impatience, at least! Arthur being out for tea and the twins with their nanny, I accepted the invitation with pleasure. As I entered, another carriage drew up, and a couple of a certain age stepped out and entered the house behind me. Mrs Darwin's maid took all the shawls and wraps, and we settled down in front of a roaring fire. Children ran in and out, tea was brought in and poured, various cakes were served, and introductions were made all around.

Professor Francis Darwin, I learnt with some excitement, was a naturalist, and Professor Carl Correns from Tübingen his guest in Cambridge!

'I am very honoured to meet you,' the eminent professor said to me in that respectful and somewhat weighty tone that a German accent always appears to lend to the English language.

'And I to meet you,' I said with an enthusiasm that he probably found surprising. 'My husband was at your lecture on heredity, and what he told me has made me very eager to meet you and learn more about it.'

'So, you have a scientific mind?' he answered pleasantly. 'It is something of a rarity to meet a woman with true scientific curiosity in the tradition of old, such as the legendary Marquise du Châtelet.'

'I am honoured by the comparison!' I laughed. 'I have heard about the marquise, who brought the discoveries of Newton to the scientists of the French court. It is said that she studied day and night. I only wish I possessed such capacities!'

'Yet you are interested by the sciences, and perhaps often like to meet and discuss with the scientists who work or visit the university?'

'Yes, well,' I said. 'I do get very curious about some of the discoveries I learn of through my husband. I admit to a certain interest, even if my understanding must necessarily remain superficial. But I was particularly intrigued by what my husband described to me of your lecture. I must say that heredity is a topic that fascinates me deeply. However, he was only able to tell me just enough to whet my appetite for more, without giving satisfactory answers to any of my questions.'

'Perhaps I can do better,' responded Professor Correns with delighted gallantry. 'At any rate, I am quite ready to try, and where I fail, my colleagues will certainly help me.'

Mrs Darwin was chatting quietly with her sister-in-law during this conversation and Professor Bates was standing at the sideboard together with the two Professors Darwin. Mrs Bates, seated on the same sofa as myself, was following our conversation without participating.

Professor Correns settled into an armchair that

he drew up nearer the sofa. I took advantage of his proximity to examine him more closely.

He looked no older than Arthur, and his eyes were of a bright Teutonic blue with a merry twinkle. He seemed to be playing at a very entertaining game, yet there was an air of melancholy behind his laughter. I found him an intriguing and attractive personality, but my desire to know about his science was stronger than my desire to draw him out.

'Well then,' I said, 'let us see if you can possibly explain the secrets of heredity to an ignorant being such as myself.'

He sat back and smiled.

'Part of the secret of heredity is beyond my own knowledge,' he said, 'and another part must always remain mysterious to us humans because it is dependent on no other laws than the laws of chance, which as you know are unpredictable. I don't know if you are aware that the laws of chance give precise predictions only over very large numbers, but never over a single occurrence of some event. For example, if I flip a die, I cannot make any prediction about which number will come up, but if I flip it six thousand times, I can predict that the number of times that a one will appear will be quite close to one thousand. Do you see?'

'Yes, I do see,' I said. 'I see it for a die, because there are only six possibilities and we know them all and we know that there is an equal chance for any of them to occur. But it doesn't seem possible that those simple rules could apply to a situation as complex as that of heredity in living beings, where it would seem that the number of possibilities are absolutely endless and impossible to enumerate.'

'Very true, for complex living beings like humans. But there are much simpler living beings whose study has allowed us to understand the grand discovery, namely that the rules of chance governing the dice are the same identical rules which govern heredity; it is simply the number of possible combinations which is infinitely greater.'

I paused to think for a moment.

'Well,' I said, 'I can conceive somehow that such a thing might be true. It seems to us that the possibilities for two human beings to create another one are endless, but perhaps, as you say, they are really only in the many millions and that seems like an infinite number to us because we cannot tell the difference. Theoretically, I can see that what you are saying might be the case. But I must admit that I have not the faintest idea of how, even having conceived of this theory, it could possibly ever be proven.'

'It takes a genius, madam,' said the German professor with a sudden ponderousness, and I glanced at him in surprise, wondering if he could possibly be using this term in reference to himself. But no. This sudden earnestness was of that which is inspired by the contemplation of an extraordinary phenomenon.

'I will tell you how it was done,' he explained, 'but I must first tell you by *whom* it was done. It is a surprising story, and a sad one. The story is about a monk in a monastery in Brünn who, some thirty-five years ago, published a paper which was misunderstood and utterly ignored and forgotten, until I myself discovered it barely one year ago – and it has changed my life, so that I now consider my scientific mission to be the bringing of this seminal work to the light of day!

'The story is about a monk who asked himself the same question that you are asking about the secret of heredity, and who actually devised a way to make a scientific investigation of the answer, by studying plants in the monastery garden! It is the story of a monk who spent years making the most extraordinary, intelligent controlled experiments and painstaking notes of the results, then analysing their mathematical meaning with the brilliance of genius, to come to a final result. A result which is, to my mind, one of the most astounding scientific discoveries of our century, in no way inferior to Charles Darwin's theory of natural selection.' Here he broke off and glanced at the men at the sideboard, hoping, no doubt, that he had said nothing to offend the sons of the eminent naturalist. But they were paying no attention to him, so he went on.

'And finally, it is the story of a monk who, on becoming the abbot of his monastery, ceased to pursue his research, and whose notes were burnt at his death by his successor, who had no understanding of the genius contained therein. His name was Gregor Mendel, and it has been the crowning glory of my professional life to be the one to rediscover that old, forgotten published paper, the only remaining trace of all his careful work, and to recognise its potential importance. I gave myself the task of reproducing his experiments in order to confirm his astounding theory, and have met with total success. And therefore, I can now trumpet the work of Gregor Mendel to the entire world: *heredity is governed by the laws of chance*! A sentence which must be properly understood, of course, since to the layman it may sound like heredity is a matter of chance. But that is not what is meant at all; the laws of chance, which are mathematically known as the laws of probability, are strict, and they govern heredity according to fully understood rules. This, by my reproduction of Mendel's work, has now been definitively proven!'

'The descent from theory to experiment is always liable to render a theoretical idea more accessible to the layman's mind,' I said. 'Would it be possible to describe your experiments?'

'Nothing could be easier,' he said. 'The experiments themselves were so simple that you could do them yourself, if you were interested. They are based on the careful study of pea plants. Do you cultivate vegetables?'

'I do, in fact,' I said, glancing automatically out the window at the Darwins' garden, whose wintry aspect left all visions of peas and the usual tomatoes and beans entirely to the imagination. 'At least, I do in the springtime, but nothing is happening there now, unfortunately.'

'But still, I will tell you how the experiments are done, and you can try them for yourself. But please do not forget to pay careful attention to the fact that the beauty of the theory is not in the experiments themselves, but in the fact that Mendel was able to see that he might be able to deduce the secret laws of heredity from making sufficiently many of these experiments, and carefully observing the results. He never claimed to understand *how* the traits are passed from one generation to the next – that delicate mechanism still remains beyond our knowledge. But he created an experiment to test the laws governing the frequency at which certain given features will be inherited by the offspring, and this is a shining example of genius.'

I agreed to bear this in mind. Professor Francis Darwin, catching the mention of plants even from some distance away, now came towards us and sat down to listen.

Professor Correns continued, 'Mendel began by making a careful examination of the common pea plant, *pisum sativum*, that grew abundantly in the monastery kitchen garden, and he noticed that, unlike the human being, in which each physical trait (for instance, the colour of the eyes) can take a myriad of different shades and hues, many distinguishing traits of the pea plant took just two possible forms. For instance, the flowers of the pea plant always grow either at the top of the plant, or on the side, never both. The plants are either noticeably tall or noticeably short; there does not seem to be the possibility of every kind of height, as with humans. The colour of the pods on

77

a given plant are either all green or all yellow, never some of each or some strange greenish-yellow combination, and the pods themselves are either smooth or pinched in between each pea. Finally, the peas themselves are either green or yellow, either round or wrinkled. Mendel studied these properties, and the first observation he made was this: if you take a single pea plant and write down all of its properties (for instance, tall with flowers at the top, smooth green pods and round green peas), and you take a pea from this plant, plant it and observe the plant that then grows, it will have all the same properties exactly, and so on down the generations.'

'So in fact, a pea plant is a creature that has but a single parent,' I observed. 'I was wondering about that. Does Mother Earth really play no role in the genesis of the new plant?'

'None at all. The pea is naturally a monoparental plant practising self-fertilisation, but it can be made to have two parents by the method of cross-fertilisation. This is the experiment that Mendel made.'

'He was not alone to make such experiments,' interjected Francis Darwin suddenly. 'My father did many such, over a period of years, and even published a book called *The Effects of Cross and Self-Fertilisation in the Vegetable Kingdom*.'

'But of course,' rejoined Professor Correns placatingly, then added, 'your father's book is a classic of the subject, and his methods are certainly similar to those of Mendel. Cross-fertilisation and breeding of plants has been practised by gardeners for hundreds of years. Mendel's research took place several years earlier than Darwin's, of course, since he published his article in 1865 and that already followed years of research, whereas your father's book, if I am not mistaken, appeared in 1876. But that is not the point. Mendel's particularity was the mathematical study of the results, and the mathematical theory he devised to explain them. It is in this that he differed from all who preceded and followed him in the study of cross-fertilisation of plants.'

His father's honour saved, Francis Darwin subsided, and, with the true interest of the scientist, prepared to listen as attentively as I to the German professor's explanations.

'To return to your point,' he began, 'Mother Earth certainly plays a role in the genesis of plants, since a plant could not be born and grow without nutrients. But she plays no role in their hereditary properties. Father Plant, Mother Earth – it is a beautiful analogy, but it is not correct here. There is a proper analogy within the pea plant itself to the role of both mother and father, and it takes place within the flower. You see, within the petals of the flower of the pea plant, like most common flowers such as crocuses and tulips, there are two organs, the pistil which is the centre part, and the stamens which are the tiny stems containing a little yellow spot on the top of each. It is the stamens which play the role of the male organ, as their pollen ferti—?'

The professor's voice ground to a halt as his attention

was drawn to the strange behaviour of my neighbour upon the sofa, Mrs Bates. For some moments already she had been fanning herself vigorously with a Chinese fan decorated with pagodas and flying herons, from which depended a green tassel decorated with a bead, and now she leant back, closed her eyes and slipped into a near faint. Her pale lips murmured something that I didn't catch, since I was paying attention to the maid, who was already hastening forward holding out smelling salts. I took them and agitated them under Mrs Bates' nose, and she revived somewhat and remonstrated in a voice of deep dismay.

'I cannot stand it – such language! I have never heard such a conversation. The stamens – the male – indeed! I cannot bear it – I am sorry – I am not accustomed . . .'

Her voice trailed away in a show of weakness, but her husband, rushing forward to her aid, added his protests to hers.

'Whatever have you been saying to shock my wife so deeply?'

'Oh, the conversation took a turn – dear Thomas, I know that it is science, but I really could not hear it!'

'Well, it shan't go on, my dear. Would you like me to take you home?'

'No, no,' said Mrs Darwin soothingly. 'Here, dear Mrs Bates, do have your tea, it will revive you in a moment. We shan't have any more scientific conversation, shall we? Let us all speak of ordinary things!'

Calm returned to the company, and everyone present was

relieved that the moment of tension had passed. Everyone, that is, except for myself. I was overcome by a great wave of anger and frustration, so powerful that it risked entirely ruining the atmosphere of a pleasant social occasion, and leaving an unpleasant trace and strained relations behind. My delight at being asked to tea had been uniquely due to the possibility of having my questions answered, and now the tea party had transformed itself into an obstacle blocking my way to the knowledge I so dearly wanted. Even though Mrs Bates' fainting spell was genuine enough, I could not help feeling that there was something hateful about it – something artificial and untruthful; not that she herself was counterfeiting her emotion – I did not think that of her – but yet how in Heaven's name could the words 'male organ', pronounced in the most abstract scientific manner, on the subject of the stamens of a flower, cause such an effect upon a woman who was a wife and very probably a mother? Whence exactly came the shock to her nervous system upon hearing those words? Certainly not in the actual fact of the existence of the corresponding object! What hypocrisy, that the pronunciation of a word should cause a shock where the thing itself presumably caused none! I was truly suffused with rage and unable to pronounce a single word, for I saw that not only was Professor Correns' fascinating discourse destined to be interrupted, but there should be no chance of its being resumed at any time during the course of the party, which at once became a dreary duty that I must perform, puppet-like, while hiding my feelings to the best of my ability.

By a miracle of the same kind of intuition that had allowed him to sense the importance of Gregor Mendel's published but utterly unrecognised work, Professor Correns detected my thoughts and drew me aside.

'I perceive your deep interest in these questions,' he said, 'and that you do not suffer from the sensitivity of certain English ladies with regard to certain somewhat delicate questions. Or perhaps it is that you, like myself, belong to a new and younger generation. So, I would propose, if you wish, that we meet again, perhaps to take a quiet walk through one of Cambridge's lovely parks, and discuss these things in privacy and at leisure. It would afford me great pleasure to do so.'

The world returned to rights, and I felt a great smile of gratefulness spread over my face as I accepted joyfully and fixed a date that unfortunately could not, due to other obligations, be nearer than two days hence. But the professor's understanding compensated for the delay, and, thanks to his words, I was able to resume the tea-drinking and the now relentlessly proper and correct conversation that ensued, with everyone gathered round the tea table together, and nothing left to chance, the husbands apparently not ready to abandon their wives once again to the unknown dangers of science.

CHAPTER SIX

*In which Vanessa reads a book in German
and one chapter in particular*

The art of automatic writing, I wrote, painstakingly translating the foreword to Dr Bernstein's book in the hopes of developing an honest interest in the material, and thus providing myself with a perfect reason to ask for an introduction to the good doctor at the very next SPR meeting in London – *is one of the most mysterious and ill-understood phenomena of our time. This is partly due to the many aspects of the phenomenon and the deep divergences of opinion of observers as to its origin and meaning. The major trends of popular beliefs could be listed as follows:*

1. Swindle, pure and simple, for the gain of attention or even financial advantage.

2. *Communication from otherworldly spirits whether dead, distant or planetary.*

In this case, two currents of thought are to be noted:

   2.a. The communication is made in order to carry messages from the spirit to our world, through the medium;

   2.b. The communication is made in order for the all-wise spirit (possibly identified with the Lord or one of his angels) to teach the medium, if she is willing to listen, hidden but important aspects of herself.

3. *Fragmented impressions produced from the unconscious brain, not unlike the images produced in dreams. In this case again, two possibilities present themselves, as for dreams:*

   3.a. Haphazard and fragmentary reproductions, in arbitrary arrangements, of sights, physical experiences, or mental experiences (such as anxiety over a particular coming event or over a type of event in general) from the daily life of the subject;

   3.b. Mental constructions which are totally meaningful according to a logic which is different from that of the conscious mind, but which merely requires possessing the key to unlock its mysteries entirely.

The purpose of the present volume is, by the study of various cases, to indicate that true automatic writing does exist, independently of the many cases of imitation for purposes of gain, and to provide some case histories that may provide evidence for the last of these interpretations. In spite of intensive personal study of one of the cases presented in this book, the author has not yet discovered the key to unlock the meaning of her writings, yet so strong is the impression of hidden meaning that the author is convinced that all who read the writings selected here must share it, and he writes this book in order to present it to the world, in the hopes that some more experienced or more enlightened colleague may use it as a springboard to reach the ultimate truth.

Each chapter of the book was devoted to a different case history, but from the first few lines of each, it was clear that the doctor had not personally analysed most of the cases, if he had even actually met them. Thus, his ability to link their writings (often quite coherent in themselves) to a deeper meaning connected to the unconscious personal life of the writer was in the majority of chapters limited by his lack of knowledge of even the quite basic facts of that life. For this reason, it made sense that the final and longest chapter should be devoted to the one case that was actually a patient of his own: a British subject named Lydia K. I skipped over the other chapters and went straight to Lydia K.

I treated Lydia K. for a period of nearly four years, of which she spent the first part residing in my clinic for mental patients, and then the final years in my home, for I came to the conclusion that she did not belong in the clinic, being in no way insane, but a very lovely young woman.

Over this period of time, I grew to know her extremely well, in spite of the fact that my study of her case was somewhat handicapped by the fact that she had been forbidden to speak of her family or to give her true name. I communicated with the family through her legal guardian, who checked regularly on her well-being through the visits of a deputy who was sent to the clinic on a monthly basis, and also came regularly in June to bring Lydia home for the annual summer holidays. The family was clearly desirous of keeping her identity entirely secret. She had been instructed to refuse to answer any questions whatsoever about the subject, whether it be on her name, her parents, her siblings, or her more distant relatives. Aided by a natural tendency to discretion, she kept these promises faithfully, no doubt as convinced as the rest of the family of the shame that her 'illness' or 'abnormality' might afford to what I imagined must be a noble or prominent family. Throughout the time she spent in Basel, she was known to me as Lydia K., the K. standing for the name of her guardian, a name very widespread in England. I was quite certain that this name was not her real name, for she sometimes did not react to it very naturally, yet I never knew her by any other.

Lydia's greatest desire in life was to please others, and possessing a naturally sweet and compliant disposition, she was able to follow her family's directives and the requirements of my own treatment perfectly insofar as they did not enter into conflict with each other. When they did, she invariably chose to keep faith with the promises made to her family. Since she was a ward, I supposed her to be an orphan, and she eventually confirmed that this was the case, telling me that her father had died when she was four and her mother when she was fourteen. Apart from these bare facts, I was left in the most complete ignorance of many facts of her childhood that, I am certain, would have aided me to come to a deeper understanding of the ailment that afflicted her.

Yet even without such information, I believe that as the years passed I was coming closer and closer to some kind of comprehension, and, at the same time, her own writings were evolving in interesting ways, although to a superficial eye they may not have appeared significantly different from those she produced from the very beginning of her stay at my clinic.

Although the guardian, Mr C. K., steadfastly refused to give me the information that I felt I needed to know on the subject of Lydia's family, he was desirous that she should be cured, and willingly answered various other questions that I asked him during the course of an exchange of correspondence that lasted throughout the four years of her treatment (I never met him personally). He told me, for example, that according to the family she had no noticeable peculiarity of writing before reaching the age of fourteen, apart from a tendency to occasionally mar the margins of her copybooks with stray words, phrases or lines of poetry, but nothing which could in any way cause alarm, although to a trained mind these might have served as the first indications of the direction that the subsequent abnormality was to follow. Lydia herself told me that as a child she had no consciousness of writing the stray words and was usually quite surprised to see them there when her governess had corrected her work. However, there was no cause for concern, and Lydia was able to complete her education altogether normally; indeed she was a cultivated and well-read young person.

At the age of fourteen, coinciding in her case with the onset of puberty and (as I eventually learnt) following the death of her mother, Lydia's tendency to absent-mindedness while writing began to increase noticeably, until it became necessary to stand over her and call her attention repeatedly to the matter at hand whenever she had to perform an ordinary writing task such as a letter or invitation. A moment's inattention on the part of the governess would result in sentences turning, seemingly of their own accord, into something quite different from what was intended: snatches of poetry, confused images and the like. This tendency continued and intensified in spite of (perhaps partly because of) repeated scoldings and punishments, until Lydia could no longer take pen in hand without slipping into a state in which her hand alone functioned and her will could inject no sense at all into the process. By the age of nineteen or twenty she had reached a state of complete inability to write anything on purpose.

From our discussions I became convinced that, in spite of appearances, Lydia's slow slide into automatic writing after her mother's death represented a progressive relief from repression rather than a descent into confusion. This reasoning was the first step towards my conviction that by her writing she was expressing inner thoughts that were totally inaccessible and incomprehensible to her conscious mind, and from that point on, my efforts were all bent on understanding the message itself. I believed that if I could understand it, I would hold the key to understanding the reason for which the message had been mentally suppressed, and something of the mechanism by *which the human brain is able to accomplish such a feat. Everyone has the experience of forgetting something just when it is needed, only to have it spring into the mind at some entirely irrelevant moment, proving conclusively that the fact in question has not really been forgotten by the brain at all, but was only made temporarily unavailable. This phenomenon in itself is not mysterious, or, at least, it is familiar to everyone, but the mechanism which puts into direct opposition the brain's intention of hiding something with the soul's urgent desire to express that same thing, and the manifestation of this struggle by such rare and extraordinary phenomena as automatic writing, are mysteries, the unlocking of which would lead us deep into the secrets of human psychology.*

The patient came to me in the autumn of the year 1870, at the age of twenty-four. She had previously been living at home. I was not sure what particular event had motivated her suddenly being sent for treatment after six years of a stable although strange condition. It occurred to me that the family probably saw her condition as an obstacle to marriage, for which she was in every other way entirely suitable, being a sweet-natured and very presentable young woman with polished manners. In the absence of any contact with pen and paper, it would have been nearly impossible to notice anything at all peculiar about her, were it not for a tendency to dreaminess and a certain lack of ability to reason efficiently, but these are of course traits shared by many young women and in no way prejudicial to her marrying happily and raising a family. Later, when I learnt that Lydia was an orphan, it occurred to me that she may have become a burden on her siblings for some reason, perhaps due to their own marriages into other families.

I began Lydia's treatment simply by a series of examinatory sessions, during which I gave her pen and paper and observed her writing with no interference.

The sight of pen and paper produced an immediate although scarcely visible effect on her; her eyes developed a dreamy look, almost as though they were covered by a film, and she appeared to look inwards inside herself. She confirmed to me that she saw and heard nothing while writing, nor could she recall any thoughts that went through her head. She spontaneously wrote for periods of time that would typically last from one to several minutes, after which she would appear to awaken. When she read what she had written, she used to shake her head with a laugh, exclaiming 'What nonsense!' in a casual tone I felt certain that she had been taught, probably by family usage. Her writings were all very similar to each other in tone and in vocabulary, with a very small number of continuously recurring themes. Here is one example from the earliest days of her treatment.

Sky arches overhead, clouds over trees, world is large, world is vast, sky covers all, world and sky contain all. Nothing is more secret than any other thing to the eye of God, which knows and sees all equally like the sky covers all equally. God the Father made that which is Natural and that which is Unnatural thus the Unnatural is as natural as the Natural and pain is as natural as joy and all comes from the Father. Joy and abomination are both expressions of the love of the Father. Not one thing is right and one wrong but all are equal being sent by God as they are equal under the sky.

Attempting to analyse writings such as this one together led us far along the path of religious investigation, as we explored the writings of Calvin and the roots of Protestantism. However, Lydia repeatedly told me that these writings did not express her own consciously-held religious and moral views, and that she was herself shocked by reading 'Not one thing is right and one wrong but all are equal' which in no way corresponded to the manner in which she had been brought up. She was occasionally tempted to believe that a spirit from outside herself was dictating such words to her, but her belief in this theory was and had always been tempered by the complete absence of any kind of self-identification of the said spirit (unlike in many of the other cases cited in this book). Of herself, Lydia made no attempt to comprehend her own writings, dismissing them as nonsense as observed above.

Having obtained a grasp of her habitual procedure when writing, I began to make a series of very gentle experiments with her. My goal early on in the treatment was exclusively one of curing a peculiar and rare disease for which no kind of treatment had yet been developed; I was not, at that stage, as profoundly fascinated by the disease itself as I later became. In the desire to restore to her, little by little, control over her own writing, I began by suggesting that she include certain specific words in her texts. Before handing her the pen and paper or even showing them to her, I would impress upon her that she should attempt to write down a certain word, for example 'house', as many times as possible within her text. However, these efforts bore no fruit whatsoever. The moment the pen was in her hand, she lost contact with the conscious world and all memory of my request to her was effaced.

The next strategy I adopted, after some weeks of trial and reflection, had more success, although of an unpredictable and confusing nature. By its very nature, this technique could only be used rarely, as it could be easily recognised and I did not wish her to know my intentions. It occurred to me that if her writings were reflecting a repressed reality, then perhaps if I gave her some knowledge purposely destined to be somehow repressed, echoes of it might emerge in her writing. I decided to make her the confidante of a secret – not an important one, of course; indeed one that I invented for the occasion – yet I told it to her with no reference whatsoever to its relevance to her treatment, but rather as though I wished to ask her advice, and I repeated to her many times the necessity for complete secrecy and discretion, which she of course whole-heartedly promised. The story I told her was one of a slightly embarrassing skin ailment, asking for her opinion as to whether I should inform my wife of it, or visit a doctor. In order to perceive the traces of my effort, I chose a topic – 'skin' – which had not yet made an appearance in any of her writings.

I was immediately rewarded by the emergence in the following treatment sessions of the new word in her automatic writing, yet so disguised as to keep the secret perfectly. The word 'skin' now appeared occasionally, but in contexts not even remotely associated to the secret I had confided to her, and so disguised that, had I not been especially on the lookout for it, I would have missed its presence entirely.

Truth is what comes from God and not what we ourselves believe is the truth for we are subject to error.

Whatever comes to us from God is the truth and our difficulty is to distinguish truth from error, truth from Him and error from ourselves. This is the only task and not distinguishing the wrong from the right, the pain from the joy, the outer from the inner for these are one so long as they come to us from the Source. We have a body and there is the world and we perceive it as the inner and the outer, our skin is the frontier between our sense of Inner and our sense of Outer yet this is an illusion for within us there are elements of the outer and outside of us of the inner. All Truth is outer, all Lies inner. On the Day of Judgement, the Truth will emerge. When man rips the fabric of God's Truth then only then is he Evil. Before condemning a man for Evil be certain that his thoughts and deeds were not sent to him for a purpose beyond our understanding.

In style and essential content her writings were as before. Only I could be aware of the introduction of an entirely new word into the mental processes that produced them. In order to verify my findings, I repeated this experiment a few times, but at quite long intervals so as not to make the patient aware of my proceedings. Each time, some fundamental word or words from the secret emerged in a different context in her writing.

By this time, Lydia had been with me for more than one year with no noticeable change in her condition. Standard exercises geared towards

a practical outcome of allowing her to write
something in a conscious manner systematically
failed as soon as she took the writing instrument in
her hand, be it pen, pencil, or any other implement. I
tried to fabricate such peculiar writing instruments
for her as should continue to attract her attention
and keep her in a conscious state during the writing,
but had no success in this venture. Using chalk
in front of a blackboard, she fell into her usual
trance and covered the blackboard repeatedly at
a tremendous speed, writing again and again over
what was already written without any erasures. I
once believed I was on the brink of success when
I suddenly asked her to trace the letter A with her
toe in the sand. I saw her listen to my request and
attempt to obey; her foot made some disjointed
movements, something vaguely triangular
emerged, but she was so acutely troubled as to fall
in a kind of faint directly afterwards, somewhat
discouraging me from trying the experiment again.
I did so, nonetheless, one further time, after having
obtained her agreement; in her normal state, she
even spoke humorously about the possibility of
her learning to write with her foot, but the exercise
once again turned awry as she underwent a kind
of seizure, her limbs becoming rigid and her eyes
rolling upwards, before falling into an unconscious
trance during which time she sank to the floor and
her hand made rapid although illegible gestures of

writing in the sand until she awoke a few minutes later.

By the time Lydia had been in my clinic for two years, I had come to the conclusion that there could be no possible cure for her without coming to a complete understanding of what was causing her writings; in other words, their hidden meanings. At the same time, I began to feel that it was entirely useless for her to live in the clinic together with the patients suffering from serious mental problems when she was quite normal in her everyday behaviour. It began to seem to me, although this was perhaps in my imagination and a consequence of a certain worry, that the clinic was having a negative effect on her mental state, and that she was becoming stranger and more dreamy and absent-minded there, and even more distant from ordinary reality, so I determined to restore her to a normal daily life by taking her into my home, which I did with the consent of my wife. She lodged in a room at our house, embroidering, reading, and singing. She sang extremely well; astonishingly, in fact for a young woman who had never had music lessons, as she told us. For the rest, she accompanied us on our walks and outings and took her meals with us, while I continued to hold regular writing sessions with her, now more in order to probe the secrets I felt convinced her writings were revealing than to effect any kind of pragmatic cure in which I no longer believed.

In the summer of 1874, her family sent for her to pass the holidays with them. She had returned home for the summer each year since she first came. All seemed entirely normal – yet I was never to see her again.

I never received any further explanation. A man was sent to fetch her things, bearing a short note to the effect that the treatment was to be terminated, and that was the last I ever saw or heard of one of the most fascinating cases it has been given to me to encounter in the whole of my career.

CHAPTER SEVEN

*In which Vanessa is treated to a fascinating discourse
on Mendel's theory of genetics*

Having told Professor Correns to come and pay us a
visit on Wednesday afternoon, I had left the garden gate
invitingly open, and upon hearing his step upon the path
at three o'clock precisely, I hurried out to greet him. He
was looking all about him with an air of great pleasure.

'The poetry of your garden, Mrs Weatherburn!' he
said admiringly.

I dearly love my garden, which is quite ample
compared to others along Malting Lane, stretching up
the side of the house to the street as well as behind the
house. In spring and summer it is a riot of flowers and
sunshine. January, however, is not usually the season at
which I most appreciate it. Thanks to the clemency of

Cambridge weather it is very green, but the taller plants tend to wilt sadly and have an air of awaiting the spring with the same glum patience I sometimes feel myself when the wintry weeks stretch on for too long. But Professor Correns had already spotted the nearly-empty vegetable patch at the back, in which nothing remained but a few blackened and broken stems.

'Ah,' he said, hurrying over eagerly to have a closer look. 'Yes. I see that you do know peas.'

'Just the ordinary type,' I said.

'*Pisum sativum*,' he said. 'That is exactly what my own research was concerned with. Having cultivated them, you probably noticed that the peas produced are sometimes green and sometimes a yellow colour; also that they are sometimes round and sometimes wrinkly.'

I had never paid much attention to these details, and dared not mention that the peas that I harvested for the enjoyment of a summer day's gardening were generally shelled by Mrs Widge. But my conscience was relieved by calling up the image of the dishes of roast mutton that she fondly served us, accompanied by our own garden peas and tiny carrots. Yes, a few were wrinkled and the colour of the peas was not entirely even. Although if any peas looked too yellowish, I suspected that Mrs Widge might actually throw them away. However, I nodded vigorously, and seeing that the professor was on the point of launching into a discourse, I asked him whether he would like to come indoors.

He looked up at the sky, then at the house through the

open door of which the wild shouts of the children could be heard, and then suggested that as it was a particularly lovely day for January, we could perhaps take a turn. The idea did not displease me, and hurrying indoors to put on hat and wraps, I called out to the children's nurse that I was going for a walk and hastened quickly out again before they had time to cling to me with a show of wild protestations performed uniquely for the histrionic fun of it, which tended to redouble in intensity in the presence of outsiders.

'Let us walk about the Lammas Land,' I said as we started down the lane. The professor accompanied my steps, looking around him with unmitigated delight.

'It is like a country village here,' he said. 'It is almost difficult to imagine that we are but ten minutes' walk from the busy colleges.'

'Less than that, if you count Newnham,' I said, pointing towards Sidgwick Avenue. 'It's just a two-minute walk that way.' But Professor Correns was not interested in Newnham College. Reaching the end of the lane, we entered Laundress Green, and I began to do the honours of the place, pointing to the public house on the bridge and to the back of the Darwins' granary with its little white balcony, but he seemed to have something else on his mind. As we crossed over a small bridge under which the river runs sluggishly through the fen grasses, he turned to me with an air of secrecy, and I thought that he was going to pick up the interrupted conversation about the mating habits of pea plants, when instead he said in a hushed tone,

'Rumour has it that last year you discovered a body floating in this place.'

'Oh!' I said. For many months I had been unable to cross the Lammas Land without recalling the events surrounding that murder, but of late that association had begun to fade away under the influence of other more recent events. 'No, no, rumour exaggerates. I did not find the body, I merely helped in understanding the facts that had led to its being there.'

'But it was here?'

'Not quite. It was more over there, I believe. Caught in the reeds and grasses.'

'I have heard that you are regularly involved in detective activities,' he went on, and I noted in his tone respect mingled with a curiosity of which he was slightly ashamed but unable to completely repress. The enquiry in his blue eyes was intense and alive with intelligence. Normally I loathe talking about these things, or perceiving the prurient interest they occasionally arouse. But I did not feel that now, and I became aware with a blush that it was because his interest was not directed at the grisly tales of murder, but at myself. This sensation was unusual and, to be quite honest, not unpleasant. In any case, it provoked in me an uncharacteristic expansiveness, and I found myself telling him not only about the girl who had been killed, but, to my own surprise, all about Sebastian and the source of my sudden interest in heredity. And by this circuitous route, having crossed and circled the Lammas Land and Laundress Green from top to bottom, edge to edge and bridge to bridge, we found ourselves naturally back at the subject which had first brought us together, and caused such emotion to Mrs Bates.

'You were telling me about heredity in peas,' I said.

'Of course! Exactly. I was telling you that the stamens of the flower function as the male,' he responded at once, launching into a lecture with the natural flow of an experienced professor, 'and the pistil functions as the female organ, which is fertilised by the stamens in the following manner: they shed the yellow powder that you can see upon their tips, the pollen, onto the pistil, and that fertilises it and allows it to produce a pea pod containing peas.

'Now, if you allow the flower to self-fertilise and obtain a pea pod, from which you extract a pea which you then use as a seed for another pea plant, you will, as I said earlier, obtain a pea plant having characteristics identical to the parent plant; green or yellow, round or wrinkly and so forth. That is because, in this case, the mother and father are from the same plant, so of the same type. Such plants are called purebred, and they carry the strains of their characteristics from generation to generation, exactly as one might see certain characteristics carried down in strains of purebred horses or dogs, for example.

'What Gregor Mendel wished to do was to see if it was possible to comprehend whether the transmission of visible features in peas and the role of the pollen and the pistil is governed by a discernible theory. To separate the role of pollen and pistil, he cross-fertilised plants of different strains.

This is a technique which has been practised by farmers for many, perhaps hundreds, of years: it consists in opening the immature flowers of the pea plant and cutting off the stamens, and then using a small brush or even the fingers to remove pollen from a different plant and brush it onto the immature pistil. One then carefully closes the flower petals and leaves the whole situation alone until the pea pod emerges, after which one can study the properties of the individual peas in the pod, and then plant them and observe the properties of the plants they produce. He was a monk, if you recall, in Brünn, and had all the necessary time and leisure to do as he pleased in the monastery garden, and the approval of his superior as well.

'In order to carry out numerical observations, Mendel repeated his experiments on many hundreds of plants, crossing the same type with the same type, for each of the many possibilities, again and again, observing and counting the results. What had been believed at first – that crossing a plant with green peas and a plant with yellow peas could produce a plant with either green or yellow peas (regardless of which parent was green and which yellow), and that it was merely a matter of chance – turned out to be false. In fact, crossing purebred strains yielded very clear and observable results. Considering just the property of the peas being green or yellow, he saw over a great number of experiments that crossing two purebred green plants could only produce green plants, and crossing two purebred yellow plants could only produce yellow, whereas crossing a green and a yellow invariably produced a green.

'He then proceeded to mate purebred plants with those of the second generation of mixings, and now he observed something new. Mating a purebred green with a green that was actually of green and yellow parentage produced only green offspring, but mating a purebred yellow with a green of mixed parentage produced green exactly half the time, and yellow exactly half the time. As for the mating of two mixed plants, the result was a green offspring three-quarters of the time, and a yellow offspring one quarter. Can you guess the rule? It is a purely mathematical question by now!'

I stopped and leant my elbows on the railing of a bridge, ruminating over the pattern he was describing. He stopped next to me, and extracting a crumpled envelope from his pocket together with a stub of pencil, he drew the following diagram.

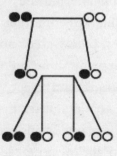

'Look!' he exclaimed. 'This is Mendel's stroke of genius, and the picture explains it all! Each organ, whether stamen or pistil, must contain two *markers* of some kind, which can be either green or yellow. From the stamens only one of the two can pass to the offspring, and from the pistils again only one, and these are selected by random chance! In a purebred green plant, both markers will be green for the stamens and the pistils, so, if they are crossed, they can only pass green markers to the offspring, and for purebred yellow it will be the same. But when you cross the plants – then what happens to a plant with one green and one yellow marker?'

'Well,' I said, 'you claimed that crossing a green and a yellow purebred always creates a green, so I am obliged to conclude that a plant with one green and one yellow marker must be green.'

'Logically spoken!' he cried and again looked at me with an undue measure of admiration. 'Mendel called these markers *alleles*, and the fact that green and yellow together make green, he described by saying that the green allele is dominant and the yellow recessive. Thus, of the four possible father-mother combinations green-green, green-yellow, yellow-green and yellow-yellow, only the last one will actually show yellow peas – so only one quarter of the offspring, on average, will be yellow! But the mixed plants will contain alleles that are totally invisible when observing the plants themselves, but that will affect a certain number of the offspring, according to the laws of probability. Generalise this theory to all possible physical traits, and you have the entire theory of their heredity and the manner in which they are passed down through the generations.'

'Is that mystery not contained in the nature of the

alleles?' I said. 'They seem to hold the secret of it, whatever they are.'

'We do not yet know their precise nature,' he said confidently, 'but we will. They are some kind of purely physical entity, microscopically small and carried within each living creature. When we have sufficiently powerful microscopes, we will perhaps be able to observe them physically. As to the mechanism that ensures that each creature carries a pair of alleles and passes exactly one of them to the offspring, that is also a physical reality. The power of Mendel's theory is that it proves that the choice of which allele passes down proceeds according to the laws of probability. For the rest, the only mystery that remains is how God could fabricate machines as utterly complex and fascinating as living creatures surely are. And the question of God's power will no doubt remain forever beyond our grasp.'

'You mean that human beings must be content to be satisfied with the physical explanation, as long as it is complete.'

'For myself,' he said, 'between the physical description of the alleles, and the mathematical description of their behaviour, it is the theory that I find the most interesting. Can you imagine that Mendel understood why, when a yellow pea plant is crossed with a purebred green, they will have only green offspring, but exactly one quarter of the grandchildren provided by mating those offspring will be yellow? And how many typical human characteristics of heredity are explained by that same observation?'

'You're right – that is striking,' I said, my thoughts reverting suddenly to Sebastian. 'I have often heard that many traits are seen to "skip a generation", and to pass directly from grandparent to grandchild without being visible in the parents. Do you think that Mendel's theory could really explain it?'

'But it is certain!' he said. 'For one particular example of such a thing, one might say that it could be due to many complex combinations of heredity, but when such a thing is perceived very generally, there is no doubt that it must be interpreted as a consequence of the theory.'

'This is one of the most fascinating things I have ever heard,' I declared. I was bemused and seduced by it all: it seemed so very revealing, so daring, so deep and yet so fundamentally simple – and so patently true! 'But still,' I went on, 'there is something I don't understand. If your theory explains the hereditary transmission of physical features – and I quite understand that human features are subject to a great many more variations than pea plants, and therefore the number of possibilities is gigantic, yet the mathematical laws governing them would be the same – what about the transmission of non-physical attributes?'

'You mean such as character?' he asked.

'Yes. Such as often-noted family tendencies such as a quick temper, or a high intelligence. Or – or musical gifts.'

'The question is both deep and subtle,' he said, 'and I have pondered it myself a great deal. I have finally arrived at the conclusion that, in spite of appearances, there is no way to be certain that these traits are not just as much consequences of a physical disposition as visible features are. Could not a musical talent be a consequence of a physical superiority of the ears, causing more acute appreciation of sounds that already seem beautiful to everyone?'

'But surely the love of music, the feelings of emotion connected to art and the ability to communicate them are more than just a fine ear,' I said.

'Can we be certain? Could not an emotional, artistic temperament be a consequence of a more fragile heart, thus more easily and more strongly moved, again, by visions that are considered lovely by all? Could not a tendency to rage be due to some physical quality of the brain or the body?'

'We do speak of "hot blood",' I replied thoughtfully. 'Someone, somewhere, must have had an intuition of your claim that character traits are purely physical, to invent such a phrase. Yet it shocks my feelings!'

'It shocked mine also, at the beginning,' he said. 'And, of course, it is true that education can be another powerful vehicle for transmission of certain things between the generations, but not this kind of thing. Certainly, Mendel's ideas go beyond and even against many received notions about character. Yet I have come to believe in them absolutely. If I see any remarkable resemblances between any two members of a family, I now attribute them automatically to heredity, and begin to reflect upon what physical peculiarity they might reflect.'

'I suspect that if I think about it enough, I will soon begin to do the same,' I admitted. 'It is too convincing. It opens up new vistas of possibilities – albeit slightly frightening ones. But now that I understand it, I cannot help believing in it. Even before I have had time to get used to it.'

'That is because you are a very unusual young woman,' he said, taking my arm.

CHAPTER EIGHT

*In which Vanessa attempts to understand
what the suicide note might have meant*

'Vanessa! It's me! I'm visiting at home for a few days
– I simply had to see how you were getting on!' Rose's
delightful face beamed at me from the doorway. The
afternoon sun shone on her thick, wavy hair, once
gold, now burnished to the colour of ripe honey. Her
whole being radiated joie de vivre; the kind of happiness
that simply comes from inside, with no cause and no
explanation; some people are born happy and the
happiness wells up inside them no matter what the
circumstances. I felt how lucky it was for Rose, and for
those around her, that she could express her feelings in
music.

'I was going to write to you,' I told her. 'Do come

in. It's nearly teatime.' As I spoke, a tornado stormed through the front room in the form of the twins, who flung themselves bodily upon Rose, one clinging to her legs and the other attempting to scale the vertical surface of her back with the aid of her hair, which immediately came down.

'Rose! Rose! Rose!' they screamed in a cacophonous medley. I had already noticed with pleased astonishment how deeply they were attached to her, even though they rarely had occasion to see her; still, she had known them from the earliest moments of their existence, and in their little minds she was as familiar as their own nursery. It was a charming feature of their love for her, that they were able to sit silent and attentive through an entire concert of cello music, if only it was Rose who was playing.

'Dear me,' I remonstrated, trying to pull them off her as they shouted for her to come up to the nursery to see their newest toys. 'It seems we will not get any calm if we have tea at home. They won't stay upstairs if they know you're here. I propose a bargain,' I added, grasping each twin firmly by the arm in order to get its complete attention. 'Rose will play with you in the nursery for half an hour, and then Rose and Mamma will go out to tea and you will have yours in the nursery with Nurse.'

'I should love to,' said Rose warmly. 'It is amazing how they grow each time I look away for a few moments!' And she sailed off up the stairs, towed like a little ship by two eager tugs. An unseemly racket was immediately heard to proceed from the nursery, but I forbore to interfere.

Half an hour later I collected my things and went to fetch Rose, causing something of an uproar, which was fortunately soon quelled by the sight of three severe adult faces combined with the sudden production of a sponge cake for nursery tea. Rose and I took ourselves outside, and walked across the Green to a tea shop I was fond of, tucked away in Little St Mary's Lane.

It was not until tiny sandwiches, scones, jam, cream and a steaming teapot had been set before us that I undertook to tell Rose something of what I had learnt, and to ask her the questions that were troubling me. I recounted to her the entire tale of my Swiss adventure, and she listened intently, but at the end of my tale she sighed.

'I only wish he had really heard something on that evening!' she exclaimed. 'But I simply can't pick out anything special from what you describe. If only the doctor you haven't seen yet told him something special. But probably that would be too much to hope. For the rest, it sounds so banal that I'd have died if I had been there. Sebastian loved that kind of attention, though. He basked in it, he really did. He always wanted to be the centre of attention; always centre stage.'

I looked up quickly.

'You almost sound as though you didn't like him,' I remarked.

'No, no – I didn't mean it that way! I loved him, really. How could I not? Everyone did. He was so magnetic. He had such energy, and when he looked at you the effect was tremendously strong. He was ardent like flame. He made you feel drawn up in the whirlwind of his life when he paid attention to you, and everything seemed possible. Sebastian really reached for the stars, Vanessa. He wanted the fame and the wealth and the success, but only to laugh over. What he really wanted was to play music the way no one ever had before. I know what I'm trying to say even if it isn't coming out right. I should love to be able to make you see what he was like. He was inhabited by a kind of devil. I don't mean something evil, but something wild and strange, uncontrolled, that drove him, that made him too beautiful, too attractive, too irresistible from the outside, but that was burning him up inside. You know, there were times when he really seemed a little out of control. He could actually be a bit frightening, because he reacted to things so strongly and violently sometimes. He really needed to play the violin, to play out that thing that was inside him. The violin is really the devil's instrument, isn't it? Because it's also wild. Can you imagine the devil playing the harpsichord?'

'No, I suppose not,' I said, 'but perhaps I should have thought of him playing the drums.'

'Drums express the savage within us, not the devil,' she said, smiling. 'Anyway, this is all a digression. I wanted to tell you something about Sebastian. You know, I'm glad he was engaged to Claire, because that made it impossible for me to fall in love with him. I mean, it helped me keep my distance and protect myself. Otherwise, I might very well have fallen in love with him, and that wouldn't have been good at all.'

'Why not?'

'Because of the centre stage thing.' She blushed. 'Claire was content to be his shadow and to pour all her love for him into her music, which she offered to him as the supreme gift. She is enormously talented, but her interpretations were largely adapted to his. For the trio, of course, we all adapted to each other to some extent, and I found his approach exciting and experimental, and also very beautiful. But when I play sonatas for piano and cello, I don't want to be upstaged by the pianist. I want to play them *my* way. I want someone who will share my ideas and help them bloom, without sacrificing either my ideas or his. Playing with Sebastian helped me discover many things about music, but not much about myself. And that's what I will really need from the person I fall in love with. I don't think I could do what Claire did.'

'If one is lucky, one's husband can be remarkably good about letting one be what one truly needs to be,' I said philosophically, spooning up some cream. I had a fleeting feeling of guilt which, upon closer examination, turned out to be a mixture of a suspicion that Arthur, while indeed being remarkably good, was making something of a sacrifice in letting me do quite so very much as I pleased with regards to detective work, and a feeling that I oughtn't to be enjoying such a delightful tea without the twins. But I ignored it firmly.

'Enough about me,' said Rose eagerly, pouring herself another cup of tea and smiling at the waitress who hovered near her elbow with a pot of hot water. 'Now that you've told me what you found out, tell me what you think! Do you have any ideas? Have you put two and two together?'

'Not yet,' I admitted. 'I don't know enough. It doesn't make sense to me yet in the least. I have been thinking over the possibilities, but none of them seem to be particularly supported by the facts.'

'Well,' she said, 'let's hear them.'

'I asked myself what kind of thing Sebastian could have found out about himself, and I decided we could divide the possibilities into two types: on the one hand, he found out something about his own character – for example, by a spontaneous reaction to some event of which his higher self disapproved; on the other, he could have found out something purely factual about himself – for example, that he was suffering from some illness.'

'That makes sense,' she said. 'Well said. It's an important distinction. Pity he didn't say more in his note. *Please try to understand* – what a thing to say, as if one could!'

'Perhaps he tried to say more, but found himself unable to explain,' I suggested. 'His note does sound a bit like a beginning, as though he had meant to say more, and then gave it up as a bad job. Well, that is our task, isn't it? To find out what it may have been. So, returning to my classification, I want first to try to imagine what kind of thing might have provoked Sebastian to feel negatively about himself. Does anything I've said give you any ideas?'

'No. Really not, I'm afraid. You know, I simply can't imagine Sebastian feeling really badly about himself. Even if he discovered some feeling inside him that he didn't know about, he would be more likely to observe it with fascination, even with delight. He really loved living, Vanessa. Much more than with morality, he was concerned with life itself.'

'But surely, if it were something really bad, he could hardly feel delight.'

'Well, but what could possibly be so very bad? He discovered that he liked to smoke opium? He fell madly in love with somebody else? He committed a crime? And liked it, perhaps?'

'Such levity! No, nothing I've learnt indicates that anything of that sort happened. But I was wondering about the fact that Herr Hegar was reluctant to schedule a concert of your trio playing the Beethoven Triple Concerto.'

'That was a pity, to be sure. But if Sebastian were to kill himself over not being able to play such a concert, then the concert would be even more impossible than it already was. That makes no sense at all, Vanessa!'

'Oh, I wasn't suggesting that he felt disappointment. I was wondering if he thought of himself as betraying the trio, by accepting to return and play other concerts without you. Perhaps he realised that he would actually be able to sacrifice the trio for the sake of ambition, and disliked observing such a trait in himself.'

'But Vanessa, surely you don't think it would have been a problem if Herr Hegar had preferred to invite him back alone to play some virtuoso violin concerto instead of the Beethoven? Of course we'd have understood. It was just an idea, that Beethoven concert. The musical world is like that. You play the concerts that you can; it's no use crying over those you can't.'

'I suppose so. But you don't think that Sebastian might have been troubled inside by the knowledge that he risked always keeping his wife in what she might perceive as a subordinate position, professionally?'

'Vanessa – have you looked around you? Do you know any couples in which the wife is not in a subordinate position? I know we've just entered the twentieth century, Vanessa dear, and that we both expect great strides in the advancement of women from it! But I think you need to give it a little time. We've had it for less than a month!' She laughed, and so did I.

'You mean that Claire would not have expected anything different?'

'Of course not. Claire would probably have stopped playing concerts once she had children, and stayed at home, teaching them their scales.'

'Does that really go without saying? Will you do that?'

'Well . . . no, I don't think I will. A woman doesn't absolutely *have* to, you know. There are some exceptions. You've heard of Clara Schumann, the wife of the composer? She went on playing concerts while having eight children and then losing her husband first to madness, then to death. She never stopped playing publicly until she was seventy! She died just a few years ago. And yet, you know, it can't have been easy for the children. And Clara too considered herself subordinate to her husband, musically speaking. He composed, she interpreted. She longed to compose, but she didn't have the time because she needed to play to support the family. Crowds adored her, and she adored her husband. Well, why not? She was famous, she was celebrated, she enjoyed the limelight as much as anybody, and yet her husband came first. That corresponds to the idea of the perfect couple, doesn't it? I do wonder if the twentieth century will eventually change that ideal, or not.'

'So you think that Claire would have accepted that Sebastian pursue a grand career in music, at some point leaving her behind, without any resentment?'

'Without resentment towards him, in any case. Surely women sometimes feel a little resentment against their destiny in general. But Claire is not much of a fighter. Believe me, Vanessa, Sebastian did not kill himself over such a thing.'

'I do believe you.'

'But then, what other possibilities exist?'

'Perhaps he fell in love, and committed some mad act on the way home from Switzerland?'

'You think he might have done that? But then, I think he would simply have broken off his engagement to Claire. He'd have written to her – why, now that I think of it, he'd have written just what he did write. *Darling Claire, how can I say this to you? I've found out something about myself – I can't go on with it any more. I'm sorry. I'm so sorry. Please try to understand.* He might have written exactly that!'

'But you've forgotten the most important part, the bit about cursed inheritance and the danger of taking risks. If this idea is right, what would he have meant by that? Could Sebastian's father have been a known philanderer?'

Rose burst out laughing.

'Oh dear. No, I'm afraid not. From what I've heard, poor Mr Cavendish was a very upright old gentleman afflicted with gout. He was ill and in pain for many months before he died. Sebastian says he was always correct and just, and he does remember him with respect, even though he was a rather cold and distant kind of father. He never played with Sebastian as a boy or anything like that, and always talked about improvement. Still, though, he encouraged him to excel and allowed him to follow his bent and study music when so many other fathers would have wanted him to study law as he did himself. He said that if that was Sebastian's choice, he would have to make his own way in the world, but Sebastian says he didn't mean this disapprovingly; he thought it was good for a young man to make his own way in the world. He left nothing to Sebastian when he died, by the way. His will left all of his worldly goods to his wife. I don't think it was an awful lot, though. Sebastian says they were wealthier when he was a child, but the family fortunes declined badly, and they live very simply now. But Mrs Cavendish is to be married next summer, to Lord Warburton, the gentleman who accompanied her to the memorial concert.'

'Really,' I said. 'That will improve her circumstances. Still, though, what if her first husband was a rake in his youth, and then settled down?'

'If that was the case, Sebastian knew nothing about it. I can promise you that, because Mrs Cavendish is awfully keen on keeping up appearances. She would never have told him such a thing, even if she knew about it herself. No, I can't believe that Sebastian suddenly discovered that he had inherited libertine tendencies by meeting some lovely maiden on the way home in the sleeping car. You know, if he had had a tendency to fall in love easily, we would have known about it already. It's not as though he wasn't surrounded by female admirers. He wasn't like that, and even if it happened once, that would prove nothing.'

'I suppose so. Oh dear. Anyway, I hardly believe that such a trait can even be inherited. I suspect it's more of a caprice of nature, or else an act of rebellion against a strict upbringing.'

'So, we have to exclude this possibility as being as unlikely as the previous one.'

'Well, then. Who else might Sebastian have inherited

anything from? Who else was in his family?'

'No one that he knew,' she said. 'Mr Cavendish's parents died long before Sebastian was born. Mr Cavendish's father was a merchant, and I recall Sebastian saying that he felt he had nothing in common with his father's side of the family. And he had no aunts or uncles, no sisters or brothers. It was just his mother and him.'

I set down my teacup and leant back. 'We seem to have run out of ideas as to what he might actually have learnt about himself and considered as inherited,' I said. 'Let's think about the other idea: he realised something quite different – not a feeling, but a fact. A dreadful fact of some kind; something he simply couldn't live with.'

Rose giggled nervously.

'I'm sorry, Vanessa. Sebastian is dead, and he was so much a part of my life, in a way much deeper than just friendship. He brought me a passionate intensity of music making that was a miracle each time. I miss him more than you can imagine, musically. Whenever I play with John instead of Sebastian, it simply hurts inside. Yet this whole conversation is making me realise that I'm just not able to take his suicide seriously. I simply can't face that it really happened, or make myself understand that there must have been a reason. Everything you're suggesting seems outrageous, ridiculous, out of the question! What could he possibly have discovered that could have such an effect? The more you make me think about it, the more it seems absurd!'

'Could it have been something to do with his violin? I heard that he inherited that from his grandfather.'

'Oh yes. He loved his violin. It was an extraordinary instrument, just right for his playing, although sometimes he would have wished for more power. But he could produce strains of madness on this one. It went so well with him. It had a lion's head instead of the scroll. Have you heard about that? That was just the kind of thing that appealed to him; something peculiar, mad, different, full of energy. A roaring lion instead of a dainty scroll. That was Sebastian all over.'

'Perhaps he discovered that the violin was stolen?' I suggested. 'That it didn't really belong to him?'

This time she laughed outright.

'He died because he couldn't face life without his violin? Or because he was going to be flung into prison for the rest of his life on account of his grandfather's theft? No, I'm afraid not. The violin was offered to Sebastian's grandfather by a patron, because he was an incredible violinist. It was quite common in those days; it still is, for that matter. It went to Sebastian's mother, and she gave it to him. It really was his.'

'Well,' I said, 'you say he inherited nothing from his father, but at least here we have an inheritance from the grandfather. What else did he inherit?'

'Don't say that he inherited his gift – he used to hate it when people said that and he would deny it outright. That's rather odd, now that I think of it. I wonder why he cared?'

'I have heard about that. Yes, it is striking; the refusal to accept what everyone noticed. Perhaps that might be the key. It's a pity I know so little about the nature of musical talent.'

'I have an idea,' exclaimed Rose eagerly. 'You should come with me to the Royal Academy once, and talk to my professor. He often talks about musical inheritance! I think he has heaps of ideas. Oh, Vanessa, he is a marvellous, luminous man; a darling, but also a genius. You would love him. He is certainly the best person to talk to about this. And now that I think of it, we can try to arrange for you to meet Sebastian's professor as well. Who knows what you might learn from him?'

'I should love to meet them,' I said. 'But the problem seems very difficult. I hardly know what to ask them. I must admit, I am sorely puzzled.'

'Please don't give up!' she exclaimed. 'Please, Vanessa, do go on trying to understand! He deserves it. He loved Claire; he loved children – he wanted lots. He was so vibrant. It must have been something enormous to take his life away so suddenly. We do have something to go on – after all, he *did* kill himself, so there *was* a reason – it really does exist! Please, do go on trying to understand. I think I'll never really rest until I know. And for Claire it's a matter of life or death. She's like a ghost with not knowing. Please don't give up!'

'I'm not going to,' I said firmly. 'Absolutely not. I shall be in London next week for a meeting of the Society for Psychical Research. Yes, I know it's strange, but I'll explain it later. Anyway, when I come I shall visit you as well, and you shall take me to meet your teacher. I promise, I'm far from giving up. As you say, the reason most definitely exists, and we have only to find it!'

CHAPTER NINE

*In which Vanessa attends a meeting of
the Society for Psychical Research,
sees some very strange things, and hears their explanation*

I hastened into the large lecture hall, removed my wrap, which was unpleasantly damp from the disagreeable sleet falling steadily outside, and slipped into one of the last remaining empty seats, situated modestly near the back of the hall. The president of the Society for Psychical Research stepped onto the stage, introduced himself as Mr Frederic Myers, and began to say a few words on the subject of the presentation about to take place.

'What is the purpose of our Society?' he began, very pertinently, as I thought. 'Why, faced with the scepticism and derision of the public, do we pursue against all odds a direction of knowledge guided by observations which suffer from their irregularity, their doubtfulness and their frequent infestation with the forces of vanity and dishonesty? What, ultimately, is our goal?'

He paused and glanced around challengingly, then continued.

'Starting from various standpoints, we are endeavouring to carry the newer, the intellectual virtues into regions where dispassionate tranquillity has seldom yet been known. First, we adopt the ancient belief, implied in all monotheistic religion, and conspicuously confirmed by the progress of modern science, that the world as a whole – spiritual and material together – has in some way a systematic unity: and on this we base the novel presumption that there should be a unity of method in the investigation of all fact. We hold therefore that the attitudes, the habits of mind, the methods by which physical science has grown deep and wide should be applied also to the spiritual world. We endeavour to approach the problems of that world by careful collection, scrutiny, testing of particular facts; and we account no unexplained fact too trivial for our attention.[1]

'We are exceptionally lucky today, ladies and gentlemen,' he went on, 'to have the opportunity of welcoming to our premises one of the world's most fascinating and impressive mediums: Mademoiselle Hélène Smith of France! Mademoiselle Smith discovered her amazing talents eight years ago, and since that

[1] Actual words of Frederic Myers, president of the SPR in 1900, cited from the preface to the book *From India to the Planet Mars* (1899) by Th. Flournoy.

time she has provided us, the students of the spiritist world, with an incredible wealth of information from abroad, from the past, from the dead, and most recently and extraordinarily – a phenomenon truly unheard-of hitherto – from the planet Mars! As Mademoiselle Smith is presently in contact with spirits from Mars, you will very likely hear, when she appears on this stage and allows herself to be led into a trance, actual words of the Martian language, together with their translation into French by a Martian spirit. I myself will stand here to the side, out of the way, and write upon this large board, as silently as possible, the English translation of the French for your benefit.

'Following the session, we will hear two analyses of Mademoiselle Smith's visions, one by famed spiritualist Mrs Ellen Jackson from the United States of America, and the second by Professor Theodore Flournoy, expert in psychology and psychophysiology, from the University of Geneva. I beg you, ladies and gentleman, to welcome Mademoiselle Hélène Smith!'

I felt an expression of total mystification painting itself upon my face as Mr Myers described the medium's accomplishments, and I noticed the same expression reflected in many of the faces around me. Yet equally many were upturned towards the stage with every sign of delight and rapt attention. I firmly put aside the voice of reason that screeched with dismay within me. I do believe that Arthur and his scientific friends have had too much influence over me of late. I *know* there is much in life than can startle even the most rational of scientists.

But – Mars?

The audience applauded politely as the curtain at the back of the stage parted, letting through a tall and striking woman with black hair piled high in a manner befitting an earlier century. This woman greeted us with reserve, then took her place in an easy chair that Mr Myers pushed forward for her, and closed her eyes. The electric lights on the stage and in the hall were dimmed until her outline was blurred in the shadows. Only a tiny light remained, brightening the board upon which Mr Myers was to write his translations. This gentleman then approached the medium and laid his hand upon her forehead, reciting the following words in French with a strong British accent:

Pose bien doucement ta main sur son front pâle
Et prononce bien bas le doux nom d'Esenale!

He spoke the name of Esenale with the strong emphasis of one who calls for a person, then removed his hand from the lady's forehead and walked quickly and silently to the edge of the stage.

A great sigh proceeded from Mademoiselle Smith's lips, and in a ringing voice, she proclaimed:

'*Cé évé pléva ti di benez essat riz tes midée durée!*'

There was a short silence, then Mr Myers called out: 'Esenale! Please translate into French!'

'*Je-suis-chagrin-de-te-retrouver-vivant-sur-cette-*

129

laide-terre!' emerged, in a foreign-sounding staccato, from the mouth of the medium. Mr Myers hastily wrote: *I am sad to find you still living upon this ugly Earth.*

'*Mitchma mitchmon mimini tchouainem mimatchineg masichi-nof mézavi patelki abrésinad navette naven navette mitchichénid naken chinoutoufich,'* she burst forth suddenly, and then, spinning out of control, she continued so rapidly that one could only catch syllabic snatches such as '*ték . . . katéchivist.. méguetch . . . kété . . . chimék'.* At length her voice slowed to nearly a stop, and in a sepulchral tone she clearly enunciated:

'*Dodé né ci haudan té méss métiche Astané!'*

'Translate, Esenale!' shouted Mr Myers quickly, into the moment of silence that followed these words.

'*Ceci-est-la-maison-du-grand-homme-Astané!'* stuttered the medium. *This is the house of the great man Astané!* wrote Mr Myers. And then she fell completely silent. Her eyes stared up at the ceiling with a weirdly empty expression, and occasionally her body was shaken by strange shudders, or she made peculiar motions with her hands. The audience waited in transfixed silence as the minutes passed. After perhaps a quarter of an hour, during which the attempts of the more impatient spectators to while away the time by whispering together were sharply quelled by Mr Myers holding up his hand like a severe schoolteacher, she stirred, and slowly awoke. Mr Myers hurried forward with a glass of water, from which she weakly sipped, then she sat up and looked out at us as though astonished to find herself in such a place.

'Will you recount to us what you saw?' he asked her respectfully. She answered in a lovely, musical voice totally unlike that which had pronounced the words we heard before.

'I stood before an astonishing house of a shape and colour I had never seen before. A man of dark complexion emerged and took me by the hand and led me away. I knew that this was Astané. I saw before me a landscape and some peculiar people. I was on the border of a beautiful blue-pink lake. A bridge with transparent sides formed of yellow tubes like the pipes of an organ seemed to have one end plunged into the water. The earth was peach-colour; some of the trees had trunks widening as they ascended, while those of others were twisted. Later a crowd approached the bridge, in which one woman was especially prominent. The women wore hats that were flat, like plates. I do not know exactly who these people were, but I had the feeling of having conversed with them before. Astané went onto the bridge. He carried in his hands an instrument somewhat resembling a carriage-lantern in appearance, but which, when pressed, emitted flames, and which seemed to be a flying-machine. By means of this instrument the man left the bridge, touched the surface of the water, and returned again to the bridge. He took me by the hand and led me back through the emptiness of space.'

Upon this, the lady arose from her seat, crossed the stage, and arriving in front of the board where Mr Myers had noted down the two brief Martian sentences that had been translated into French, she proceeded to make a drawing of a square house of unusual shape, with decorations like battlements at the top and strange trees on either side.

'This is the house I saw; the house of Astané,' she told us in quite a normal tone. She smiled with pleasure and modestly inclined her head as the audience burst into spontaneous applause and Mr Myers led her off the stage to some quiet place, no doubt, where she could recover her strength over a cup of strong tea.

A moment later, another woman appeared upon the stage, and was introduced to us as Mrs Ellen Jackson from Connecticut. She took her place confidently behind a lectern that was quickly pulled forward in place of the easy chair. Dressed to the height of fashion in a tailor-made suit with a sailor collar which firmly structured her rather generous forms, she began to speak with an American accent, a loud voice, and a degree of enthusiasm typical of our visitors from the other side of the Atlantic but which is rarely or never visible here in England, where its original freshness has been blunted, perhaps, by the passage of too many centuries. Mrs Jackson assured us that Hélène Smith was the most astonishing medium she had ever encountered, and this in a long tradition of association with the most reputed mediums of America, including herself.

'When I found,' she told us emphatically, 'that poor Hélène was having to work in a department store for her living, standing behind the counter for up to eleven hours each day till her health was worn to a thread, I said to myself, "Something must be done about this!" I was travelling across Europe to hear all the most famous mediums from over here, and what I heard from Hélène left me just utterly spellbound, as you probably are right this minute. I simply couldn't let such a treasure go to waste selling gloves and scarves, I thought, with all her knowledge of secrets withheld from the rest of us! We need to hear everything that Hélène has to tell us! And I want to tell you today that I have decided to free dear Hélène from the need to earn her living, thanks to my own good fortune which has enabled me to support people in need wherever and whenever I find them. I want to say that I've helped many a fascinating medium reach the apex of her talent, and none of them has ever seemed to me as worthy as Hélène Smith! People such as she are contributing to the advancement of knowledge beyond anything that science can achieve! Worthy as our astronomers are, they have not been able to reach as far as the planet Mars, and I never thought I would know what goes on in that mysterious place during my lifetime. I'm not going to talk about any kind of analysis of what Hélène says, because it doesn't need any. I am certain that it is all quite literally true. I have had enough experience of spirit communication to know about the invisible reality it reveals, and that it can tell us about places beyond the reach of science. Hélène's visions represent the only chance we have to learn about the planet Mars! And that's why I have offered Hélène the means to pursue her mediumistic activities without constraint, for the rest of her life! *Vive Mademoiselle Hélène Smith!*' And upon this, she burst into a spontaneous applause into which the audience joined with a general feeling of laughter and astonishment.

As we clapped, Mr Myers returned to the stage from the side, accompanied by a short professorial gentleman with a pointy beard. This was Professor Flournoy, specialist in psychology and psychophysiology from the University of Geneva: the very man who had discovered the amazing talents of Hélène Smith, or at least, revealed them to the world. Having been close to her for six years now, and having thus had the opportunity to observe every detail of the development and evolution of her visions, he had recently completed a book upon the subject, containing a full analysis of her visions and of the Martian language that spoke through her mouth. This book was to appear very shortly in print, and as Mr Myers informed us with some pride, we were now to be the first to hear some of the most significant parts of its contents.

Professor Flournoy greeted Mrs Jackson with a slight bow and, turning to the audience, pronounced a few words of grateful recognition for her grand and generous gesture. She thanked him, and proceeded to sail off the stage in a stately manner with Mr Myers, upon which the professor began his speech.

'The first task which investigators of obscure mental

phenomena set themselves is, naturally, that of separating and sifting the real, actually existent facts from the mass of fraud and deception created by mercenary charlatans. These, aided by the easy credulity of the simple-minded, have contrived so completely to bury from sight the true phenomena, that for a long time now the intelligent public has utterly refused to believe in the existence of any real phenomena of the kind, but insisted that everything when fully probed would be found to be mere delusion, the result of trickery and fraud.

'Probably no scientific fact since the dawn of modern science has required so great a weight of cumulative evidence in its favour to establish the reality of its existence in the popular mind than have the phenomena in question. I am glad to be able to say, however, that this task has finally been accomplished!

'Mademoiselle Smith is a high-minded, honourable woman, regarded by all her neighbours and friends as wholly incapable of conscious fraud. Moreover, she has been subjected to the closest surveillance on the part of a number of eminent physicians and scientists of Geneva for more than five years past, while Mrs Jackson, the famous medium from Connecticut whom we have just had the honour to hear, has been subjected to an even closer scrutiny by the Society for Psychical Research for the past fifteen years.

'Yet in spite of the fact that this society has announced its willingness to become responsible for the entire absence of fraud in both cases, there still remain a considerable number of ultra-sceptical persons who persist in asserting that fraud and deceit are at the bottom of, and account for, all this species of phenomena.

'The endeavour to explain these mysterious phenomena by scientific investigators has resulted in their adoption of one or other of two hypotheses, namely:

'1. That the phenomena are really of supernormal origin and emanate from the disincarnate spirits of the other beings, who return to earth and take temporary possession of the organism of the medium, talking through her mouth and writing with her hand while she is in a somnambulistic state.

'2. That the phenomena are the product of and originate in the subliminal consciousness of the medium.

'The first theory, exemplified by Mrs Jackson's earlier address, adduces as the essential argument in its support the frequently observed occurrence of mediums in trances speaking languages or expressing information that they do not know and cannot possibly know in their ordinary lives.

'The second theory, instead, credits the subliminal consciousness of the true medium with quite extraordinary powers of knowledge, memory, invention and understanding. When I first began regularly attending the séances of Hélène Smith, I hesitated for some time before coming to a final conclusion about which theory best describes the phenomena I then saw, and of which you have all been a witness today. In my present lecture, I will defend the hypothesis of the second theory.

'Let me attempt to explain why, by first saying that of all the traits that I discover in her tale of Martian romance – which consists in several dozen sessions similar to that which you witnessed today, but greatly varied and containing very little repetition of information – the most salient feature is undoubtedly this: *its profoundly infantile character*.'

The audience gasped collectively. Surely this was unheard-of insolence, stated so bluntly in the hallowed circles of the SPR!

'The candour and imperturbable naivety of childhood,' continued the professor, ignoring the noise, 'which doubts nothing because it is ignorant of everything, is necessary in order for one to launch himself seriously upon an enterprise such as the pretended exact and authentic depictions of an unknown world. An adult who is at all cultivated and has any experience of life would never waste time in elaborating similar nonsense; Mademoiselle Smith less than anyone, intelligent and cultivated as she is in her normal state.

'In general, it is the sitters who gather as much as they can of the strange words pronounced by Mademoiselle Smith in her states of trance, but, as you have just seen, that is very little, since Hélène, in her Martian state, often speaks with a tremendous volubility. Moreover, a distinction must be made between the relatively clear and brief phrases that are later translated by Esenale, and the rapid and confused gibberish the signification of which can never be obtained, probably because it really has none, being only a pseudo-language.

'Although as you saw, Hélène can preserve a certain memory of her visions in the waking state, and make reproductions of some of the things she saw, her verbo-motor hallucinations of articulation and of writing seem to be totally incompatible with her preservation of the waking state, and are invariably followed by amnesia. Hélène is always totally absent or entranced while her hand writes mechanically, and she is not aware of speaking Martian automatically, and does not recollect it. This incapacity of the normal personality of Mademoiselle Smith to observe at the time or remember afterwards any of her verbo-motor automatisms denotes a more profound perturbation than that which she experiences during her reception of visual hallucinations. For this reason, it is not surprising to me that her visual experiences bear an obvious resemblance to those which surround her in her ordinary life: the Martians closely resemble the human beings of our own planet in their appearance, and their houses and trees are mere fanciful variations upon ours.

'The Martian language, produced in a state of deeper trance leaving no memory behind, appears far less similar to anything familiar to us. Yet proceeding by analogy, I determined to inspect it more closely to see whether, in fact, it was not actually much more similar to Mademoiselle Smith's native French than it appeared on the surface. I began by a complete examination of the strange alphabet in which she wrote down the Martian sentences during her experiences of automatic writing.

'Now, it is not always easy to represent a language and its pronunciation by means of the typographical characters of another. Happily, the Martian, upon detailed examination and in spite of its strange appearance and the fifty millions of leagues which separate us from the red planet, turned out to be in reality so near a neighbour to French in both alphabet and syntax, that one can only conclude that either French-speakers are astoundingly lucky in having a language that is so close a neighbour to Martian, or that Mademoiselle Smith has invented the Martian language entirely, based on her intimate subliminal knowledge of her mother tongue. Let me give two simple examples supporting my claim that the pretended Martian language is nothing but an infantile travesty of French: it will suffice for you to contemplate for one moment the two sentences spoken in Martian here in this hall, whose translations are written upon the board before you:

'*Cé évé pléva ti di benez essat riz tes midée durée!*'
'*Dodé né ci haudan té méss métiche Astané!*'

'If you compare these sentences to their English translations, you may already be struck by a general similarity in sentence structure, compared for example with that of the Chinese. However, a moment's examination will show you that their relationship to French is yet one degree closer, in that the French translation admits of a word-by-word correspondence! Take for example the first sentence, rendered in English as "I am sad to find you still living upon this ugly Earth", which is as good a translation from the French as can be expected. But consider now the actual French as it proceeded from Hélène's very mouth: "*Je suis chagrin de te retrouver vivant sur cette laide terre!*" Here, each word in Martian has its exact equivalent in French, and, as a further indication, we note that the short words "*de*", "*te*", "*sur*" in French correspond to equally short monosyllables in the Martian. Comparing the French and the English of the second sentence reveals the same peculiarity: whereas "This is the house of the great man Astané" will not allow for a word-for-word correspondence, the French "*Ceci est la maison du grand homme Astané*" does, thanks to the contraction of the two words "of the" into the single French "*du*" which, remarkably, also exists in the Martian "*té*".

'If I add that the consonants which appear in the Martian language correspond very exactly to equivalent consonants in French, and that I have verified these claims on a great number of other Martian sentences pronounced over the course of dozens of séances, this will explain why I have been led to the inescapable conclusion that the Martian language is nothing but French, metamorphosed and carried to a higher diapason.

'Now, my argument would not be complete if I did not have a theory justifying, at the same time, the complete dissimilarity of the individual Martian words with those of the French, for it must be acknowledged that there is no trace of parentage, of filiation, of any resemblance whatever between the Martian and French vocabularies.

'But in fact, this apparent contradiction carries its explanation in itself, and gives us the key to Martian. This fantastic idiom is quite evidently the naive and somewhat puerile work of an infantile imagination, which had the idea of creating a new language, but which even while creating strange and unknown words, caused them to run in the accustomed moulds of the only real language that it knew. The Martian of Mademoiselle Smith, in other words, is the product of a brain or a personality which certainly has taste and aptitude for linguistic exercises, but which never knew that French takes little heed of the logical connection of ideas, and did not take the trouble to make innovations in the matter of phonetics, of grammar, or of syntax.

'The process of creation of Martian seems to have consisted in simply taking certain French phrases as such and replacing each word by some other chosen at random. That is why not only the order but even the structure and number of syllables of French words can be recognised in many Martian words.

'Yet the search for originality inherent in the creation of new language represents an effort of imagination with which Mademoiselle Smith must certainly be credited. Homage must also be rendered to the labour of memorisation necessitated by the making of a mental dictionary. She has sometimes, indeed, fallen into errors; the stability of her vocabulary has not always been perfect. But, finally, after the first hesitation and independently of some later confusions, it gives evidence of a praiseworthy terminological consistency, and which, no doubt, in time, and with some suggestive encouragement, would result in the elaboration of a very complete language.

'The preceding analysis of the Martian language furnishes its support to the considerations which the content of the romance has already suggested to us in regard to its author. To imagine that by twisting the sounds of French words a new language capable of standing examination could actually be created, and to wish to make it pass for that of the planet Mars, would be the climax of silly fatuity or of imbecility were it not simply a trait of naive candour well worthy of the happy age of childhood.

'If, however, one takes into account the great facility for languages known to have been possessed by Mademoiselle Smith's father, the question naturally arises whether in the Martian we are not in the presence of an awakening and momentary display of a hereditary faculty, dormant under the normal personality of Hélène, and from which she has never profited in an effective or conscious manner. It is a fact of common observation that gifts and aptitudes often skip a generation and seem to pass directly from the grandparents to the grandchildren, forgetting the intermediate link. Who knows whether Mademoiselle Smith, someday, may not cause the polyglot aptitudes of her father to bloom again with greater brilliancy, for the glory of science, through a brilliant line of philologists and linguists of genius?

'Let me insist once again upon my total conviction that while everything learnt from Hélène's visual and auditive hallucinations is a pure production of her subliminal consciousness, thus revealing the infantile elements which all of us carry deep within and which rarely or never emerge in our conscious state, I do not for one moment suggest the slightest effort at fraud or conscious manipulation on her part. Knowing Hélène as I do, I would lay down my honour as a guarantee that she is totally unaware of the tricks her subconscious is playing upon her, and hears and sees the messages exactly as though they proceed from the exterior. And above and beyond this statement, I would also beg to observe that while clearly containing, as I have shown, all the hallmarks of the infantile subconscious, her inventions reveal tremendous and impressive powers of creation and imagination which can only lead me to have the greatest admiration for a brain able to produce such a wealth of visionary material and, furthermore, unlike most, able to find its own startling and unusual manner of bringing this material to its conscious attention when it usually remains unrecognised, or expressed only through the confusion of dreams.

'It is hardly necessary to add, in conclusion, that the whole spiritistic or occult hypothesis seems to me to be absolutely superfluous and unjustified in the case of the Martian of Hélène Smith. Autosuggestibility set in motion by certain stimulating influences of the environment amply suffices to account for the entire Martian romance.'

He stopped speaking and laid his papers down upon the lectern. But poor Professor Flournoy – his carefully thought-out efforts had fallen largely on deaf ears! None of the enthusiasm which had greeted Mrs Jackson's address was expressed now, and it was only due to an extreme of courtesy that scattered and unenthusiastic applause was heard at all, while a couple of voices even cried out observations such as 'Shocking!' and 'Boo!' He gave a resigned smile, bowed slightly, and left the stage.

I remained in my seat as people stood up all around me, collecting their scarves and wraps. My head was spinning with the ideas set in motion by the professor's speech, which so remarkably pulled together the ideas that had been knocking about loosely in my head. Subliminal consciousness, unconscious infantile impulses emerging in states of trance, their expression by automatic writing, the role of heredity – even the mention of heredity from the grandfather that I had so lately discussed with Carl – or Professor Correns, rather. I sat turning these notions over in my mind, trying to find out what notion within them was tickling my brain, until I suddenly realised that the room was nearly empty, and only a few grey-bearded men remained clustered together near the door! I recognised

Professor Flournoy and Mr Myers amongst them, as well as the famous Sir Oliver Lodge. But what about Dr Bernstein, the man I had come here to see! I jumped out of my seat at once. Had I in my stupidity let him disappear?

CHAPTER TEN

*In which Vanessa meets a Swiss doctor of psychology
who recalls something that might
or might not be important*

Approaching the group, I addressed myself to Sir Oliver,
reminding him of the circumstances in which we had
last met. He hesitated for a moment, then laughed as the
recollection struck him.

'Mrs Weatherburn – of course! Delighted to see you
here. So, you have become a believer!' he exclaimed with
enthusiasm. 'As I remember, you used to be something of
a sceptic. Am I not right?'

'I was,' I said diplomatically. 'But now I realise that
we are surrounded by mysteries that science is not yet
able to explain. Today's demonstration was particularly
fascinating. I had read about automatic writing, but never

witnessed it. In fact, ever since reading this book I have greatly wished to meet its author,' I added, extracting Dr Bernstein's volume from my muff and showing it around.

'Why, then you are in luck,' he said, 'for the very man is standing in front of you,' and he indicated the gentleman next to him, short of stature, wearing the pointed beard that all doctors of psychology seemed to feel the need to sport as a badge of their identification with the ideas of Dr Freud, and smiling in surprised amusement at being so suddenly and so anxiously sought. Sir Oliver kindly performed the necessary introductions.

'To tell the truth, I wished to speak to you on a very particular matter,' I confided to the doctor in a low tone as soon as the general conversation about the day's events had died down somewhat, and the other gentlemen had taken up their canes and umbrellas in preparation for departure. 'If you are willing, perhaps we could talk in private for some moments?'

'But certainly,' he replied, casting me a glance bright with interest, and he led me out of the lecture room into the front hall of the building. After a glance outside, where freezing sleet continued to pour down as it had been doing relentlessly since the morning, he led me across the hall into a smaller, empty room equipped with desks and a blackboard.

'We shall be quite quiet here,' he said kindly. 'Now, do tell me how I can be of service to you.'

'Do you remember a concert in Zürich at the end of December, in which you heard a violinist named Sebastian Cavendish?'

He started visibly and looked at me with an entirely new expression. Clearly he had not expected this: Frau Bochsler must not have had the opportunity to tell him about my visit to her. Although he controlled it carefully, his reaction struck me as quite strong; there was a tension, a sudden attention that intrigued me greatly, and something fleeting in his eyes. What was it? A stab of pain?

I also took care to show nothing particular, but I felt very alert. The more so since the man, a trained psychologist, must probably know more about my thoughts and feelings than an ordinary person would. It was not, of course, that I had anything to hide; only that I preferred to remain in the shadows, as it were, observing while providing no food for observation. A difficult task before a man who looked at one like a mind-reader.

'Of course, of course,' he said in quite a natural voice, belying the palpable strain I noticed in his jaw and shoulders. 'A beautiful concert, quite unforgettable. I read about the sad death of the young artist in the newspaper a short time afterwards. A terrible loss.'

Ordinary words, and yet how significant they sounded in his mouth. Was this simply the way of all psychologists, to bring out the deeper meaning behind the everyday?

'The reason I am here,' I explained, 'is that his family has asked me to make some attempt to understand why he killed himself. You know that it was a suicide?'

'I read it,' replied the doctor, 'but I know nothing more.'

'Neither do they,' I told him. 'You see, all appeared to be going wonderfully well in his life. He was engaged to a lovely young woman, his career was brilliant, he was a beloved and successful artist. He left a note, however, which seems to indicate that he learnt something deeply troubling about himself in those final days before his death. His mother and his fiancée seem to have no idea what that thing could possibly be. Yet it was something terrible enough for him to take his own life, without even choosing to share it with them. They have remained stunned by it all.'

'That seems hard,' he said softly. 'He really gave no explanation?'

'All he said in his note was that he had found out this terrible thing, and could not go on. The only clue is that he used the words 'cursed inheritance' and said it was too dangerous to take risks with it. His fiancée is quite desperate. She has asked me to find out, if I can, exactly what it was that he discovered in those last days. I am trying to follow his traces step by step during the last days of his life, and to speak to everyone he spoke to then, in the effort to discover something, anything at all, out of the ordinary. I have already been in Zürich, and with the help of Frau Bochsler I have talked with nearly everyone who attended the party at her home that followed Sebastian's concert. You, however, were away, and as Frau Bochsler remembers seeing you having an animated conversation with Sebastian, she encouraged me to try to meet you here.'

'I see,' he said slowly. 'I see. Yet you have also read my book.' He came to a complete stop.

'Frau Bochsler gave it to me,' I told him, 'and I did read some of it, particularly the chapter about your own patient, Lydia K. It was fascinating. But I admit that that is not the reason why I wished to see you. I am sorry,' I added, taking his silence as a sign of disappointment.

'No, no,' he said. 'That is not why I ask you whether you read it. It is because of something that did happen, on that evening at Frau Bochsler's.'

An electric tingle traversed me.

'I cannot possibly see how what I said could have any connection to the young man's suicide,' he went on. 'And yet, it was strange. Perhaps it was wrong of me to mention it to him, but, you see, I was violently excited and moved by his physical appearance. I really do not think I am dreaming when I tell you that he bore a remarkable resemblance to a person I once knew well. To Lydia K., in fact.'

'He resembled Lydia K.!' I exclaimed, truly surprised.

'Astonishingly, to my eyes,' he replied, 'although there is no one else who could verify my feelings on the matter. But I will tell you that I could hardly take my eyes off him for the entire evening. He was a lively young man, full of laughter. It was only when he remained calm and stationary that the resemblance sprang to view; when he was talking and laughing, it ceased to be visible to me. Thus, I felt the need to stare at him continually, in an attempt to catch him at those moments when he should be listening attentively, in order to question and confirm what I was seeing again and again, a hundred times.'

'Did you think there was a chance that it was a family resemblance?' I asked.

'Naturally I did! If you have read my book, you know how much I searched for Lydia after she disappeared from my life. No, what am I saying? Of course you cannot know that – obviously I did not write about it in the book. But I can tell you now that I wrote many letters to Mr Charles King, her guardian, and called at his house in London more than once in the years after she was taken away from me. But he neither answered my letters nor received me, and I was unable to find out the true identity of the ward who had been using his name. He died five or six years later, and with him my last hope of finding her. But the dream of seeing her again someday has never left my heart. She was a most interesting person; a most extraordinary case.'

'And you talked to Sebastian about this?' I said, much excited. Surely, after the violin, here was yet another tale of inheritance arising out of the mists of time.

'I did, and I mentioned the name of Lydia King, but he had no knowledge of any such person, not even of the Christian name Lydia. Everyone in the room was referring to the fact that Sebastian was the grandson of a famous violinist named Joseph Krieger, so I even suggested to him that Lydia Krieger might have been her true name, but he told me that his mother's name was Tanis, not Lydia; he knew of no Lydia. My gently

151

probing questions revealed that his mother had not the slightest peculiarity in writing, nor any strong physical resemblance to her son other than a general effect of height and bearing, and also that she married in 1869, before I ever met Lydia.'

'How did he seem when he reacted to your remarks?' I asked. 'Shocked or surprised?'

'Not at all. Slightly amused and not particularly interested,' he said. 'I believe he actually remarked that it was rather a pity that there was no Lydia in his family, for he had always regretted being the only child of a widowed mother, and would have much appreciated the sort of extended family filled with grandparents, uncles, aunts and cousins that some of his friends enjoyed. But he certainly did not say this in a tragic manner. He was not a tragically minded person, but one more inclined, I should say, to laugh off adversity.'

'And that is all you told him? Only that you noticed a physical resemblance to a Lydia King you once knew, who would be in her fifties at the present time? And you asked if he was acquainted with any such person?'

'Well, I told him a few words about how I had known Lydia and what kind of patient she was, and that I had lost sight of her long ago and often wondered what had become of her.'

'And he did not appear especially moved.'

'No. Perhaps he would have been more interested if his attention had not been solicited by so many other admirers that evening, but it is certain that what I was telling him did not strike any particular chord.'

'You are a psychologist,' I said thoughtfully, 'you are used to reading human reactions. You do not think it possible that what you told him actually had a stronger effect than what he showed? That it really did provoke a deep inner disturbance? That it meant something to him which he was able to successfully hide?'

'Unless he was one of the greatest actors in the world, and able to control himself so completely in a situation of which he had no previous warning, I should have to say that that is completely impossible. His reaction corresponded in every way to that of a person who had never heard of any Lydia, K., King, Krieger or otherwise. I think I can state with certainty that the name simply meant nothing to him, and neither did the mention of automatic writing. He seemed perfectly unfamiliar with the phenomenon, probably viewing it as no more than a fad which fascinates the kind of person who attends meetings such as today's in this building.'

'But that "cursed inheritance",' I persisted. 'If, stimulated by your remarks, he did make enquiries, and discovered that he was related in some distant way to your Lydia, might not the cursed inheritance then refer to madness?'

'But Lydia was not mad! She was as sane as you or I – or as Sebastian himself – outside of her trances. And he was not likely to consider himself mad, either. Gifted with a wild and creative imagination he certainly was, but without a trace of hysteria or any other mental disease. Unless, perhaps, he too was subject to trances?'

'I have heard absolutely nothing of the kind,' I admitted.

'Then I cannot see what it could have meant to him. No, however we turn it around, it seems quite impossible to me that our conversation could possibly have led to his suicide. I would be most surprised to learn that he had even gone so far as to make enquiries. He did not seem to take the idea of a connection between Lydia and himself at all seriously.'

'And what about you? You must have been very disappointed by his reaction,' I said.

'Not by his reaction, but by the plain fact that he knew nothing,' he admitted. 'For me, on that evening when I saw his face and the traits that reminded me so strongly of her, I knew a moment of ecstatic hope that was then dashed. I did not say this to anyone, of course. But Lydia was like a shooting star that once traversed my life, illuminating everything, and then lost forever. Nothing has ever been the same for me since then. Nothing.'

I squeezed the old man's hand as I shook it goodbye, for the sadness in his eyes was deeper than tears. To my surprise, he squeezed mine gently back.

'I have never spoken of all this to a living soul,' he said. 'Not a single person has known of my feelings for Lydia. For years after she went, I hoped for some message from her. Of course, she could not write, but I thought that perhaps she might manage to have a message conveyed to me someday, through another person. But nothing came, nothing but the years of silence. And then suddenly, from out of the chaos and turmoil of existence, an echo of her face was flung up at me from an unexpected source – and now it is lost again.' He sighed deeply, and added philosophically, 'Surprising physical resemblances can occasionally occur as the result of pure chance. I have been told more than once that I myself greatly resemble Sigmund Freud.'

'That is just because of the beard,' I said.

'The beard and more,' he replied with the ghost of a smile. 'Inheritance is not merely something passed from parents to children, you know. Its consequences spread through entire countries, entire races. You must not give it too much importance.'

But Sebastian did, I thought, as I forced my way out of the front door into the blast of icy wind that hurled itself inside the building, as though for shelter. Something about inheritance was important enough for him to die for.

CHAPTER ELEVEN

In which it is stated that suicide is selfish
and that the cello is an instrument for women

'Professor Wilcox?' Rose said timidly, opening the door a crack, once her preliminary knock had produced a rather sharp 'Come in!' in response.

'Come in.' The professor was sitting at a desk laden with papers, mostly musical scores, in the process of making annotations on one of them with a pencil. He wrote with his right hand; his left, turned palm upwards, was agitated by a continuous wiggling of the fingers which I momentarily took for a disease before suddenly comprehending that he was playing an imaginary violin, visualising fingerings that he was then transporting onto the score by means of tiny numbers. He looked as though our arrival was something of an unwelcome interruption, I thought, but then surely the worry lines etched into his forehead indicated a state of more general strain than that caused by our momentary apparition.

'We're very sorry to bother you,' said Rose politely, 'but my friend is trying to help Sebastian's family – Sebastian Cavendish – and we thought . . .' Her voice trailed off suddenly at the sight of the hostile storm gathering upon the professor's face.

'I have no interest in discussing Sebastian Cavendish,' he said shortly.

Abashed, I was on the point of melting meekly away, and I am sure that Rose did not mean to be insolent. The sudden 'But why not?' that sprang from her lips echoed nothing but a most sincere reaction of bewilderment.

Professor Wilcox stood up and, bracing himself on his desk with his two fists, leant forward to add emphasis to his chopped-off words.

'Why not?' he repeated coldly. 'Why not? Has it ever occurred to you that there is no act more indicative of utter egotism, selfishness and cruelty than suicide?'

There was a brief pause, during which Rose and I glanced at each other and each perceived that such a thought had never crossed either of our minds. A shocking, iconoclastic notion, this, cutting across the accepted – and surely not entirely mistaken – view of the suicide as having been harassed to his death by the unbearable weight of inner or outer circumstances.

'I spent years of my life nurturing Sebastian,' Professor Wilcox was continuing, the muscles of his face strained.

'I invested countless hours, limitless effort, unspoken depths of feeling in that boy. And if I, a teacher, can say this, think for one moment of his mother! So much devotion, so much love, so much care went into him. What right had he, on the edge of manhood, on the very cusp of the fruition of all our dreams, to throw it all away? I don't want to speak of it. I don't even wish to think about it. Did he have a single thought for anyone else before rushing into that mad act? Probably not. What Sebastian did has thrown me into a mental state of disgust with teaching that I will take months or years to overcome, if I ever succeed.' He glared at us for a long moment, and finally spat, 'I wish never to hear his name again,' leaving the clear impression that the name was ceaselessly before his troubled mind.

There was no possible rejoinder to this argument, so bitter and yet so undeniably justified. All of my eager questions faded upon my lips, and we could think of nothing better to do than murmur confused apologies as we hurried simultaneously out of the room in a swish of mingling skirts, and closed the door carefully behind us. Only when we had put an entire corridor and staircase between ourselves and the intensity and resentment of the wounded teacher did we stop to breathe.

'Oh dear,' said Rose, not knowing whether to laugh or cry.

'Oh dear, indeed,' I said. 'Oh dear, oh dear. I do hope the others won't be like that.'

'But they might, for he really is right in a way. From

his point of view, I mean. I do see that now, although I would never have thought of it before.'

'I believe it takes an egotist to see into the heart of an egotist,' I observed sagely. 'Performing musicians, star soloists like Sebastian or his grandfather, must necessarily have a strong ego, otherwise they would not be able to lead the life they do, or even to desire it.'

'I suppose so,' she assented glumly. 'At any rate, that was absolutely useless, and very disagreeable to boot. I wonder who else would know? Oh, I have an idea, if you feel courageous. We'll go straight to the Director. He's a very formal person, but really he's a dear at heart, and surely he can't feel quite as personally involved in it all as Professor Wilcox does.'

She led me to the Director's office, where we were told by a forbidding secretary that the Director was out and that in any case he could only be seen by appointment, and asked what the object of our visit was to be.

'It's about Sebastian Cavendish,' Rose began. The woman looked up sharply, and repeated the name in a questioning tone. It struck me that everyone in the school knew Sebastian or at least knew of him, and that much might be learnt from speaking to them.

By a stroke of pleasing good fortune, the outer door opened at that precise moment, and the Director entered just in time to hear the secretary repeat the name.

'What about Sebastian?' he asked, without any formality at all.

'Oh, Professor Mackenzie,' she said, her stiffness

melting slightly in a flutter at having been observed unexpectedly. 'I was just about to make an appointment for you with these two young women. I recognise you,' she added in Rose's direction. 'You are a student here, are you not? Rose Evergreene, I believe.' She ran her pen down the pages of the appointment book that lay open upon the desk before her, searching for an empty spot.

'You wished to speak to me about Sebastian?' the Director said, coming nearer and ignoring the secretary and her book.

'Yes, Professor Mackenzie,' said Rose quickly, 'you see, we . . .'

'Come into my office, why don't you,' he interrupted, and, passing behind the secretary, he unlocked and opened the door to his inner sanctum, ushered us through, and closed it behind us. I remained for a moment staring at the beauty and luxury of his office, which contained as many artworks as a museum. Exquisite vases stood upon tables and paintings lined the walls: portraits, Flemish still-lives, and a pastoral scene by Watteau. The professor caught my eye.

'The paintings honour the role of Director of the Royal Academy of Music,' he said with a smile. 'They belong to the Academy and to this office, whoever occupies it. Directors come and go: the paintings remain.'

There was a kindly modesty in his remark that made me smile as I took the seat he offered me. Rose took a deep breath and began to explain to Professor Mackenzie that she I and were making an effort to understand the reason behind Sebastian's suicide.

'But my dear,' said the professor, 'attempting to discover the cause of a suicide is a difficult and thankless task. It may so easily be that there is no precise cause, but a general state of depression and despair. Or,' he added, no doubt noting the contrast between his description and the impression that Sebastian had left on people, 'it can be a consequence of hidden, inner doubts. I do admit that although I knew Sebastian but little as an individual, having encountered him only in the contexts of my classes, I would never have guessed that his life would end this way. It is a tragedy for him and for the Academy, and I would not be averse to understanding better what occurred. But I do not see exactly what you are trying to do, and even less how I can be of help to you.'

'I am particularly concerned by the fact that he spoke of inheritance in his last note,' I told him. 'Since it seems there can be no question of money involved, I believe that he must have been speaking of something more personal, more intimate; something about himself, and I particularly wanted to find out more about his grandfather, the violinist Joseph Krieger.'

'Ah yes,' he said, 'I recall now hearing that he was Joseph Krieger's grandson. Quite right. An interesting point. Krieger was the greatest soloist in England in his time. I never heard him, of course. He must have died just about the time when I was born. But his performances were still spoken of twenty years later. Indeed, even today they are remembered as legendary, although there must be relatively few people alive now who actually heard him.'

'It is possible that Sebastian was referring to something personal about his grandfather and not merely his reputation as a violinist, with which he must have been familiar all his life,' I said. 'That is why I was hoping to discover someone who had personal memories of the man and his family.'

'The professors here are all too young for that,' he said. 'But someone here may know someone . . . wait – you give me an idea. When I first came here as a student in 1862, I studied with Prosper Sainton, a Frenchman who came here from Bordeaux. He had been my father's teacher also, and I recall that he had known Joseph Krieger quite well at one time. In fact, he had cultivated his acquaintance assiduously at the time when he was involved in the establishment of the popular concerts. They were friends for a time, and then I believe that they quarrelled. Now, what was it that he told me about Krieger? Wait, it is coming back to me. Something about adoption. Did Krieger adopt a child? Was that what it was?' He blinked, lost in the effort of memory. 'A little girl, perhaps? Do you know anything about this?'

'Well,' I said, 'Sebastian's mother was Joseph Krieger's daughter.'

'Quite right, of course she was. Possibly my vague

memories on the subject of adoption may concern that lady.'

'Perhaps we could ask Professor Sainton?' I said hopefully.

'Oh, he died ten years ago,' said the professor. 'But do you know, he left all of his musical papers and writings to one of the professors here, Hans Wessely. We hired Wessely in 1889; Sainton was already an old man then who no longer gave lessons, but he came here often and followed the musicians of the Academy with great interest. They became very close during the last months of Sainton's life. Wessely tells me that there are some interesting things amongst the papers that Sainton left behind; many years' worth of reflections on the teaching of orchestral musicians, and other recollections. Why don't you ask him? If it can be of help, I will write him a personal note requesting him to show you whatever he has. If there really was an adopted child, the circumstance may be mentioned in private papers or letters. I don't see how you can do any better, for anyone alive now who knew Krieger would have had to have been very young at the time, and would probably not have been a familiar of his household. I remember Sainton's telling me that Krieger was quite standoffish and could be downright unpleasant.'

He wrote the note, sealed it and gave it to us, and we set out into the corridors once again, now in the direction of Professor Wessely's office. But he was not in, and his door was closed and locked.

'Bother,' said Rose, 'but fortunately I know that he will be here the day after tomorrow. He teaches on Thursdays.'

'Urgh,' I said. 'I am so impatient to see the old papers that might talk about Joseph Krieger. Well, I will just have to wait. You know, it makes sense that Mrs Cavendish might have been an adopted child.'

'Does it?' she said, surprised. 'I shouldn't have said so! Everyone connects Sebastian's talent with his grandfather – and he wouldn't even really have been his grandfather after all!'

'That's true,' I rejoined thoughtfully. 'But there was one person who always refused to make that connection. Do you see?'

'Oh? Why, yes, I do see – you mean Sebastian himself! I know he always denied that his gift could have anything to do with inheritance. After we talked about this in the tea shop, I decided that he must have been resentful of its being attributed in some way to family, like a person who would prefer to earn his own fortune rather than merely inherit one.'

'Well, that might have been what it was,' I said, 'but I'm not sure. I mean, I've never met anyone who had inherited a family fortune and denied it when it was mentioned. Family heritage is usually a source of pride. Think back, Rose. Do you think there's any possibility that Sebastian might have been aware all along that his mother was an adopted child?'

'I see now that that's possible; it does seem as though

he was hinting at it, though he never said it outright,' she admitted. 'But if his mother didn't want it known, he would have respected that. Pity it's such an embarrassing question to put to Mrs Cavendish directly. That's annoying; she must know the answer, but we can't ask. He might have told Claire – but no, he can't have. If she had known that, she would have known that the cursed inheritance couldn't come from the grandfather.'

'But this raises a whole new set of possibilities!' I said suddenly. 'Perhaps he unexpectedly found out something about his *mother's* real parents!'

Rose gave her head a little shake.

'I can't get that idea into my head,' she said. 'Everyone always associated him with Joseph Krieger. Oh dear, I don't know what to think. I have an idea, Vanessa – do let's go now and see if *my* professor is in. He's a cello teacher, of course, but he's old, he's been here for ever so long, and I think there isn't much that goes on here that he doesn't know. And he's so lovely! Come – let's go and find him. He's a marvellous old gentleman. I adore him. It's true what Professor Wilcox was saying about gratefulness, you know. I hadn't thought of it for Sebastian, but for myself, when I think about all that Professor Pezze has done for me – and more than that, all has given to me of himself – I can't even think about how he would feel if I died. He's like a darling grandparent, only even better because he transmitted all that music to me out of choice, out of a love that didn't come into being because of any bond of blood. The love of the teacher for the student is something different, perhaps even deeper in some ways. Oh, I don't know how to explain it. But it's something strong that builds you up and stays with you for your whole life. Here we are. Listen – he's in! That's his cello sound. He may be almost seventy, but he still has such energy in his playing. Oh, I do love him!'

She knocked, and flung open the door at once without waiting for an invitation. The white-haired professor holding the cello turned his face to the door, and it lit up immediately with an expression of delighted pleasure.

'Rose, Rose! You do not come to see me so often any more!' he exclaimed with a warm voice and a strong Italian accent.

'I'm sorry,' she said contritely, while the blooming womanliness of her seemed to melt away, leaving the place to a loving little girl.

'What have you been doing lately? I have not seen you since your recital with the sonata of Grieg, but I heard wonderful zings about your Beethoven,' he said. 'Ah, and your trio.' His face grew suddenly sad, but not with a tragic look; rather, with the sadness of an old man who has seen a great deal already, and is prepared to endure more as the years go on.

'You were doing a beautiful work wiz the trio, Rose,' he went on, the music taking the major place in his mind, above the sordid realities of life and death. 'The last time I heard you there was much, much progress since one year ago when you began! Eet was all much more harmonious in style. You worked hard to tame the wild one, the lion, did you not? You must teach him that his voice ees not ze only one, yes? And to bring forth the storm hidden inside the timid miss at ze piano, and to find her hidden passion. I felt it, zat if Sebastian was ze energy driving the trio, you were ze glue which bound it togezer. It was wonderful work, Rose. *Brava!* Eet ees terrible zat it has finished so. What will you do now? Find anozer violinist?'

'Oh, I don't know!' A point of impatience crept into her tone. 'Claire wants us to play with John Milrose. He says he shouldn't, and can't replace Sebastian, but it's obvious that he wants to, and Claire wants him too. It's all wrong, Professor Pezze. John's style goes well enough with the old Claire, the way she used to play, but she's come so far since then! I don't think we can make a go of it with John, but I don't know how to tell them what I really feel. Oh dear. I do wish I didn't have to be in this situation!'

'No, you must not do eet eef eet ees so, Rose. Better to cut eet short sooner zan later.'

'But that would hurt Claire, and I can't hurt her right now, Professor. She is already devastated! Oh dear, oh dear. But don't let's talk about me. See, I've brought you a friend, Mrs Weatherburn from Cambridge, on purpose to meet you.'

'Yes, I see. How do you do, Mrs Wezzerburn? Eet ees a pleasure. To what do I owe such a rare honour as a visit from Rose, in company even? You are a musician?'

'No, no,' I said blushing, 'although I love music.'

167

'No, she isn't a musician, but she's trying to understand about Sebastian, Professor Pezze.'

'Understand what?'

'Understand why he died. I mean, why he killed himself. You see, we don't understand.'

'But one cannot hope to understand such zings,' said the old man, giving the same argument that we had already heard more than once that day, but with a air of gentle philosophy. 'Ze boy was perhaps disappointed wiz something. It happens so often, sadly. Ze young people, zey do not always zink.'

'But he wasn't really, Professor. It's very strange. But Mrs Weatherburn really wanted to ask you some other questions. Questions about music, and about musicians. For example, about Sebastian's grandfather. Did you know him?'

'Joseph Krieger, you mean? I encountered him once or twice, yes, when I was young.'

'What was he like?'

'What was he like? He was . . . vain, domineering, proud, hard, and brilliant. One who must always be at ze forefront of everyzing. You could not approach him wiz friendship. He zought he was always right, knew everyzing best. He was a very difficult man. His students at ze time, I recall, suffered sadly at his hands. When zey could not stand it any more, zey would sometimes come here, to ze Academy, to get a decent education.'

'Did you ever play with him?'

'I? No, no. No one played wiz him. He played no

chamber music. Only grand concertos wiz ze orchestra, or else solo upon ze stage.'

'But he played well?'

'Oh yes, he played marvellously, if you like zis way of playing. A little bit wizout a heart. Passion, yes, but no warmth of ze heart. For virtuoso playing, he was of ze very best of his generation. Zey say he had some gypsy blood in him, alzough he came from Germany. I don't know if zat is true, or if it is just a story he liked to spread to mark his difference wiz all ozers. Ze violin is a dangerous instrument, you know. It is a devilish instrument as we have known since Tartini, ze greatest violinist of his time, actually saw ze devil playing incredible music upon ze violin and wrote it down. Ze violin sometimes sheds somezing of its dangerous character on ze violinist. When ze capacity is too great, zere is some danger.'

'You think the cello is fundamentally different, then?'

'Oh, yeeeees. Ze cello ees completely different! Fundamentally, you know what?' The old man leant forward with a gleam in his eye, as though to confide to us a most humorous secret. 'The cello ees a woman's instrument,' he whispered, and sat back squatly in his chair, his pudgy hands resting on his short thighs, which hardly jutted out farther than the round stomach which rested comfortably upon them. His eyes twinkled merrily. 'Zat is what ze people do not yet realise – no! Zey zink because eet ees big, because eet has a deep voice, eet ees an instrument for men! Zey forget zat ze cello sings wiz ze voice of thrilling tenderness – ze woman's voice! Zey forget zat ze low, sweet tones are feminine; ze loud, brash tones are masculine. And ze women are practically forbidden to play it, are zey not? In ze Academy, one hundred cello students, how many women are zere? Two – only two! And why is zis? I will tell you why. It is because you must hold ze cello between ze knees. *Knees?* But in zis country, ze women may not have knees; zey are not allowed to admit having knees!'

He sat back in his chair again, and a mellow laugh rippled forth.

'Not to mention ze word *between*,' he added. 'Zis word, I zink, evokes ze worst of sin to ze English. But you will see, or perhaps you will not see . . . but zings will change wiz time, zings will change. One hundred years from now, I will bet zat all ze cellists will be ze women, and ze men will be playing ze drums and ze trombone.'

'That would be lovely,' said Rose decidedly. 'Vanessa, do ask him our question.'

'How can I put it?' I said thoughtfully. 'Professor Pezze, can incredible musical talent arise in a person whose family is not at all musical?'

'Certainly,' he said. 'Zere are many examples. Rose, eet ees so wiz you, no?'

'And what about the opposite,' I went on. 'If the parents are musical, how likely is it that the children will be?'

'It happens,' he replied, 'but eet ees not certain. Zere are examples of entire families gifted wiz unbelievable gifts. You know Manuel García? He was our professor of singing here at ze Academy until he retired just a few years ago. He lives nearby still. You have seen him?'

'I have,' volunteered Rose. 'He's awfully old, isn't he?'

'He is 95 zis year, he taught here until he was 90! Can you imagine? But did you know zat his sister is ze famous soprano, Pauline Viardot? And zat his ozer sister is the legendary Malibran?'

'Really! Why, how can that be? La Malibran – she was famous sixty or seventy years ago, wasn't she?'

'Yes, but she was a young zing when she died, no older zan our Sebastian, I zink. Her sister Pauline is still alive, but very old. Zeir parents were both singers, you know. And ze children of Pauline Viardot, zey are all fine musicians also. Zere is a talent which is inherited wizin an entire family. You see? Yet on ze ozer hand, musical parents can have children wiz no talent at all. I have seen some here, sadly. The parents force zem so zat zey can play, but zere is no real talent. And zen, many times I have seen ze gift pass directly from grandfather to grandson. Just as in ze case of Joseph Krieger and Sebastian Cavendish. Or perhaps, who knows, it may be zat the children of Joseph Krieger were also filled wiz talent. I have some memory of hearing zat he would not have zem learning any music. It does not surprise me. He wanted always to be ze focus of attention himself. I cannot imagine his taking ze time to teach his children, or taking ze risk zat zey might become so brilliant as la Malibran, more famous zan himself. Who knows?'

'What if you found out that Sebastian was not really

Joseph Krieger's grandson after all?' Rose said. 'We think he might not have been – we heard a rumour that his mother was adopted. Would that surprise you?'

'Ha? *Davvero*? You heard such a zing? No, impossible! Zat would be really astonishing.'

'Why astonishing? You told us that talent can spring up anywhere,' she said.

'But not een this case, surely! I heard zem both, you know. Fifty years apart, I heard zem both. Perhaps not many people have. Ze same bearing, ze same attack, ze same flair, ze same technical prowess. Krieger not Sebastian's grandfather?' He shook his head doubtfully. 'If he was not, zen ze whole zing is truly a miracle.'

CHAPTER TWELVE

*In which Vanessa suddenly puts two and two together
and finds that it might make five (or even six)*

Two days later, I crossed Hanover Square, turned into
Tenterden Street and entered the imposing square door
of the Royal Academy of Music quite by myself for
the first time. I almost felt something of a fraud as I
walked through the hall and up the stairs, following
the directions that Rose had given me to locate her at
the end of her trio rehearsal. All around me, students
passed carrying all kinds of instrument cases, some of
shapes so lumpy and irregular that I could hardly guess
at the identity of the instrument inside. A tall young
man carrying a tiny box that probably contained a flute
accompanied a diminutive girl lugging a contrabass
taller than her companion. Feeling oddly naked with

nothing but my handbag, I walked along briskly, trying to look quite as though I belonged there, and soon reached the padded door where Rose had told me I should find her.

I stood outside the door and cocked my ear. Faint strains of music filtered through, muted and lovely, facilitating the necessary wait, for I did not want to interrupt the musicians at their work. Crossing notes and fragments wafted through the corridors from all of the different doors along it. I found the place pervaded by a stimulating atmosphere of hard work and deep concentration. My own thoughts were in something of a whirl, for Rose was to accompany me to visit Professor Wessely, and armed with the kind note scribbled by the Academy's director, I thought to be allowed to have access to the private diaries and letters of a musician who had known Joseph Krieger closely and well.

The idea that Tanis Cavendish might have been an adopted and not a natural child of her father intrigued me to the highest degree, and I longed for some kind of confirmation. I stood there in the hall thinking it over, and trying to remember what the old Swiss violinist Herr Ratner had said about the Krieger family. He had spent about two years visiting the house regularly for lessons, I recalled, but he could hardly remember Krieger's wife; he had called her a self-effacing person, a remark which might have been a deduction as much as a memory. He had also said that Joseph Krieger had no sons, for if he had, Herr Ratner might have found employment as their musical tutor. But there had been only daughters, Herr Ratner had recalled.

Until now, I had not taken any particular notice of these words, taking them to mean nothing more than the expression of Joseph Krieger's not being childless, yet having no sons. But now, I wondered suddenly. *Daughters?* Might it not be possible that Herr Ratner remembered daughters, because there really were daughters, and not just one daughter? And had Professor Mackenzie not quoted Sainton as saying that Krieger had not had his *children* trained in music? It could be just confusion or poor memory, of course – but could it not also mean that Sebastian's mother Tanis might have had a sister? And if she had, what were the chances that that sister's name was nothing other than *Lydia*?

I made a rapid calculation of ages in my mind. According to Dr Bernstein's book, Lydia had been twenty-four in 1870: she would be fifty-four today. Mrs Cavendish must be of much the same age.

My heart began to beat as a mental scene began to unroll itself before me. There was the party in Zürich, in Frau Bochsler's padded, plushy parlour, filled with pillows and little porcelain objects. There was Dr Bernstein, telling Sebastian with eyes full of memory about a woman called Lydia, of nearly the same age as Sebastian's mother, whom he resembled astonishingly. I saw Sebastian smiling indulgently, having never heard a word about the existence of any such person, and paying

175

scant attention, probably putting it down to coincidence or to the faulty memory of a romantic old man. And later on, at that very same party, there was Herr Ratner, chatting away with the young star of the evening, telling him this and that about how he had once known his grandfather – and mentioning *daughters*.

Why should he not have mentioned them that evening, as naturally as he had mentioned them to me? And if he had, then might not the very same idea have sprung into Sebastian's mind as now sprang into mine?

I knew nothing of Sebastian's family, but he had lived near his mother for his entire life, and must have been sensitive to her every mood, reserved and cool though she was. If my idea was right, if Tanis Cavendish had had a sister whose existence had been concealed from her son, then how would she have reacted when he asked her, in all the innocence of childhood, why he had no aunts, uncles or cousins as his friends all did? She would have kept her secret if she wished, of course, but as for the underlying minuscule tensions that invariably accompany a lie – who is better equipped to detect them than a mother in her child, or a child in his mother? I smiled to myself, remembering a time not days ago when, upon being asked, little Cedric had asserted with a broad smile of angelic beatitude that *of course* he had already cleaned his teeth. How was it that I was able to laugh at him without the slightest feeling of doubt, and tell him to stop telling untruths and to go and clean them at once? I could hardly even define to myself what made me so certain; it was not that he had looked sly or shifty, it was far more subtle than that: some elusive, inexpressible difference between that cheery smile and his usual one. Might not Sebastian have felt a similar minuscule pinprick when his mother told him that she had no family at all? Without ever having the slightest indication of the contrary, he had probably dismissed it from his mind. But perhaps the two facts he had learnt almost simultaneously that night had suddenly made that pinprick blossom into a full-fledged doubt, accompanied by an urgent desire to *know*!

The door before me opened and Rose looked out into the corridor.

'Oh, Vanessa, you found the room!' she exclaimed. 'You didn't need to wait out here. You'd have been welcome to enter. Do come in.' The dark-haired, solidly built young violinist that I had already seen, John Milrose, was standing with Claire, his hands on her shoulders, and was talking to her softly and seriously, his eyes locked into hers. Rose's glance followed mine and she shrugged, with a faint air of annoyance.

But Claire wrenched away from him when she saw me, and hurried over, her hand outstretched.

'Mrs Weatherburn,' she said. 'Rose says you have found out some things, but she wouldn't tell us anything till you came! Oh, I did so want to see you. Do you think you understand what might have happened? I'm sorry,' she added, recovering her manners, yet with a nervous stammer still causing her voice to shake, 'I have barely even asked you how you are. And about – about your expenses. Rose says you have been travelling. Of course I will—'

'Please, do not even think about that now,' I said firmly. 'We can discuss it at the end. I do have some things to tell you, although nothing is yet certain. But I am continuing to discover new information.' In a few words, I told her about Lydia K., then about the mention of daughters in the plural, and the possibility that Sebastian had made a connection between the two things. She looked doubtful.

'But you say that he didn't pay much attention to what the doctor told him,' she said, biting her lip. 'You really think—'

'There is one more thing,' I interrupted. 'We learnt yesterday that there seems to be some rumour, some possibility, that Sebastian's mother may not have been the true daughter of Joseph Krieger, but an adopted child. Rose and I were wondering if it is true, and if Sebastian knew it, and if that fact could perhaps explain the way he always used to deny that he had inherited his musical abilities from his grandfather. I wondered if you knew anything about that. I thought perhaps he might have told you, if he told anyone at all.'

Her startled glance reminded me of a wren.

'I—no,' she began. 'No, I didn't know that. He never told me. But you know, I wonder – it's strange, because he did hint at something of the kind, now that you mention it. He made some remarks once or twice, but I never paid any attention, because I thought it was just his way of declaring his independence. You know, from the all-dominating grandfather thing.'

'Quite. However, it has occurred to us that, if true, this piece of information might completely change the meaning we have been giving to the words "cursed inheritance",' I said. 'We were thinking that he might have found out something about his mother's real parents, perhaps.'

'Yes, I see. Yet I still don't understand why he should have cared so dreadfully, whatever it could have been.'

'I only wish we could confirm that his mother really was adopted,' I said, 'and that Sebastian knew about it.'

'He did,' said John Milrose unexpectedly, coming nearer to us. He had been standing aside, out of politeness, but he could hear everything we were saying, and as Rose and Claire seemed to consider this perfectly acceptable, I did as well.

It was far too early for Claire to even think of falling in love again; it was obvious that Sebastian still reigned over her heart, but it was also clear that John had an interest in helping her in any way he could to recover her peace of mind. It had not occurred to me, though, that he might know anything intimate about Sebastian that had not been confided even to Claire.

I was, however, mistaken. John explained to us how Sebastian had told him the truth some months earlier, when they had entered into a serious argument on the subject of hereditary artistry.

'He was actually angry with me for insisting,' he

admitted, 'and that's why he told me. His mother had told him the truth because of what happened at his debut concert, his very first solo concert with orchestra. He was just thirteen, and after the concert dozens of people came and told him that he was the worthy heir of his grandfather and that it was easy to see where his gift came from. He said that after they were all gone he actually cried with rage; no one was talking about him – it was just Joseph Krieger, Joseph Krieger, Joseph Krieger, like he didn't even exist, like he was nothing but a reincarnation. That's when his mother told him that it wasn't even true, that Krieger was not his real grandfather because she was an adopted child. She said he must never tell anyone, but should always keep that knowledge inside himself to give him strength.'

'So that's it,' I exclaimed, astonished to have so suddenly obtained an answer from this unexpected source to one of the many questions that assailed me. 'Did he say whether he knew anything about his mother's real parents?'

'He said she didn't know and didn't wish to,' he replied. 'Actually, I believe he regretted telling me about it, afterwards. Not that he cared much himself whether people knew, but it isn't a thing one spreads about really; and then, his mother did not want it to known. It was not that she drew any special pride or glory from being the great violinist's daughter – she never behaved in that way at all – but still, with her engagement to Lord

Warburton, questions of family were taking on a certain importance, what with Warburton being a proponent of Galton's eugenics and all. Sebastian asked me to keep the secret for his mother's sake, so I never mentioned it again.'

'But Sebastian's note didn't make you think about it at once?' cried Rose in amazement. 'I mean, the words "cursed inheritance" – I'd have thought of that right away, if I'd known what you knew!'

'He wrote those words in his note?' he said in surprise. 'I had no idea. Claire never showed it to me. I thought I had understood that he hadn't given any explanation at all.' He put his arm around Claire's shoulders, as though to defend her from the cruelty of such an empty message. Rose hoisted her cello case over her shoulder.

'Oh dear,' she said, 'it was probably silly of us not to think of asking you before. I do hope we haven't missed too many opportunities like that. Of course, there's Mrs Cavendish herself, but we simply *can't* ask her about this – and anyway, it's probably true that she doesn't know much about it. We think the best place to find out would be from older musicians who knew Joseph Krieger. We're going to chase up a source right now. Come, Vanessa, let's go see if Professor Wessely is free.'

She led me through the halls in the direction of his office.

'Urgh,' she said, 'John Milrose annoys me. It's not nice of me, and I don't even know exactly why it is, but the way he's pressing Claire with his feelings – can't he see that it's much too soon? It's in poor taste. Sebastian died barely a month ago!' With the energy of irritation, she knocked vigorously upon the door. No response, however, was forthcoming.

'I know he's here today,' she said, and she hailed a young man passing by with a violin case slung over his shoulder.

'Professor Wessely is teaching in the grand studio right now,' he told us, consulting his pocket watch. 'It's on the ground floor to left. But he won't like being interrupted. He hates that, you know.'

'We'll just wait until he's free,' said Rose, and down we went, to a very grand door that seemed to indicate passage into an unusually elegant room. Through this door we heard a few notes, which were quickly interrupted by a long string of remarks in heavily accented English. Rose knocked gently and opened the door a crack.

The studio was indeed large, with a burnished parquet floor covered with remarkable carpets, portraits upon the walls, and an immense shining grand piano before which sat a woman, her fingers on the keys, waiting for instructions. To my surprise, the student was just a little boy no more than ten years old, with a bony, sensitive face, a large nose, deep eyes sparkling with intelligence and a violin that looked too large for him. I was alarmed at Rose's boldness and half-expected a sharp reproach at our interruption, but the professor, a dynamic man in the prime of his life, smiled cordially.

'Ah yes,' he said, 'that is quite perfect. Please, do

come in and sit down. Wolfe, you will play the Tartini for these visitors. Enter, enter,' he added, beckoning us forward and ushering us to two of the brocaded chairs that surrounded the walls. 'This is my youngest student: Wolfe Wolfinsohn, from South Africa. An extraordinary youngster. He will play for you the Devil's Trill.'

Rose poked my arm. It was the very piece that her professor had mentioned! The small boy slid into the performance with a theme so wistful that it brought to mind images of infinite sadness and nostalgia, interrupted once or twice by strident chords indicative of a sudden spurt of rage. Just as I was allowing myself to be lulled by the spirit of this part, he launched into something quite different; a kind of dance of Puckish sprites which leapt and laughed without a stop as though they were rushing all over the room. After a few minutes of this, the air was suddenly filled with wrenching chords, like sobs torn from the very entrails, ending with a tragic weeping. Then began the real madness, accompanied by the gentle touch of the woman at the piano, whose role, essentially a series of soft chords, served to accentuate the wild peculiarity of the violin music, which now soared and dived, slowed and rushed forth again, leapt and above all trilled – lengthening the whole notion of trill from the usual pretty ornament to a terrifying, unending cackle of diabolical laughter, twisting agilely in and out of the realm which links beauty and madness. It ended with a single note repeated manically again and again to distraction – and then the burst of a grand farewell.

Rose and I began spontaneously to clap, and heaped praise upon the young artist. Rising, we then thanked the professor for having given us the opportunity to hear this extraordinary student, and asked if there might be a moment when he could see us privately. He seemed quite pleased and gave us an appointment in his office upstairs for six o'clock. Closing the door behind us, we emerged into the grey, chilly day and bent our steps towards a nearby tea room. My excitement had been stimulated to fever pitch by the wait, but even more so by the music itself, which was obsessional, possessing. I hurried Rose inside and ordered tea, and we set to discussing the events of the day.

'Do you think Mrs Cavendish was really adopted, or did she just tell Sebastian that in order to console him?' Rose asked.

'Oh, I think it must be true. I can't imagine that anyone would invent a thing like that. There would be plenty of other ways of learning to deal with Sebastian's feelings, and this one might become rather a burden in the end, what with his hinting it but not feeling right about saying it openly.'

'That's true. It would be a very odd thing to invent. But you do see why I still think it might be possible?'

'No. Tell me.'

'Why, it's because of what Professor Pezze said about Sebastian's resemblance to Joseph Krieger. I wouldn't believe it from anyone else, perhaps, but with him – it would be the first time I ever put even one syllable he pronounced in doubt. He knows and feels music right through every fibre of his body. It would be astonishing if he were wrong about this.'

'Well,' I said thoughtfully, 'but he did know beforehand that Krieger was the grandfather – it's not as though he deduced it just from seeing Sebastian play. So perhaps he had a prejudice in his mind.'

'You don't know Professor Pezze. It's simply inconceivable that he could imagine some musical relationship that doesn't really exist!'

'Sebastian – the grandson and yet not the grandson,' I said, and suddenly a great flash of light burst blindingly into my mind! 'I have an idea, Rose! Perhaps Sebastian was not actually his mother's son, after all! Perhaps he, too, was adopted! Maybe his real mother was Lydia K – and maybe she really was Krieger's own daughter!'

So excited was I by this seemingly incredible discovery that I could hardly breathe. I tried to remember exactly what Dr Bernstein had written about Lydia K. She had left Basel when she was 24 years old, and it was in the summer of 1874.

'Exactly how old was Sebastian?' I asked Rose.

'He was twenty-four.'

'So he would have been twenty-five this year; he must have been born in 1875. That would be the reason why she never returned to Basel! It's possible, it's very possible. It would explain so much!'

'You mean that you think that the Kriegers might

have adopted Mrs Cavendish even if they had a daughter of their own? Why would they do that?'

'There could be any number of reasons. Perhaps close friends of theirs died and left an orphan child behind. Rose, I believe we are getting closer to the truth. Just think! Here's Sebastian, denying outright that he can have inherited anything from his grandfather, and certain that he's right, because he knows that his mother is an adopted child. Yet people keep mentioning it, perhaps people like Professor Pezze, people he trusts, so he can't help but be puzzled somewhere deep inside. On that evening in Zürich, he unexpectedly receives indications that his mother might have had a sister whom he resembles remarkably and whose existence was completely hidden from him. Do you not think he might jump to the conclusion that the mysterious Lydia could be his real mother – and also the real daughter of his grandparents? I can imagine that such an idea would send him rushing to try to discover the truth!'

'Oh, Vanessa, it all hangs together – it's very possible!' she cried. 'If only we could find out more.'

'Well, perhaps we will. Hopefully, we will be leafing through Prosper Sainton's papers in less than an hour.'

'Hum. We'd probably better be prepared for disappointment,' she warned wisely. Who knows what Professor Wessely might have done with his old papers – who knows if he even actually really kept them, or whether they might not be somewhere unavailable, like

186

in his far-off home in Hungary. And even if we find them, who knows whether they contain anything more than remarks about music – or boring information like "Saw J.K. today" – or even worse, no information about Joseph Krieger at all!'

'Stop, stop! We must be optimistic!' I answered firmly, calling the waitress over to pay for our tea.

'All right, we shall be.' She stood up and gave her head a little shake. 'But Vanessa, there's still something I don't understand. If this new idea is right, then Sebastian couldn't have discovered anything dreadful about his mother's true parents. I mean about Mrs Cavendish's true parents. What I mean is, if he realised she wasn't his real mother, then no matter who they were, it wouldn't matter to him. Not in terms of the "cursed inheritance", at any rate.'

'No, that's true,' I agreed. 'This would change all of that. If we're right, it was Lydia K he was concerned with.'

'Still, though. Even if our theory is true, no matter how angry he might have been to discover that his mother had hidden it all from him, I simply can't see why he should kill himself over it!'

'The "cursed inheritance",' I said. 'I wonder if somehow, he found out something terrible about Lydia herself. I wonder what happened to Lydia? If her sister adopted her baby, it could be that she died—'

'—or went raving mad! Could that be it?'

'It could. And yet, even if she did—'

187

'—no matter how dreadfully, it still doesn't seem like a reason for Sebastian to take his own life! It doesn't, Vanessa. No matter what happened to her, it doesn't. Does it?'

'No,' I admitted. 'No, it doesn't. There's still a lot we don't know.'

Unspoken words remained in the air as we gathered up our things and left.

CHAPTER THIRTEEN

*In which the logical progression of ideas
encounters an obstacle*

When we arrived at the eminent music teacher's office at six o'clock precisely, we found his door standing welcomingly open. He was inside, bent over a musical score in the company of the small boy we had heard earlier, and they were studying it together with animation. Professor Wessely looked up as we entered, waved us to some leather chairs, and packed the boy off, carrying the music and his violin, to go and practise it by himself.

'I am so glad that you have come,' he said. 'Young Wolfe is an exceptional child. I believe that he may be the greatest talent I have ever seen among my students; perhaps the greatest that the Royal Academy has ever seen. You heard his playing. It is astounding for a boy of ten. With proper teaching and nurturing, I believe there is no limit that he may not surpass.'

Rose and I glanced at each other, slightly surprised.

'He is quite wonderful,' she agreed. 'We are really delighted to have had the opportunity to hear him play. Now, what we—'

'The search for some kind of financial support is not easy,' the professor went on firmly. 'People are not used to such cases nowadays. But this is something really special. When I was a child in Hungary, there, at that time, there were children who were able to work and learn like this child. I do not say they necessarily possessed the same gift. I myself, for instance, realised as I grew up that my vocation was to be a teacher; that passing on to students the wonderful secrets of technical accomplishments and the splendid approach to musical interpretation that I had learnt from the best of the Hungarian teachers, laden with all of their traditions, was my true destiny in life, and not to play solo upon the grand stages of Europe. But the devotion, the inspiration, the effort I devoted to the violin as a child – these have all but disappeared in our modern time. Young Wolfe is the first child I have seen of the young generation to possess this kind of depth. It would be impossible to choose a more worthy object of aid and support.'

He paused expectantly, but we did not know what to say in the face of what was turning out to be quite an embarrassing misunderstanding. Apparently the professor had been expecting possible sponsors to come and hear his prodigy, and had taken us for them. This was unfortunate, as neither Rose nor I commanded the kind of finances that could cover the support of a young child over a period of years, however deserving.

'Wolfe comes from South Africa,' Professor Wessely said, deciding to pursue his effort in the face of our silence, 'and he arrived in this country on the recommendation of his teacher there, who wrote a letter to me explaining that no teacher in the country could do justice to a talent of this magnitude. He has come with his mother, leaving father and siblings behind. But the mother is not sure that she should stay; helping this gifted youngster deprives the others of a mother, but returning to them would leave this one nearly in the situation of an orphan, although of course I would look after him as much as time would allow me to do so. In the meantime, however, they have barely enough money to survive. That is why it is so important to find some person who will accept to offer the gift of a scholarship. I believe that that person will be gratified, in just a few years, by seeing young Wolfe Wolfinsohn become the name of one of the legendary violinists of the new century.'

I sat calculating a number of possible but unsatisfactory remarks in my mind and discarding them all. But Rose began to speak, and I realised as I listened that she had had a stroke of genius which might just turn out to be of benefit to everyone, as well as satisfying our immediate purposes.

'Unfortunately, we ourselves are not in a situation to be able to provide the amount of financial help that Wolfe would need,' she said kindly, 'but the reason we are here is because we are acquainted with someone who is in such a situation, and who, we believe, seeks an opportunity to do some good in the musical world, having recently undergone a terrible loss. I am speaking of Mrs Cavendish, the mother of Sebastian Cavendish. You know about him, I presume?'

'Mrs Cavendish! Of course I know of the terrible tragedy,' he replied. 'The poor woman. Is it possible that she can be thinking of helping others at a time like this? That would be very courageous of her, indeed.'

'It is something of a consolation, or perhaps, I should better say, a manner of actively expressing her grief,' said Rose smoothly. 'It is not something she is determined upon yet, merely a vague idea, and, as you can imagine, she is not in a state to search out the possibilities for herself. You are acquainted with her?'

'I am not, although I have seen her more than once, at the recitals and auditions here,' he replied. 'Naturally, I knew her son and even coached him in the occasional chamber music group when he was a student. A phenomenal talent, although not so astonishing an early-bloomer as Wolfe, and perhaps more brash than deep in a certain manner. But that is merely according to my taste and my tradition. Sebastian is a great loss to the future of British violin playing, there is no doubt about that. I will write to Mrs Cavendish.'

I paused at this, wondering whether our inventions might not end up by getting us into trouble, but it was impossible to back off now. And even if she disliked the idea, I could not imagine Mrs Cavendish answer the professor's request otherwise but courteously. 'There is another thing,' I gabbled, in a hasty desire to steer the conversation away from scholarships. 'You probably know that Mrs Cavendish's father was the late Joseph Krieger.'

'Yes, I have heard that,' he assented, his interest aroused.

'Well, having lost her father as a very young child, she has always been interested in learning anything she could about him, and now, at this dreadful time, it seems she has vaguely had the idea of beginning to write his biography.'

Rose glanced at me quickly, then added, 'It would be a way of remembering family ties, and those who have passed away.'

'I quite understand,' he said, looking as though he didn't, which was perfectly natural, given the hasty and haphazard nature of our inventions. I quickly handed him Professor Mackenzie's note.

'The Director told us that you may have quite a lot of interesting information about Joseph Krieger in your possession,' I explained, 'amongst the private papers of Prosper Sainton. He remembers that they used to be friends, and then quarrelled.'

'I have heard that Joseph Krieger quarrelled with

everyone,' he murmured. 'It would not make much of a topic for biographical writing.'

'But he had a family, many important acquaintances in the musical world, and innumerable concerts and interesting encounters and experiences,' I improvised. 'Professor Mackenzie thinks that Prosper Sainton may have written about these things during the period of their friendship.'

'It is possible,' he said. 'I have not read much of his private papers, I must tell you honestly, because they are mostly written in French. From the little I have seen, they may be historically quite interesting. It has been one of my long-standing projects to find a French student to properly read and classify them for the Archives of the Academy. Do you read French?' Upon our both nodding breathlessly, he pulled out his watch, glanced at it, and said, 'I must go and teach for one hour now. An extra lesson for a student who has not been working well lately. I would not wish the documents to leave my office. May I entrust you with them here until my return?'

We assented with alacrity, almost unable to believe our luck, as he opened the cupboard directly behind him and extracted two large piles of disordered notebooks and papers. Much of the heap consisted of annotated musical scores and exercises. He swiftly separated those out and put them back, leaving us with a large quantity of yellowed envelopes addressed in the scratchy copper-plate of fifty years ago, and more than a dozen notebooks covered with writing in a crabbed but legible hand.

The moment the door had closed behind him, Rose took up a handful of papers and said,

'Well – our first worry has melted into thin air. Now we just have to hope that Monsieur Sainton was a terrific gossip at heart!' And she set to examining the letters in the envelopes with a great speed that was no doubt due more to the three or four summers she had spent at chamber music festivals in the mountains of France than to the rudiments of French grammar that I had dutifully inculcated into her as a child. Not to mention the helpful fact that, unlike the diaries, at least half of the letters were actually written in a language we both spoke fluently.

I took up the notebooks, and soon found that as I became used to the old Frenchman's handwriting, the speed of my ability to spell out his words increased. I put aside everything concerned with the years following Joseph Krieger's death, and concentrated on the earlier ones, going through them from the year 1844, in which Prosper Sainton had first arrived in England. I saw immediately that the diaries were a wonderful place to look for information. He wrote in their pages no more than once or twice each month, but when he did, he described concerts, encounters and anecdotes in a breezy and amusing tone which made me suspect that he was perhaps doing it with a view to writing his memoirs one day. And a fascinating book they would have made. The names of musicians and composers, familiar and unfamiliar, filled the pages as he followed their careers: he had known Berlioz, Alkan, Chopin, Mazas, Liszt while at the Paris Conservatoire, and followed their careers all through the years, attending their concerts in London and playing their orchestral music. He described leading his orchestra in the position of concertmaster through innumerable concerts, of which the most unforgettable, he wrote with an eager hand, was an extraordinary performance of Beethoven's violin concerto conducted by none other than the great Mendelssohn himself, and performed by a boy of twelve whose name, Joseph Joachim, returned repeatedly in the pages of the diary. I searched in vain, however, for a mention of Joseph Krieger.

Rose was the first to make a find.

'Vanessa, Vanessa, quick, look!'

I jumped out of my seat and read over her shoulder a short note written in English, in a bold handwriting whose pointed letters denoted a German origin. The note mentioned that the author had been invited to a luncheon and had heard that Mr Sainton was also to be there. 'It will be a good opportunity for us to discuss the questions you raised the other day,' it read. I turned over the sheet to read the back, and my eye fell upon the signature.

'Joseph Krieger!'

'Yes – isn't it eerie? We've heard so much about him,

and now we have something concrete: a letter from his very own hand! Look at the date; August 1848. So we know they knew each other then. Perhaps you could skip directly to there in the diaries.'

The notebooks for 1844, 1845 and 1846 having proved disappointing, I followed the hint, took up the one from 1848, and was rewarded almost at once. In that year, Joseph Krieger had played a large part in the life of Prosper Sainton. Sainton had left the Royal Italian Opera to lead an orchestra known as the Queen's Band, and he desired to consolidate the reputation of the Queen's Band by organising a series of concerts presenting the most prestigious soloists of Europe. The invitations closest to his heart, the ones he took care of personally, concerned the violinists, and detailed descriptions of his correspondence and negotiations with them filled a generous portion of the diary's pages. While they mainly sought the great soloists from the continent – Henri Vieuxtemps from Belgium, Joseph Joachim from Germany – London did provide Joseph Krieger, who was persuaded, once, twice and then a third time to perform with the orchestra, playing some of the most splendid concertos in the world, and invariably astounding the audience by following them up with encore pieces played with a virtuosity that had not been seen since the days of Paganini! Sainton spoke of the lion's head violin and of Krieger's hands and his long and exceptionally flexible fingers. I showed the passage to Rose.

'They sound exactly like Sebastian's hands,' she said, looking up at me.

Soon after the beginning of 1848, it became obvious that Sainton was courting Krieger, professionally speaking, and their contacts were increasingly frequent. Sainton managed to be at many a social event where Krieger was invited as well, and even became acquainted with the ephemeral figure of Mrs Krieger, a thin, sad, pale woman ('*maigre, triste et pâle*'), as he wrote, who seemed 'lost when not standing at her husband's side, and nervous when she was'.

A few weeks farther on in the diary, I read something which made me sit up.

'As we played for a moment with our host's delightful three-year-old daughter,' I read, 'Mrs Krieger's eyes filled with tears, which began to run down her cheeks. I felt quite embarrassed ('*gêné*') and yet very sympathetic, and she explained to me that she, also, had once had a daughter, named Xanthe, who had been very ill and died in the countryside where she had been sent to get well. Controlling her weeping with difficulty, she told me that she longed for children to love and care for. But she cannot be much under fifty, and will surely never have another. It is very sad.'

I went on and on, with Rose now reading over my shoulder, and it was in the entries for the month of September that we suddenly struck gold.

'All musical London is buzzing with the rumour that Joseph Krieger and his wife have adopted two small orphans. In my opinion, it is his wife's desire alone, but it was good of him to comply with her wishes.'

And in December, giving an account of one of the carefully organised concerts with the Queen's Band, complete with a description of Joseph Krieger's flabbergasting rendition of Mozart's fifth violin concerto (*'he played the so-called Turkish chromatic passages in the final movement with a lascivious daring that could leave no doubt as to his interpretation, if the question may still be asked about Mozart's intentions'*), he recounted seeing Mrs Krieger after the concert and asking after the children. *'She seems a different woman,'* he wrote, *'still nervous, tense and shy, certainly, but stronger. The little girls have given her a new purpose in life. I am glad for her, because she is a good woman, and deserves this happiness.'*

'Rose,' I said. 'Oh, Rose, I don't know what to think!'

'We've found Lydia,' she said. 'We simply must have. The two little girls were Lydia and Tanis. They must have been!'

'Yes,' I replied, 'but don't you see the problem? Both girls were adopted – so our idea that Lydia was the true daughter of the Kriegers must have been wrong. So even if Sebastian was her son and not Tanis' – why, it still does nothing to explain the "cursed inheritance"!'

'Oh, blow,' she said, 'you're right. We had it differently in our heads, didn't we?'

'We had thought that Tanis might be the daughter of friends of the Kriegers who had died,' I recalled.

'Maybe both girls were. Any friends of the Kriegers were probably musicians, and perhaps that would explain where Sebastian's talent came from.'

She laughed. 'If one admits that it needs any explanation at all,' she said. 'You know that Sebastian wouldn't agree. Anyway, it isn't the talent that needs explaining, it's what Professor Pezze said. He saw a *real* resemblance to Joseph Krieger, Vanessa. I can't not believe him – but neither can I see how it could be true! Oh, this is annoying – just when we were getting everything to be so plausible!'

'We simply must find out who the children really were, and where they came from,' I said, and at that moment, well before we had had time to finish reading the diaries, let alone digest the new information, the door opened and Professor Wessely came back in.

'You seem very busy,' he remarked. 'Have you found interesting things?'

'Extraordinarily interesting,' I blurted out. 'Did you know that Mrs Cavendish was adopted by Joseph Krieger and his wife?'

'Really?' He looked surprised. 'No, I didn't know that. I always assumed that Sebastian's talent came from his grandfather through his mother. It seemed something that ran in the family. I am not aware that Sebastian's mother played any instrument, but I noticed more than once that she has a profound feeling for and understanding of music. From seeing her over the course of several years at the concerts and recitals that take place here at the Academy, it was clear to me that she had a remarkable ear. In fact, I have more than once noticed her actually wincing at a wrong note, and when I say a wrong note, I am speaking of something very subtle, just the smallest bit off-colour, not something that would disturb an ordinary amateur.' He smiled. 'In any case, what importance does it have? None at all. As I told you, talent can flower anywhere, and the important thing is to nurture it once it is discovered. I am very grateful for the idea you have given me. I will certainly write to Mrs Cavendish about Wolfe.'

'Please, do not mention our visit!' said Rose quickly. 'We are acting on what we felt to be an unspoken wish of hers. She does not know of our search on her behalf, and might perhaps be annoyed by it.'

'Of course, of course,' he replied understandingly. 'Rest assured, I shall be most delicate.' He hesitated for a moment, glancing at his watch. 'I am sorry, I must lock the office and leave now. But you have been very helpful. Is there something that you would like to borrow from all this?' He indicated the papers scattered over his desk.

I gratefully took the notebooks for the years 1849 and 1850, and stowed them in my bag.

'I will take the best possible care of them,' I promised him, 'and bring them back to you tomorrow.'

He smiled again, warmly.

'They have lain untouched for a long time,' he said. 'Monsieur Sainton would be pleased, I think, to know that someone was reading them. It is important not to forget those who are dead.'

'They have much to say to us,' I agreed, but I was thinking of Sebastian, not Prosper Sainton.

'And many ways of saying it,' added Rose, and I knew her thoughts were running in the same channels as mine.

CHAPTER FOURTEEN

Vanessa takes a trip to a graveyard
that also leads into the past

I stood with Rose in the wind and cold damp which rendered even the luxurious gardens and splendid monuments of the Highgate Cemetery drab and gloomy, and stared down at the smooth earthen plot where Sebastian Cavendish reposed, his vibrant voice forever silent. The grass had been replanted, but the chill had not encouraged it to flourish, and only a couple of patches showed some straggling blades. Faded bouquets with brownish petals, tied with discoloured ribbons, still lay at the foot of the large stone cross, together with a few fresher ones. Clutching her own bunch of white lilies, Rose stood and contemplated them motionlessly.

The base of the cross was a solid four-sided block in grey stone, and in the frontal panel were carved the words:

IN MEMORY OF
JOSEPH KRIEGER
WHO DIED APRIL 10, 1850
AGED 60 YEARS

Joseph Krieger had prepared a tomb for his family, but they were not there. The other three sides of the block were bare and smooth. In front of one of them, a small wooden cross had been planted, upon which was mounted a tiny brass plate containing the words:

Sebastian Cavendish
1875–1900
Rest in Peace

'They haven't had time to carve it into the stone yet,' said Rose. 'It's such a little epitaph.'

'It's more beautiful so,' I said. 'Adding words wouldn't make it any better.'

'No one knows exactly what time he died, before or after midnight,' she went on with a catch in her voice. 'The carvers offered him 1900 as a kind of gift; that he should have seen the new century before he died.'

'That is a touching thought,' I said, and she burst into tears.

'No, it isn't,' she sobbed. 'He could have been spared those last hours. They must have been horrible.'

I had never asked about the precise circumstances

of Sebastian's death, contenting myself with the brief mention of taking poison that Rose had let fall on that first day at the memorial concert. Even now, when Rose spoke of it spontaneously, I felt inhibited about asking for details. Whatever Sebastian had taken, it would not make any difference, and I had no need to know.

If he had really taken it. Of his own will.

The thought entered my head unbidden, but not for the first time. In the last few days, it had presented itself there with a persistence that increased in proportion to the tenacity with which I pushed it away. I did not want to behave like a seeker after sensation – and yet – it did seem that the unfolding pattern was leading to discoveries which, exciting though they were and liable to cause a tumult of emotions, could not comprehensibly have led to a state of suicidal despair.

Consciously, at least, I tried to reject the idea. I told myself repeatedly that there might be, there must be, a missing link of some kind, and that I was not to jump to conclusions before knowing the full detail of Sebastian's actions on the day he died. But it lingered stubbornly in the recesses of my mind.

Someone could have been jealous of Sebastian.

Someone could have been angry with him.

Or someone could have been afraid of him, or of something he might do, or discover.

It wasn't difficult to construct mad theories. It was perhaps useless, and in any case certainly premature. But Rose's tearful words gave me an opening to find out something I had not known how to ask.

'Was it very dreadful?' I asked, taking her hand in both of mine.

'It was arsenic,' she wept. 'It was right there in the house; it had always been there. It's a terrible death, Vanessa, they say. Hours of terrible illness before you die.'

'Why on earth did he have arsenic in the house?' I asked, instantly alert. Chemists do not sell pure arsenic. Anyone in possession of arsenic may be justly suspected of planning a suicide.

'He took it from a porcelain pot on his mother's dressing table,' she said, wiping her eyes. 'She bought it in America. We went there three years ago on tour with the Academy orchestra. Sebastian was concertmaster, and we also played solo – we played the Brahms Double Concerto together. It was so exalting – I'll never forget it. The way we played that night. Oh, Sebastian!' Leaning forward, she suddenly set her bouquet of lilies in the middle of the patch of earth over the grave. She laid it down with both hands, almost pressing it, as though she could push the message of loving memory through the earth to the body below. She remained there for a moment, bent over, her hands on the flowers, communing silently. Then she stood up, her face calmer. Drawing my arm through hers, I led her towards the large entrance gate as she went on speaking.

'Mrs Cavendish came with us on the tour; she took care of some of the organisation. I suppose she enjoyed the opportunity to hear Sebastian, and also to see something of the United States. It really was great fun, and fascinatingly different, too. One of the things we found out was that American women believe that tiny doses of arsenic are splendid for the complexion. You can buy pots of it over there, and Mrs Cavendish got one. I found out later that some ladies actually do use it over here as well, but they've got to soak it off fly-papers. Personally, I should hate the idea of poisoning myself every day, but Mrs Cavendish does have a marvellous complexion for her age; she quite glows. Sebastian took the powder from her pot and put nearly all of it into a cup of coffee. He was all alone; alone and too ill to go for help.'

'He didn't want help,' I said. Again that little voice inside me argued. And Rose argued, too.

'I know why you say that, Vanessa. But he did want help – I know he did! He wasn't made to lie down and give up. Maybe his brain didn't want to be helped, but the life-force running through his veins – it must have!'

She was upset again, but she pulled herself together as a man in a black coat came towards us, holding up an umbrella against the rain that had now begun to fall, and a second one in his hand.

'It's coming down, ladies,' he said kindly, 'and it'll be worse in a minute. Would you like to take shelter in the lodge till it's over?' He looked at Rose's face and added, 'We'll make a nice cup of tea over my spirit lamp.'

The caretaker's room was stuffy, but it was not

too cold and there was a bench covered with a ragged blanket upon which we sat while he bustled about with kettle and mugs.

'You been visiting a new grave?' he asked conversationally.

'Yes, Sebastian Cavendish's,' I told him. 'The epitaph hasn't been carved yet.'

'Oh right. 'E 'asn't started yet on that one, our carver. 'E's finishing another one; a posh one it is, in the Circle of Lebanon. Someone new in a family vault. 'E'll do the Cavendish stone next.'

He glanced out of a tiny window divided into even tinier panes, dimmed with raindrops on the outside and grime and spiderwebs within.

''E was out there working this morning. I expect 'e'll come in 'ere in a minute. 'E doesn't much like the rain. Oh, 'ere 'e comes now.'

The man who entered the lodge, the collar of his rain-streaked workman's jacket pulled up over his head, was grizzled and so old that I was surprised he could still manage such a demanding task. But his knotted hands were strong. He set down a few tools and sat next to me on the bench. I squeezed over a little to make room for him, and we greeted each other.

'Sheltering from the rain, eh?' he said. 'Visiting tombs, were you?'

'Yes. And you have been working?'

'Oh yes, I have. Gold leaf inside the letters on that one,' and he smiled largely, showing a missing front tooth. 'Which is yours? Or were you just seeing the sights?'

'No, we were visiting a new one. Sebastian Cavendish.'

'Oh right, yes. I'll be doing that one next. Poor old Joseph's finally got some company.' He smiled again gappily, and took the mug of very sugary tea that the caretaker offered him, remarking sympathetically,

'Been lonely for a long time, 'e 'as.'

'The dead people here are your friends,' I said, seeing suddenly how simple and obvious this was, and how much sense it made.

'Why, of course they are,' said the caretaker. 'We know 'em all, every one in-di-vi-dually, don't we, Jack?'

'Carved dozens o' their stones with me own 'ands,' answered the carver with quiet pride. 'And no worse than the ones that came before, if I do say so myself.'

'Did you carve Joseph Krieger's?'

'No, I didn't do that one, but I saw it done. I was serving my apprenticeship then. I 'ad a good master; good technique and plenty of style. Those words will be legible for a long, long time yet. I'm going to use the same lettering for young Sebastian's.'

'What about Joseph Krieger's wife?' I asked, suddenly curious. 'Why isn't anything carved for her?'

'She's not buried 'ere,' he said, and then added unexpectedly, 'I remember 'er well. She came to the grave with 'er daughters twice a year to garden it a bit, clean it up, set in some flowers. Every year twice, she came. In the autumn, and she'd plant bulbs around the edge, and then in the spring, when they bloomed, to clear off the winter's debris. Only one kind of flower: yellow tulips. Never anything else. The *Black Tulip* novel came out that year, and 'alf the graves 'ere 'ad them on it the next spring, only it was the purple ones that everyone was planting – there weren't no black ones for real. But Mrs Krieger, she went on year after year, always the same thing: a ring of yellow tulips right around the edge and a grass plot in the middle. That's why I remember it so well. As soon as I'd see those tulip buds in February, I'd start expecting 'er next visit.'

Mesmerised by this discourse, I waited until he had stopped speaking and even several seconds after, afraid to disrupt the natural flow of his memory by insistent questions. When I finally spoke, it was just to gently repeat his words.

'She used to come with her daughters?'

'That's right. Just little things they were in the beginning, all dressed in black like their mother. Energetic little creatures, quite a 'andful they must have been and she a widow. I saw them grow from little girls into big ones and then one year they stopped coming.'

'Do you know why?'

'I didn't then,' he said, 'but I do now, for I asked young Sebastian's mother about it last month when I met with 'er about the epitaph. One of the little girls, she was. The littler one. Anyway, it seems that the Kriegers 'ad 'ad a child who died out in the country somewhere, and was buried there, and Joseph Krieger's wife wanted to be buried with 'er child.'

'I would want the same thing, in that situation,' I said.

'She might easily 'ave asked for the child's coffin to be exhumed and brought 'ere,' he said with a note of huffiness in his voice. 'The Krieger plot is for four; all paid for and everything, it is. I wonder she didn't do that. No one told 'er, perhaps. A pity. They could 'ave all been together. It isn't too late now, either,' he added. 'I told Mrs Cavendish, I did. "Why don't you 'ave your mother brought 'ome," I said to 'er, "so you can all be together?" '

'And what did she say?'

'She said they were well where they were. But I'm thinking that she wants to keep one of the places for 'erself. Save 'er 'aving to buy one, and they're getting more expensive than they were. And it stands to reason that she'll want to be with 'er son. Poor woman,' he added in a slightly perfunctory tone, a token of respect for the unofficial aspects of mourning, so much less familiar to him than the formal ones, amongst which he felt easy and comfortable.

The rain stopped and a feeble ray of sunshine gleamed palely through the grey clouds. Rose and I got up to leave, handing our mugs back to the caretaker.

'Vanessa, everywhere we go, we find out something,' she said as we made our way out of the gate. 'Now we *know* it's all true, what we read in the notebooks about the adopted children! It's not that I didn't believe it, of

211

course, but meeting someone who actually saw them does make a difference, doesn't it? The younger one was Tanis, and the bigger girl simply must have been Lydia!'

'Illegitimate children of Joseph Krieger,' I blurted out. This thought had been vaguely in my head since we had read about the adoption of both girls in Prosper Sainton's notebooks. But I had not liked to mention it to Rose; it seemed to open doors upon such a world of impropriety and sin and evil.

Rose looked at me in surprise.

'You really think that?' she said. 'But surely Mrs Krieger would not have wanted to adopt her husband's children by some mistress, and love them, and bring them up as her own.'

'You've heard of Edith Nesbit?' I asked thoughtfully. 'You know, the woman socialist – one of the founders of the Fabian Society. My friend Sir Oliver Lodge belongs, and so does Bertrand Russell, the mathematician – I met him once. She's published some absolutely wonderful children's books; I've read them to the twins. Anyway, they are all very advanced, these people, and everyone knows that Edith Nesbit lives with her husband and his mistress all together in one house, and they're bringing up the children of both women as one big family.'

'You call that advanced?' said Rose. 'It sounds to me like the behaviour of people from a primitive tribe somewhere, or from Biblical times.'

'No,' I said, 'the difference is that these women bring up their children together from their own choice. They feel that they are in the vanguard of a movement to break out of the bonds of conventional morality.'

She looked at me askance.

'You think Mrs Krieger was like that?'

'Well, not really,' I admitted. 'But she wouldn't have had to live with the mistress or even know her. Perhaps the mistress died. And she did long for little children to care for.'

'You're sure there was nothing at all in the rest of Sainton's diary?' she said hopefully. 'If Krieger had a mistress, there might have been rumours.'

'Oh, believe me, I looked,' I exclaimed. 'When I went to give back the ones I borrowed, I stayed in Professor Wessely's office for a long time and reread all the earlier ones. There's no mention of such a thing at all. In fact, to be honest, Sainton actually says that Krieger did not much like women. But I wouldn't pay much attention to that. A man can dislike or despise women and have a mistress all the same. Anyway, soon after the bit we read, where they were friends, they quarrelled. Sainton would have accepted that Krieger didn't wish to play again with the Queen's Band, but Krieger went overboard being offensive about it. So they stopped seeing each other, and then in 1850 Krieger died. Sainton just mentions it in passing, and says it was a tragedy for the musical scene of London, and totally unexpected. I remember reading in Dr Bernstein's book that Lydia's father died when she was four, so it hangs together perfectly with her having been adopted in

1848 when she would have been two and her sister just a baby.'

'And then, when Mrs Krieger finally died, she wanted to go away and be buried with her dead child,' said Rose. 'She must have left specific instructions to avoid being buried here instead. If she'd said nothing, she certainly would have been.'

'Yes. It was funny how lightly that man spoke of exhumation, wasn't it? He doesn't realise that it makes us ordinary mortals shudder.'

'I don't think that was the problem,' said Rose moodily. 'I think Mrs Krieger wanted to get away from her husband. Nobody liked him. He must have been quite horrid. Why should she lie next to him for eternity instead of being in a peaceful, quiet little corner of countryside with the child that she loved? And this way she could leave the empty spaces for the two adopted children, who had barely known Krieger and needn't feel the same way about him.'

I smiled. 'I have to say in his favour that it's nice he let her adopt them,' I said. 'He probably didn't want them at all. So you have to give him some credit, as Monsieur Sainton did.'

We left the cemetery and took a cab for the long ride back to town. I sat still, letting the conversations I had just been having run through my mind. There had been a little question in my head as Rose and I were walking away from the tombstone together, but it had disappeared underneath all the information from the

214

epitaph carver. Now it came back to me.

'Rose,' I said, 'I wonder why Sebastian was alone at home on the evening of December 31st, when everyone in the entire country was going to a party?' *Who knew he was going to be alone at home?* whispered a little voice somewhere inside me. But no – I repressed it. I was simply supposed to be finding out exactly what Sebastian had been doing all through that final day. *Yes,* came back the stubborn little voice, *and whom he was doing it with? And who might have wished that Sebastian would die?*

'He wasn't supposed to be alone at home,' she said. 'He was supposed to go to a party – Lord Warburton's grand Centennial Ball. I know it, because he and Claire and I had all three been invited to another party for the new century, but Sebastian couldn't come with us, because Mrs Cavendish wanted him to go to Lord Warburton's ball with her. Only he didn't go there, either, because he wasn't home. He hadn't been home since he had left for Zürich; he hadn't slept at home the night before, so she simply didn't know where he was. On the 31st, she expected that he would arrive or at least send a message, but he didn't, so she left by herself, thinking that he could always join them if he did get home later on.'

'She wasn't worried about his unexpected disappearance?'

'Not when he didn't arrive on the 30th as he should have. She simply thought that he had had an opportunity to stay in Zürich for another day. That wouldn't have been unusual. He was twenty-four, after all. You'd think he might have sent a telegram, but he wasn't always a particularly thoughtful person, you know. He liked to be free, and she respected that and never made him give an account of himself. On the 31st she probably felt annoyed as well as worried, as she was expecting him to accompany her to Lord Warburton's ball, and it would have been unthinkable for her not to be there, since they are engaged to be married and she was to act as hostess. Till the last minute, she thought he would turn up, but he never did.'

'So she went to the ball by herself?'

'Yes, she really had no choice, and once she was there she had to stay nearly all night. There were fireworks and dancing and a midnight supper. The guests didn't leave the party till dawn, and then she came home exhausted to a perfectly silent house and saw Sebastian's coat and hat on the hall stand, so she assumed that he had arrived too late for the ball and had simply gone straight to bed. I know all this because the police went through it with her and then they explained everything to Claire. Mrs Cavendish went directly to bed herself, and the next morning she rose fairly early and went out. Sebastian kept irregular hours and often slept late, so she did not disturb him. It was the charwoman who found him when she came in to do the daily cleaning.'

'I wonder why Mrs Cavendish employs a charwoman,' I said. 'I would have thought she would have servants.'

'The Cavendishes didn't have enough money for live-in servants,' said Rose. 'I told you about that; Mr Cavendish left too many debts when he died. Mrs

Cavendish was able to pay Sebastian's school fees, and she gave him a small allowance. He was already starting to make a living from his concerts, and they got by. They had no servants at all except for this charwoman who came in by the day, to clean the house and prepare the afternoon and the evening meal.'

'Well,' I said, 'Mrs Cavendish puts a good face upon it. She looks for all the world like an elegant lady with a personal maid to take care of her hair and her dresses.'

'She is very elegant, that's true. She must have a sewing girl in from time to time. I don't imagine she actually does her own sewing.'

'Or her washing,' I added.

'That probably gets sent out as well,' said Rose. 'It all costs less than having servants living in the house. And when she marries Lord Warburton, she'll be very wealthy and have all the service she wants. I suppose the prospect of beginning a new and much easier life cannot but help her a little at this awful time. Lord Warburton is a widower himself; from the little I've seen of them together, they seem very well suited. Of a similar temperament, somehow. Very traditional, very upright, very proper.'

'I hope all will be well for them,' I said thoughtfully. 'I suppose that the charwoman will no longer be employed by Mrs Cavendish once the marriage takes place.'

'Surely not. They'll have plenty of servants then. But I'm sure the poor woman will find another place of work. Only too many people need charwomen nowadays, don't they? And probably Mrs Cavendish will give her a recommendation.'

'I would like to talk to that charwoman,' I said. 'I really would. I wonder if you could find out, or ask Claire to find out who she is.'

'I suppose that wouldn't be difficult,' said Rose. 'But what on earth do you expect to learn from her?'

'I don't know,' I said. 'But it occurs to me that it's quite incredible what servants can know about the secrets hidden within families, and I suppose that the same must apply to charwomen.'

'Charwomen, gravediggers and who knows who else,' she said. 'You're right, of course. I'll find out about her for you.'

CHAPTER FIFTEEN

In which Vanessa meets a charwoman who
knows no secrets but a little fact
which suddenly changes everything

I stood waiting patiently outside the imposing building where Mrs Cavendish had her flat, occasionally glancing at my watch. Rose had obtained from Claire the information that the charwoman, Mrs Munn, generally arrived at the Cavendish home at eleven in the morning and left at nine o'clock, after dinner had been served and cleared away. The woman had spent ten hours of every day but Sunday, for years, probably, in Sebastian's home. There could be little, I thought, that she did not know about the family.

Rose, who had seen Mrs Munn briefly once or twice at the house while visiting, had described her to me as a small, thin woman in black. This description perfectly fit the woman who stepped out of the front door at some minutes before nine o'clock, carrying a handbag and an umbrella.

'Mrs Munn?' I said in a quiet and reassuring voice, stepping out of the shadows. In spite of these precautions, she jumped, and threw me a look of suspicion and deep annoyance.

'Certainly not!' she snapped. 'My name is Mrs Davenport-Brown, and I would be very grateful if you would take yourself away from these premises at once, and cease importuning the residents!' She stalked away in a huff, her nose in the air, and, watching her, I berated myself for having failed, in the dusk, to notice her haughty bearing and the refined cut of her coat.

Five minutes later another small, thin woman in black emerged, this one carrying a generous holdall. I took a closer look before speaking again.

'Mrs Munn?'

Startled, she looked at me with an expression not dissimilar to Mrs Davenport-Brown's. I was, however, fingering one of those notes that are, sadly, so useful and necessary to working people as to quite modify their behaviour on occasion, and I now slipped this into her hand.

'I should very much like to speak with you for a short time,' I said gently. 'I do not mean to disturb you, but perhaps you could spare me a few moments?'

'I need to get home,' she said, looking me up and down. But perhaps home was not such a very alluring

220

prospect for her, for her reluctance to accompany me appeared quite ready to be overcome.

'We could perhaps sit down somewhere for half an hour,' I proposed, and her face brightened.

'And get a bite to eat, maybe?' she said hopefully.

'Of course, if you wish! Have you not dined yet? You don't eat dinner at your work?'

'You've no idea how difficult the times are, madam,' she said, peering at me closely in the gloaming, as though to gauge whether I was of a class that could possibly comprehend her problems. 'What with my husband sick at home, it's been years now he can't walk, after his accident falling off the building at work.' She fingered her bag almost unconsciously while speaking.

'You bring your food home to him?' I guessed, observing her gesture.

'And it isn't a great deal, either,' she said defensively. 'Mrs Cavendish don't eat like a queen, she don't. A cutlet and some beans and pudding, that will be her dinner. It's next to nothing since the young man died. I don't know how we'll manage. There used to be leftovers, there did. Before.'

'Oh my goodness,' I said. 'I should like to take you to dinner. I know a perfect place, truly I do. It's very near here; just behind King's Cross. A ten-minute walk. Would you come there with me?'

'I'd like to, madam, only my husband won't know where I am.'

As we drew under a gaslight, I saw that the poor

woman looked altogether torn and distressed by my proposal. She was indeed very thin, and the prospect of a good meal must have been an attractive one indeed. I had a glimpse of a life lived on the very boundary of misery. If an extra penny ever came the way of this poor woman, she was probably obliged to spend it on having her shoes repaired or other details required in order to look at least decent enough to enter the handsome building on Russell Square.

'It should be all right if I don't take too long,' she said. 'It happens that I stay extra some evenings, when Mrs Cavendish needs it. It brings in a few more pennies, so even if supper is late on those days, sometimes it runs to a sausage. He don't mind waiting if it's for a good reason.'

We walked together to Jenny's Corner, a little restaurant that I would never have discovered, let alone dined at, had it not been for extraordinary circumstances linked to another mystery, of many years ago now. Jenny had been warm and comforting in those difficult days, and now, distinctly older and distinctly rounder, she was still warm and comforting, and her little restaurant still served the weekly round of customer favourites that had kept her making a modest but tidy profit year after year. Arthur and I went there at least once each year as a matter of friendship and of memory, and even though we were perhaps a slightly strange sight in the busy little place crowded with working bachelors, we were always made welcome in a corner and treated with a warm-hearted and spontaneous kindness that was worth more than any ceremonious courtesy in the world.

I was eager to take Mrs Munn there; it seemed to me of all possible places in London the one I knew most suited to making her feel at home and drawing her out. As we walked, talking of nothing more than the wintry chill and the difficulties of sore feet and aching backs, I saw that she was agitated by a certain anxiety, as well she might be, having no idea where we were going. However, as we drew within sight of the bustling little restaurant, from whose slightly open door emerged a cloud of steam, smoke and conversation, she heaved a pleased sigh. We entered, and a sallow girl in a checked dress and apron came to show us to a table.

'Please, bring us two of the daily specials,' I told her, 'and do tell Jenny that Mrs Weatherburn is here. I should love to greet her when she has a moment.'

Jenny arrived moments later, carrying a plate in each hand, piping hot and laden with a generous quantity of beef, gravy, mashed potatoes and green beans. Having set them down in front of us, she enveloped me in a quick hug – a tradition of many years' standing – and asked after Arthur and the twins. Then she turned to examine my guest, summed her up in a moment, and extended a plump, red hand in friendship.

'Glad to meet you, love,' she said, grasping Mrs Munn's bony one. 'Any friend of Mrs Weatherburn's is a friend of mine. Please do enjoy your suppers. There'll be pudding when you want it, and a cup o' tea if you need it.' And she bustled back to her kitchen.

Mrs Munn looked at the food with an expression of ineffable sadness. I thought of the poor remains she had packed away in her bag, which were to constitute her husband's meagre dinner. It seemed unfair, but I could not think of any way to mend it right now; one could hardly put mashed potatoes and gravy into a holdall. But here was Mrs Munn, who worked hard all day, sitting in front of a succulent and well-deserved meal looking sad, and it seemed to me that the most urgent thing right now was that she should enjoy it as much as she could. So I picked up my silverware and encouragingly scooped up a generous forkful, and was sincerely delighted to see her follow suit.

I did not attempt to enter into any explanations until the meal was finished, and Mrs Munn must have been a bit overwhelmed by it all, for she did not ask a single question. But over steaming teacups, while I was searching for the right words to begin, she spoke suddenly.

'There must be a reason, madam, for you doing all this,' she said. 'But I can't guess what it might be, not even now that I've eaten a square meal and my head is straight. You want something of me, madam, I'm certain, but I'm afraid I shan't be able to give it to you, for I can't imagine what such as I might be able to do or say could be useful to someone like you. At any rate, though, as long as you don't tell me, it's certain I won't know.' She smiled for the first time that evening, and I suddenly perceived a little glimpse of a past Mrs Munn, probably gay and laughing and hopeful that life would hold many pleasant surprises in store.

London is filled with women such as Mrs Munn; women who work so hard they are practically enslaved, who eat so little they nearly faint, and who have the sole care of helpless dependents. Surely something is very wrong with our society, which allows such a thing to be so common that no one even takes any notice.

'All I want,' I told her, 'is to know a little bit about Sebastian Cavendish. You see, his friends are very upset about the way he died. They have asked me to see if I can try to understand why he did it.'

'There, I'm not surprised,' she said. 'You've gone and asked me a question that I've no idea about. I can't tell you why he did it, madam. It's a terrible sad thing, and he died in a terrible way, too. Very sick, horrible sick all night he was. To think of anyone wanting to do that to themselves.'

'You were the one who found the body? That must have been a terrible experience for you.'

'I knew something was wrong the moment I came in the house that morning,' she said. 'It was so weirdly quiet. I saw right away that Mrs Cavendish was out, her things being gone from the coat rack, but Master Sebastian was still in, yet everything was silent. It seems to me now that it was too silent, and I knew something was wrong as I came in the door. But perhaps I didn't know it quite so clearly. I did think he might simply be

225

sleeping, as a lot of people had come home from their parties in the wee hours that night. I didn't do anything at first, but, around midday, I wondered if I should be preparing something for him to eat or not, and I just knocked on the door and opened it a crack, to check. Oh, madam, there was a terrible smell of sickness! I just made out that he was lying on his bed, but dressed in his clothes, and that something was horribly wrong! I couldn't bear it – I didn't take one step inside the room. I ran out of the flat screaming and calling for help, and the neighbours came out and they helped me; one lady gave me some smelling salts and a gentleman went in to see what it was, and then he ran for the police. I couldn't bear to take another look, not at anything, madam; not even when they carried out the body. Then I had to clean up the room, though. It was a bad way to die; a bad, horrible business. Poor Master Sebastian. Whatever made him do such a thing!'

'Had you known him for many years?'

'Going on for ten years now,' she said. 'He was a big lad already when I first came, but such a nice one. A bit wild, perhaps, about getting his own way and such, but with a good heart. Always a smile and a nice word for me, he had, and when Christmas time came and Mrs Cavendish would give me an envelope, he'd always add something from his own pocket, and a bunch of flowers, every single Christmas for ten years although I told him it was too much for a poor old woman like me, flowers in December. Every year a bunch of flowers. They were the only flowers anyone's ever given me since the day I was married. They did look nice in a jug on the table at home. Brightened up the room, they did.'

'You must have known Sebastian well after all those years. Do you really not have any idea at all why he wanted to die? Any reason at all?'

'No, madam. I have asked myself. But really, it can't have been anything that I could know about. He must have kept it very close, whatever it was.'

'Or,' I said, 'it happened because of something he found out in the last few days before he died. Some secret about the family, perhaps.'

'I wouldn't know about anything like that.'

'Really not? You never overheard any talk with his mother about anything particular having to do with the family? I do have a reason for asking. I really think that Sebastian did discover something about his family before he died.'

'I don't remember any such discussion, madam; not any kind of talk between them about anything you might call secret, or intimate. They didn't have that kind of relation together. I'd say that if they had any secrets at all, they'd most likely have kept them from one another. They weren't close like some mothers are with their sons. Mrs Cavendish is a very private person.'

'Quite. Well, did you ever happen to hear any talk about Mrs Cavendish's father? There wouldn't have been anything secret about him, I suppose.'

'Him, the old violinist? Yes, I heard him mentioned.

Guests spoke of him pretty often. When Master Sebastian was still at school, he'd often get out his violin to play for guests. I'd be serving dinner and clearing up, so I heard him many a time. What a noise he could make on that violin of his! Sometimes the upstairs neighbours even banged on the ceiling, if they thought it was going on too long.'

'And what did you hear about Sebastian's grandfather?'

'Not much. Now that I think of it, Mrs Cavendish and Master Sebastian didn't seem to like to talk of him much. Guests would ask sometimes if Mrs Cavendish had any memories of her dad, or souvenirs or pictures, and she'd say that he'd died when she was a baby and she knew nothing of him at all. She'd get a bit short sometimes when he was spoken of, though she was always polite, of course, but I don't think she much liked to talk about him.'

'Did you ever hear anything about Mrs Cavendish having been an adopted child? That the old violinist was not really her father at all?'

She looked at me in surprise.

'No, I never heard a breath about such an idea as that. Is it true?'

'Apparently it is, and it seems that both Mrs Cavendish and Sebastian knew about it. Can you not remember ever hearing anything of the sort at all?'

She thought for a while.

'Not that. But there was a feeling that the memory of the old man wasn't much appreciated. I recall as Mrs

Cavendish used to not like when visitors would say that Master Sebastian played like his grandfather. "His way of playing comes from inside himself," she'd say. I don't think she actually even liked him playing music very much at all. She hoped he wouldn't become a musician. You asked about discussions; there were some when he left school and had to choose a profession. Then he said there was no question he'd go anywhere but to that music school, and she was very much against it and tried to persuade him to study law like his father.'

'Was Sebastian's father alive then? Did you know him?'

'Why, of course he was. He only died – let me see, when was it? It was five or six years ago. Yes, he was alive when I first came, though in poor health. He suffered badly from the gout, poor man. Such twinges he used to have in his toe. I helped him bathe his feet with special salts sometimes. Terrible, the shape they had.'

'Poor man,' I sympathised. 'And tell me, what did he say about Sebastian becoming a musician?'

'He said what will be, will be, and Sebastian should do what he wanted if he could make a success of it. Mrs Cavendish didn't like it. She would have rather her husband support her point of view, I guess, but she was never one to make any kind of quarrel, so she put the best possible face on it and let him go to the music school and didn't say anything about it any more. I guess she became proud of him later, when he started to play concerts in front of people and all. At least she would keep the concert programmes on her dressing table.'

'I should think so,' I said, quite intrigued by all that I was hearing. 'I would be proud, too, to have a son who played the violin as well as that. But if the old violinist was really not her father, I suppose I can imagine that it might annoy her if people kept saying that Sebastian's talent came from him, since she knew it wasn't true yet didn't like to publicly explain why. A person can hardly go around shouting that she is adopted.'

'I don't know anything about her being adopted or not,' Mrs Munn repeated.

'I have also heard that Mrs Cavendish had a sister,' I said.

'A sister? That's news to me as well. I never saw anyone from the mistress's family. I thought it was clear there wasn't a soul left.'

'Well, I know there was a sister, but I don't know if she's alive or dead now. But I have a rather strong suspicion that Sebastian didn't know about that sister, and that he found out that she existed just before he died.'

'You mean, when he looked in the papers in the desk?' said Mrs Munn with a gleam of understanding. I looked up sharply.

'What do you mean? When did he look at papers?'

'I noticed him looking through some of his mother's papers before he went away again,' she said with an air of backing down quickly. 'It doesn't mean anything, though. He was just looking at papers.'

'Why do you say that he went away again? Why "again"?'

'Well, he had already been and gone to Switzerland with his violin, for some grand concert over there.'

'Yes, of course. But that's only one trip.'

'Yes. And he came back, and left again.'

I was so excited that I forced myself to remain perfectly still for several moments, not wanting her to be startled and clam up, realising she had said something very important. Her words constituted the very first clue I had yet obtained about the gap – the missing hours between his arrival in London on December 30th (assuming that he had really left Zürich on December 29th as it seemed that he had) and his death on December 31st. From December 30th to December 31st, I still had no idea what he had been doing with himself. And now it seemed that a clue had suddenly fallen into my lap. And such a simple one!

'When did you see him looking at papers?' I asked very quietly.

'On the afternoon of the day before the day he died. On the 30th, it would have been.'

'At home, at the flat?'

'Of course, that's where I work. Naturally he came home after his trip. I did think that after having travelled in the train all day and all night, he'd be happy to get home and just stay there, but no. He was a restless one, he was. Off again right away, the same evening, and didn't sleep in his bed.'

'And you don't know where he went?'

'No, I've not the least idea. How should I?'

'Did he talk to you at all?'

'No, only just to say "Hello, Mrs Munn, how are you today?" He didn't even call out to me when he left. And when he saw that I saw him at the desk, he closed the study door.'

'Tell me exactly what you remember. What time did he come in and what did he do?'

'I can't be so exact. He came in in the afternoon and put his hat and overcoat and his violin and his suitcase all down in the hall. I heard him come in, then I don't know, he poured himself a drink, I think, and went about the house. I heard nothing at first, being in the kitchen in the back. But after a while, I came looking for him to ask him if he'd like a bite to eat after all the travelling. He was sitting on the floor in the study with the desk drawers all open. Mrs Cavendish keeps her desk locked, but I never thought there was anything special in there, only that she kept her money inside sometimes. Not even that she'd have private letters or anything like that. It's always been locked; no one ever paid attention, that was just her way. Master Sebastian grew up in that house, but I don't think he ever bothered to wonder what was in his mother's desk, for what should be there but ordinary papers and bills and such? Still, I'll wager he knew where the key was, for she'd open the desk sometimes to take out some money, and she used to open it up to put in his school reports when he was younger. Kids are like monkeys – they know everything about their home.'

'You must know quite everything there is to know about that flat, too, don't you?' I asked innocently. 'After so many years, I mean.'

'I never knew where she kept the key before and never asked myself,' she replied. 'I never came upon it in any of my work. But I know where it is now, for Master Sebastian put it away after he put the papers back. He came out of the study and I saw him go into his mother's room, and I went in after he had gone to check nothing was out of place and I saw that the grey hatbox wasn't stacked straight on top of the striped one as always, so I looked in. It was right inside the ribbons of the black bonnet she wore for mourning. It was a clever place to keep the key; no one would ever have any reason to look inside one of Mrs Cavendish's hatboxes and come upon the key by accident. I certainly never did.'

'What did you do with the key when you found it?'

'Why nothing, I left it there, of course.'

'And you never told Mrs Cavendish that Sebastian had looked through the desk?'

'Certainly not. What business was it of mine? I never even thought of it. I mean, when I saw him looking in there, all I thought was that he was needing a bit of money quickly. It didn't seem important.'

'And then he left?'

'Yes. Well, first asked me to draw him a bath, and he bathed and changed his clothing. And then he left.'

'Did he take the suitcase with him?'

'Yes, madam, he did. And the violin, too.'

I stared at her, digesting all of this information.

'And you didn't tell anyone about this?'

'No one asked me about it,' she said. 'I don't even know why you're asking me now, madam. I can't see that it has any importance. After all, he's dead, poor young man.'

CHAPTER SIXTEEN

In which Vanessa persuades a youngster
to allow himself to be led into doubtful ways

The day after Mrs Munn's extraordinary revelations, I came to a decision: there was something that absolutely had to be done, but I could not do it by myself. I needed help, and I thought I knew just where I might find it. At least, I thought I knew, but now I began to feel slightly lost. I went past Petticoat Lane and on down the Whitechapel Road, hesitating slightly. Where was the place exactly?

Around me bustled the life of the East End, as familiar as my own past and as foreign as an exotic, distant country. Yes, this was it. I turned onto Fieldgate Street and walked along, studying the miserable surroundings, until I came to the dingy little opening to Settles Street and stopped in front of the familiar tenement house where I had once visited David and Rivka Mendel for help in solving a case, only to discover that they were more deeply involved that I could have imagined. Rivka's cousin Jonathan had been courting my dearest friend Emily at the time, and although her subsequent engagement to the brilliant young mathematician Roland Hudson had put a stop to that, they had remained friends, and she mentioned him and his cousins to me now and again. Emily was always busy, however, trying to accomplish the feat of writing a doctoral thesis in mathematics at the University of London – the only one that would admit women to such a course of work – and I didn't see her often any more. Four years had gone by since those days, and I was not even sure whether Rivka and David still lived in the same flat.

A strange woman, her head wrapped up in a turban-like shawl, answered my knock at once. She was both unfriendly and suspicious at first, and did not appear to have a particularly advanced grasp of the English language, but my querying repetitions of David and Rivka's names eventually brought forth a response. She called forth a somewhat dirty small girl wearing an oversized dress and braids, and spoke to her in her own tongue. The girl grabbed me by the hand without ceremony and towed me unresistingly out of the house, down the street and around the corner to Greenfield Street. Unable to express the full wealth of her ideas, she grinned up at mc, revealing an amusing mixture of large, small and half-grown teeth, and contented herself by repeating 'Rivka,

Rivka Mendel' and nodding vigorously. She seemed to know exactly where she was going, so I followed along, emitting a concurring 'Rivka Mendel' with a satisfying feeling that our communication was by no means as impossible as might have been thought.

At a distance of between five and ten minutes from the old place, she stopped at another house, somewhat less peeling and rickety than her own. The front door stood open and a number of small children ran in and out, their faces, hands and knees of divers shades of lighter and darker grey.

'Sammy!' shouted the spunky child holding my hand, and one boy detached himself from the group and came over to her. I stared at him, admiring the wonders of time. A long-legged and knobbly-kneed child with bright brown eyes looked up at me, and I recalled the little Samuel tumbling about his mother's knees four years ago, now a great lad of six. A smaller boy drew up next to him, and then a third, successively decreasing in size. These three listened to the girl's explanations for a moment, then the oldest one turned to me and confirmed the situation by enquiring in perfect English: 'You want to see Rivka Mendel? She is my mother. Come upstairs.'

I followed him, and the two smaller lads followed me; like a small train chugging up a mountain, we mounted higher and higher until we arrived at the very top floor, where Samuel flung open the door and shouted out,

'Someone to see you, Ima!'

'Oh!' She turned around from where she had been bending over a baby, and straightened up, her hand to her head, pushing stray locks underneath the scarf that covered it, tied up in a knot at her nape.

'Vanessa!' she cried with real emotion as soon as she saw me, and ran into my arms with such pleasure that I felt that I had almost let slip a cherished friendship by keeping away for so long.

'Are all these your children?' I asked, amazed as the little group milled about the room, too curious to disappear back down the stairs.

'Yes, four of them now,' she said proudly. 'This is our baby Esther; a precious little girl, finally, after three great boys!' She picked up the little creature, enveloped in a cloud of pink and frills as though to celebrate the tiny femininity of her, and gestured me to an armchair, while she set about with one hand preparing a pot of tea, chattering all the while about the family's improved circumstances, her husband's promotion at his bank, the new flat with its three rooms and its own water closet and bath.

'And you, Vanessa?' she asked with interest, setting the teapot on the table and adding teacups, spoons, milk and sugar.

I was mentally searching for some explanation as to the stubborn invariability in the number of my children, when she clarified the real import of her question by adding,

'Are you still solving mysterious cases?'

'Sometimes,' I admitted. 'In fact, to be honest, that is why I came. I need help, and I thought that your husband's brother, young Ephraim, might be able to do something for me.' I blushed as I spoke, for I suspected that the plan I had in mind for the said Ephraim would not please his family, were they to know about it in any detail, although it would surely appeal to the adventurous temperament I remembered him to possess from my acquaintance with him four years earlier as an 11-year-old imp of exceptional capabilities.

A look of surprise crossed Rivka's face, and she reflected for a moment, then said,

'Well, I must say that I cannot imagine anything that would please him more.' But she didn't look absolutely delighted, and went on, 'I must tell you that Ephraim has never forgotten you and your work and the help he gave you, and ever since that time he has nourished the desire to become a detective. David does not really approve of such intentions on the part of his young brother. He would much prefer him to start work as an errand boy in his own bank, and rise through the ranks. But he says that Ephraim's fantasy will probably pass before he is an adult, and, at worst, he says it is surely better than the professions of most of the people in this part of town, who run about the streets of London with boxes, hawking everything from oranges to spectacles, and never knowing if they will sell enough to feed their family on any given day. Still, though, I'm afraid David won't much like your idea.' She stopped and sipped tea, then added, 'And yet, finding out the truth as you do is a *mitzvah*. An act of pure goodness.'

Another moment of reflection, during which I remained prudently silent, and she finally said, 'I think the fairest thing would be for you to talk to Ephraim yourself. He will be home from school at any moment. In fact, he may be home already if he has not dallied too much with his friends on the road. Shall I send Samuel to fetch him? Or perhaps we could simply walk there together? It is not far, and it will provide little Esther with an outing.'

She wrapped the baby up well – clearly there was no such item as a perambulator anywhere about, nor would it have been possible to negotiate one up and down four flights of stairs – and carried her in her arms, leaving her three tiny ones under the supervision of the oldest boy of the group at play about the doorway. She bounced the child gently up and down as we walked along the lane and around the corner, and turned right and left amongst ever more of the gloomy, dirty and rickety tenement houses that lined the road. Even the flowerpots in front of the occasional window, that must have cheered the miserable aspect of it all with a few bright-coloured geraniums in the spring, now held nothing but frostbitten, blackened stalks, and the roadway itself was covered with traces of slush, grit and unidentifiable filth. Yet the streets were very lively, filled with people, young and old, bustling about their activities; some stood at the doorways of their grimy shops and others wheeled carts, all calling out their wares; adults were making purchases and arguing about the prices, children were running about, playing, getting in the way and occasionally snatching a fruit that had rolled upon the ground with a gesture as quick as a monkey's, to the tune of shouting and scolding from the annoyed vendor.

Eventually we reached the house where Ephraim still lived with his older brother and their mother, Rivka's mother-in-law, and knocked at their door, from behind which enough sounds could be heard to tell us that more than one person was certainly at home.

The door was flung welcomingly wide, and Ephraim's freckled face looked out. It burst into a spontaneous grin of pleasure at the sight of me, which unmistakably corroborated Rivka's assertions. The impish child had grown up into a red-haired young man of fifteen, taller than me now in his stockinged feet, and with something of the relaxed pleasantness of his brother David, but more of a twinkle in his laughing eyes.

'Mrs Weatherburn!' he shouted, half at me, half back over his shoulder at the other occupants of the flat.

'Mrs Weatherburn wishes to speak to you particularly,' said Rivka in a low voice, glancing at me. 'I think it might be better if she could speak to you alone, rather than go inside now. I will visit with your mother for a while, if that is all right; not for too long, however, since I've left the boys at home.' Ephraim caught on instantly, pulled on his boots, leaving the laces dragging, and ushered

Rivka inside with her baby – then he hurried onto the landing, pulling the door closed behind him.

'Better not say anything to my mother,' he said, 'she'll ask where I'm going and all. Oh, I'm pleased to see you again! I have so many things to ask you! But do tell me – how are you? What have you come for? You look very well indeed. Do tell me why you have come? Is it another mystery? Is it?'

He led me down the stairs and out of the building as we spoke, and we walked along the road. In spite of the crowd and the cold, it was certainly the best possible place for a discreet conversation, as no one had a spare moment to notice or overhear a thing, not even to mention that few of the people surrounding us had the good fortune to speak English as well as Ephraim. Like his brothers, he had been awarded a scholarship to a regular British day-school, to which his mother had wisely elected to send him instead of keeping him at the local institutions where the children studied nothing but the Bible and the laws of the Jewish religion, entirely in their own language. In my opinion this rendered them unfit to ever emerge from their own miserable corner of London, which resembled nothing more than an Eastern European village transported bodily across the continent and set down unexpectedly on the edge of the metropolis.

'I do need help,' I said, 'and I cannot think of anyone who could possibly do what I need, except for you.' I stopped and purposely heaved a melancholy sigh. 'But I am afraid you will not want to do it. It is a problem.'

'Oh, but I will!' he said eagerly. 'Of course I will! Why wouldn't I?'

'Because,' I said, 'it is unfortunately something that might appear to be both bad and somewhat dangerous. But it's in a good cause.'

'Oh,' he said, very slightly crestfallen. He appeared to reflect for a moment, and I could hardly blame him. Surely if one is going to launch oneself into bad and dangerous activities at someone else's behest, one wishes to be certain that the instigator is trustworthy. Our previous experiences together had left me with a great stock of moral credit within the Mendel family, but still, that was four long years ago and they knew very little about me. Ephraim had doubtless been brought up with strict moral values. I awaited his final decision with interest.

'But you will tell me exactly what it is all about?' he finally said, a little meekly.

I laughed.

'It's a bargain. I will, and, moreover, you are only to do what I ask if you are as convinced as I am that it is necessary, possible, and ultimately not harmful,' I said. 'What do you want to know first: the what, or the why?'

'The what,' he responded at once. 'And probably I'd better know the when, as well!'

I hesitated. In spite of my innermost conviction of the justice, the necessity and the importance of what I was about to propose doing, some fundamental inhibition still prevented me from feeling quite open and above board about going so far as to rope a young and perfectly innocent boy into my plans. Yet I felt it really could not go wrong – at least, hardly – and the danger was only slight. A vision of Ephraim tearing down the streets of London pursued by bobbies shouting and waving their sticks streamed through my head.

'If I were to ask you to commit a small crime in a just cause,' I said, 'which would very soon be made good, and in which no one is hurt, would you be able to consider it?'

'Why not, if no one is the worse for it?' he said cheerily. 'What kind of crime?'

'I need you to snatch an elderly lady's bag and run away with it as fast as you can,' I told him, 'to a secret place which I will tell you, where I will be waiting for you. In her bag is a key to a flat. If you are willing to help me, we will go there together and you will stand guard at the door while I search inside as fast as I can.'

A frank mixture of astonishment, shock, dismay and admiration gleamed into his eyes.

'Oh my,' he remarked. 'But you will you tell me what you've found, won't you? But no, before I ask that, I should ask whether you mean the poor old lady to get her things back?'

'Certainly. As soon as I am finished, you will take the bag to the lady's house and give a penny to a small boy to carry it in to her, keeping an eye on him to see that he does it at once. And I will put something inside the bag to compensate her for the disagreeable experience.

But we must make the search directly we get the key, for although I don't think she would go to the police, she might just do so if an officer happened to be passing by on his beat. And if she tells him that she is frightened because she has a key to this flat in her bag and it was just stolen, he might rush there post-haste to check for thieves. I'm a little worried about that, and so we'll have to work incredibly fast.'

'Oh my,' he said again. 'Do you know what we are looking for? Are you actually going to take anything?'

'I don't know exactly what I am looking for, but I do know exactly where to look. It won't take long, and, with luck, I don't think I will need to take anything or to leave any trace at all of my presence in the house. Hopefully no one will ever know.'

'How exciting,' he said. 'When is this all to happen?'

'Very soon,' I said. 'I have simply been waiting for an opportunity to be absolutely certain that the lady who lives in the flat will be out when I need to go there, and, as a matter of fact, that opportunity has just arisen. Next Thursday there is to be a private concert and ceremony at the town house of a certain Lord, who is engaged to be married to this lady, and she is certain to attend.'

Indeed, contrary to all my expectations, Professor Wessely's letter to Mrs Cavendish, which must have been redacted with an unusual level of tact, had met with astonishing success. She had apparently consulted her betrothed, for the result was that Lord Warburton had accepted to become the patron of young Wolfe

Wolfinsohn until his majority, and an event had been organised at which the guests were to combine such friends of Lord Warburton as might also be interested by the possibility of transforming themselves into patrons of the arts, and musicians, both eminent professionals and friends of Sebastian. Not only was little Wolfe to be publicly presented with the gift of a monthly pension, modest indeed in view of Lord Warburton's fortune but quite sufficient to cover the child's expenses, but he was to play a short concert, and there was also to be a grand surprise, revealed to no one before the ceremony itself.

Rose and Claire were of course invited, and Rose passed me her card.

'This will get you inside,' she said, 'and no one will notice a thing. Lord Warburton and Mrs Cavendish will each think you were on the other's list of guests, and there will be quite enough people present for you to remain perfectly unnoticed. Do go – you never know whom you might meet, or what you might observe.'

'So it is to be Thursday?' said Ephraim, counting off the days on his fingers.

'Yes. Thursday, at nine o'clock in the evening. We will be at our posts from eight-thirty. I mustn't miss this opportunity.'

'We shall do it all right,' he said confidently. 'But when are you going to tell me what it's all about?'

'This minute, if you like,' I said, spotting the gold and white front of a Lyons a short distance up the Whitechapel Road, along which I was trying to keep up with Ephraim's step, whose rapidity was probably representative of a half-conscious effort to distance himself from his mother, the hub of his world and the human embodiment of his conscience. I drew him inside and ordered tea and cakes, as always blessing Mr Lyons for the recent creation of these unpoetic but clean and orderly places, which offered to an incalculable number of chilled, lonely women and shy, impoverished working girls a cup of tea or a sausage roll when no other place would be safe or suitable.

Since the first Lyons had opened six years ago, they had multiplied like mushrooms all over London, thus proving the existence of a widespread, long-repressed and frustrated demand. If only there were more Mr Lyons about, I thought, to answer the multitude of other ignored needs of women; all the infinity of little needs that combined into one great, giant need to be allowed to emerge from the shadows of a uniquely private life into the sunshine of the grand world of ideas and actions. I should not grudge them their profit, and should wish all of their pockets filled with gold, if only they would be so noble as to come to our aid and free us from our prison, the bars of which are made of unsuitability, modesty and masculine decree. Poor dear Queen Victoria, as long as she continues to champion by word, act and example, the familiar concept that woman's sphere is the home and that public appearance is to be shunned, her reign will not have the honour of being the cradle of revolutionary change. But she is eighty and a new century is beginning, and we shall see what we shall see. In the meantime, thank goodness for Lyons, and for all the individual efforts of women – with particular attention to mathematicians, cellists and detectives – to thrust vibrant green shoots out from the rich soil of the private home, and let them grow and thrive in the open air.

In front of the steaming cups, I told Ephraim the story from the beginning. His life kept him at such a distance from the people concerned in my story that I felt as discreet in talking to him about them as though I had been talking to myself, or simply telling him the story of a novel. He drank it all in with passionate interest. It was much more than a mere story to him. It was an initiation.

'How dreadful to have wanted to die without explaining why. You *must* find out,' he cried, and his words and his tone reflected the sympathy, the innate curiosity, and the profound desire to understand and penetrate to the heart of things that characterises the heart of a detective. I spoke to him as to a younger colleague, he responded in kind, and my heart was pleasantly warmed with the prospect of having a willing and able travelling companion to accompany me over some of the worst humps in my lonely and disturbing journeys.

CHAPTER SEVENTEEN

*In which Vanessa causes an infraction to be committed
and commits one herself*

I stood by the long, cloth-covered table laden with sumptuous refreshments, holding the champagne flute with which a white-gloved footman had kindly provided me from a circulating tray, and trying to keep out of the way of bumping by the people who crowded all about. Everyone was eating, drinking and uttering pleasant remarks on the subject of the delightful concert to which we had just been treated, the remarkable talent on the part of one so young, the admirable generosity of Lord Warburton who was undertaking the support of the boy for the duration of his studies, and the extraordinary, unexpected and touching gesture of Mrs Cavendish. Indeed, at the conclusion of the formal words pronounced by Lord Warburton on the subject of his pleasure at being able to contribute something useful to so worthy a cause, she had stepped forward, dressed in the deepest mourning, and, with no more than an inaudible mumble, thrust a violin case into the boy's hands and then sat down again abruptly. Lord Warburton helped the child open the case and extract from it a violin so beautiful that those in the audience not familiar with it gasped as it was held up to view: the rich tones of red-gold varnish, the burnished appearance that only age could provide, and above all the extraordinary lion's head with its roaring open mouth that replaced the traditional scroll.

This, then, was the announced surprise: Mrs Cavendish had given Wolfe Sebastian's violin. The splendid beauty and generosity of this gift, from a woman so grievously bereaved, was much admired by the assembled guests. Even with all the admirable self-control at her command, I noticed that Mrs Cavendish closed her eyes momentarily as the dark rectangular case left her hands, and averted her gaze from the violin when it was shown. I thought of the recently dug grave at Highgate, and of my twins, and of the unspeakable pain of losing a child to grinning death. Mrs Cavendish's mother had also known that pain, I recalled, and a sudden urge rose up inside me to know more about what had happened to that other girl, so long ago.

The concert that followed lasted no longer than a half-hour, as Lord Warburton was no doubt wary of unduly taxing the concentration abilities of his aristocratic guests, but it displayed young Wolfe to his best advantage as he played turn by turn religious music, lilting melodies and pieces of astonishing virtuosity. His teacher sat in the front row, the new violin on his lap, fingering its wood and strings gently, listening, and nodding his head. When it was over there was polite applause, and a pair of wide double doors was opened, leading into the dining room in which the long and well-laden tables had been exquisitely prepared.

I stood by the table, trying to be unnoticeable, and kept my eyes on Mrs Cavendish. My one fear was that the emotion of the evening would prove too much for her, and that she would request to be taken home – which would have seriously interfered with my plans! I was relieved to see, however, that between the compliments of the guests, a glass of champagne, and above all the considerate and protective behaviour of Lord Warburton, who stood near her, his hand on her elbow, she appeared to be reasonably master of the situation, and to have no intention of retiring. As I waited and watched, I followed Lord Warburton with my eyes, and admired his kind air and his upright bearing.

And I wondered suddenly.

How would such a man react if told that the sister of his bride-to-be was a madwoman? A man of noble birth, who bore an ancient tradition in his blood, and a man who, according to John Milrose, was a believer in Galton's plan of eugenics, according to which the English race must be improved and strengthened by enforced sterilisation of anyone who was suspected of any kind of hereditary mental disease.

If the truth were known, he might no longer wish to marry Mrs Cavendish. Even though she was beyond the age of bearing children, such a marriage would fly in the face of his beliefs and render him a laughing-stock amongst his peers and colleagues. Might not Sebastian have been forcibly stopped from bringing the knowledge of Lydia's existence to the attention of the eugenicist Lord? My eyes, which were resting on Mrs Cavendish, moved slowly over to her betrothed.

What if, in fact, Lord Warburton had been told the truth – what if Sebastian had discovered that Lydia was still alive, hidden away somewhere, and had gone to Lord Warburton to tell him about her and demand help. What if, shocked by the discovery, Lord Warburton realised that it would render his marriage impossible, and yet simultaneously that his love for Mrs Cavendish was too strong to be denied? What if, locked in a dreadful bind, he could neither renounce nor accept his coming marriage? Reserved and aristocratic as he was, it was obvious that he was deeply enamoured, and, indeed, Mrs Cavendish was a very beautiful woman, even if some of her glow was due to arsenical treatment. This evening, she was the very picture of noble and touching grief, allied with the infinite benevolence of a goddess. Was it out of the question that he might wish to solve the problem by suppressing all possibility of the unpleasant knowledge ever being revealed, by silencing the interfering youth?

Ah, the insistent idea of murder, sneaking yet again

into my mind of its own accord, taking me unawares. Sebastian was considered to have killed himself. He *may* have killed himself. Why was I so suspicious, so doubting?

I simply could not picture Sebastian being driven to despair and self-immolation by the discoveries that were emerging, little by little. Lydia K. – Lydia Krieger, I was now convinced – had been no madder than Hélène Smith; Dr Bernstein had said so clearly. And even if she had become so – even if beautiful, gentle Lydia had somehow, in the twenty-five years since he had lost sight of her, become so uncontrollably and so incurably mad that she was now lost amongst the very dregs of humanity; those that are locked away in the deepest and most miserable dungeons of the insane asylums – even then, I still did not believe that Sebastian would go home and kill himself over it.

But!

Now, at this very instant, while standing next to the tables, my dazed eyes following Lord Warburton as he circulated amongst his guests, holding in his hand a porcelain dish edged with a ring of gold and containing a tiny silver fork and a dainty and diminutive mince pie, I suddenly had enough of mere ruminations. There was information waiting for me in Mrs Cavendish's desk drawers, and now was the very time to go and find it! Setting down my teacup, I passed back towards the double doors opening into the drawing room in which the concert had been held. On each side of these, a pair of enormously thick curtains had been gathered, leaving the opening free. As I went through the doorway, I became aware of movements within the green velvet folds. I paused for the slightest moment.

There were two people. I heard very muffled whispers.

'No! You mustn't! John, stop!'

'I love you, Claire. I adore you. Please – let me speak!'

'No! I can't – I mustn't hear it!'

I went through, but turned my head and glanced back as I left. Claire hurried out from the curtains alone, her face flushed with confusion and distress, and walked unsteadily towards the tea table. I waited until John Milrose followed her, a long moment later. His face was grim, but also determined.

John Milrose was so in love with Claire that he couldn't even bring himself to respect her grief, let alone the memory of his friend.

He, too, had a reason to wish Sebastian out of the way.

My mind was out of control, it seemed, in a turmoil of wild suspicion; terrible, generic suspicion that seemed ready to be directed upon anyone who happened to pass in front of me. This was quite unacceptable! I hurried outside, and immediately took a cab and directed it to Russell Square. An unbearable pressure seemed to work upon me from within, and Mrs Cavendish's desk drawers took on, in my mind, the features of the Oracle of Delphi. I did not know what I should find there, and perhaps when I found it, I would not understand it. Yet it hardly mattered, as long as there was *something*.

I stood in the garden in the centre of Russell Square, sheltered from the drizzle underneath a large umbrella which further served to hide my features from the occasional passer-by (who in any case was too occupied with dogs on leashes or squalling children to care), and looked over at Mrs Cavendish's building, to see if I could spot young Ephraim lurking in the shadows, ready and waiting according to our plan. It was not easy to see in the darkness and rain, but I could just make out the occasional movements of a dim figure in a nearby doorway. The appointed hour was drawing near.

At nine o'clock the door opened, letting out a shaft of light that reflected in a thousand twinkles on the rain-shimmering pavement. Out came Mrs Munn – I made sure it was really she – and paused to reach into her large holdall and extract an umbrella, which she opened before setting off along the side of the square.

Yes! A swift and silent shadow was following her, at a short distance.

The two figures disappeared around the corner, and there was nothing for me to do but wait, whilst imaginary pictures of the events that were to take place thrust themselves into my mind in richly coloured contradictions. Here, Ephraim attacked the poor old lady, accidentally throwing her to the ground in his haste, and then stopped to raise her to her feet, drowning in humble apologies, his natural politeness smothering all the nefarious intentions I had so carefully introduced into his innocently boyish mind. There, the poor woman unexpectedly hailed a passing omnibus and hopped nimbly inside, taking Ephraim by surprise and leaving him standing empty-handed under the pouring rain. Finally, I imagined him succeeding in snatching away the bag and hotfooting it back towards Russell Square, pursued by Mrs Munn's shrieks of 'Stop thief!', several angry passers-by and a bobby, all of whom would stop directly in front of me and stare squarely into my face while Ephraim handed me his booty with a sheepish expression.

Lost in these visions of distress, I never even heard a sound as Ephraim actually approached me in reality. His step suddenly sounding in my very ear caused me to jump out of my skin, and I turned around with a gasp. The boy handed me Mrs Munn's capacious bag in silence, his expression a mixture of relief, guilt and sadness.

'Ah, thank you,' I said, somewhat absurdly.

'It was much harder than I thought it would be,' he said, following my hurried steps out of the garden and onto the street. 'I mean, it was very easy, in fact. I simply snatched the bag from her hand and ran. She cried out something, but there was no one around. I didn't even have to run fast. But I thought I wasn't going to be able to bring myself to do it. It's awful, awful. I can't believe I just did this to that poor old lady. I thought I wasn't going to be able to. I didn't realise that there was such a big, strong thing inside me trying to stop me. I thought I wasn't going to be able to make myself do it. It was so mean. I feel so bad.'

Water streamed down his face, but as he was absolutely dripping with rain, I made no assumptions, but laid my hand gently upon his arm.

'We will get it back to her and make it up to her,' I promised. 'Just as soon as I'm finished here. Come quickly, now.'

'But she has to take a 'bus and she'll not have the fare,' he sniffled.

'I know. I'm sorry. But Mrs Munn has lived through much greater difficulties in her life than this. It's not such a catastrophe. She will manage. Come now, we may have only a few minutes. Quick!'

We crossed the road together and Ephraim stationed himself in front of the door of the building as a lookout, ready to rush up and call me to come running out the very moment he should spy anyone approaching. I climbed the stairs, quickly removed my wet wrap and boots, and laid them with my umbrella outside the flat so as to leave no traces at all inside. Then I located the key with my fingers inside Mrs Munn's bag, unlocked the door without difficulty, and entered Sebastian's flat for the first time.

The flat was eerily quiet. I knew it would be empty, yet the silence was disturbing – though a sudden or mysterious noise would certainly have been worse! In my stockings, I stepped down the corridor, passing the open doors to the parlour on my left and the dining room on my right. Farther down, the doors were closed. I tentatively opened the first one, then closed it again quickly, then opened it again. So this was Sebastian's room.

It perfectly neat and perfectly clean, but probably no more so than it had been on a daily basis even during his life. I raised a corner of the quilted cover laid upon the bed, and saw that it was laid over the bare mattress; the bed had been stripped. But a music stand in the corner, books and music on the shelves, and clothes in the closet, spoke for the heart that had beat in this room.

I had no time to contemplate it further, although I would have liked to absorb something of the personality that had left its traces there. I went out and peered into the next room: it was the study. Leaving the door ajar, I finally found my way into Mrs Cavendish's bedroom.

Like the rest of the flat, the room was a compromise between the style in which it had originally been furnished, some decades earlier, and a nature more attuned to a sort of stark simplicity in which two words would never do when one was enough. The heavy furniture spoke of another time, but their smooth surfaces were bare of the vases and pictures that must have once been crowded upon them. The heavy bed curtains were drawn back and held by thick braided ropes, opening to view what had been conceived as a secretive, cosy nook. Upon the dressing table, which was covered with a piece of plain white damask, were laid ivory brushes, combs and mirrors and a modest selection of pots and flasks. I lifted the lid of a porcelain pot with a shock, but it contained only the most ordinary powder, surmounted by a tiny puff. Of arsenic, there was none to be seen. I supposed that Mrs Cavendish would hardly have kept the pot, even if the police had returned it to her, which was most unlikely. Upon the washstand next to the dressing table stood a large porcelain bowl and jug, perfectly white, the latter filled with fresh water. The whole room denoted a struggle between the clutches of the dim, heavy styles of the past – an echo of collector's objects all crowded together could still faintly be felt in the dense but faded garlands of the wallpaper and the intricate fruits and leaves carved on the wardrobe doors – and a striving for absolute simplicity and purity. Something about it was tremendously revealing. I felt as though I had had an unexpected glimpse into Mrs Cavendish's very soul.

But there was no time to waste, and I dragged a chair to the wardrobe and climbed upon it to reach the hatboxes perfectly stacked upon the top. The grey one was, as Mrs Munn had told me, on top of the striped one, and during the few seconds it took me to lift it down, I worried myself into a panic over whether she might have moved the key. I knew something was wrong the second I touched the box, for it was too light. My fears were confirmed as soon as I opened it. The box contained no hat at all, only a crumple of protective tissue paper.

Stupid me – why had I expected to find the hat here? Had not Mrs Munn specifically said that the key was tucked into the loops of ribbon on the black hat that Mrs Cavendish wore for mourning? Obviously, she hadn't been wearing it on the day that Sebastian came home, but, just as obviously, she was wearing it today. In fact, I had seen it not more than an hour ago atop her beautifully arranged silvery blonde hair.

I fingered the tissue paper, and the tiny key dropped into my hand.

In a wink, I was out of the room and in the study, where I unlocked the drawers and began to go through them with feverish haste, listening all the while for Ephraim's warning cry.

With an efficiency partly born, I admit it, from a certain amount of practice, I rifled through the contents of one drawer after another. Unsurprisingly, Mrs Cavendish's papers were perfectly organised, everything classified in carefully arranged folders of bills, household affairs and correspondence, through all of which I anxiously flipped, until in the very bottom drawer I finally came upon a single slim folder containing an exchange of no more than a dozen or so letters. No sooner had my eye caught sight of the letterhead on the top of each than I grew cold and shivered, while the letters themselves burnt my fingers.

Holloway Sanatorium, Virginia Water, Surrey was printed in beautifully calligraphed letters across the top of each page. The name of Lydia Krieger jumped out at me at once, a blinding confirmation of everything I had guessed.

It did not take long to read them all.

In 1875, Mr Edward Cavendish, brother-in-law to Miss Lydia Krieger, became her legal guardian in the place of Mr Charles King, who had played that role since the death of her mother. The reason given was that Lydia's mental deficiency necessitated a continued guardianship, and that, given certain events that had transpired while she was his ward, Mr Charles King found that he could not provide the necessary surveillance and desired to relinquish his responsibility.

Mr Cavendish took the decision to consign Lydia Krieger to the Holloway Sanatorium, an institution specialised in the care and treatment of mentally deranged patients. The fees charged and paid by Mr Cavendish proved that the sanatorium was not intended for members of the poorer classes. These monthly fees had been paid by Mr Cavendish for nearly twenty years, until his death in 1894. The individual bills had not been kept, but only a complete yearly financial statement whose figure gave me a clearer understanding of what had happened to at least a significant part of Mr Cavendish's money, both before and after his death. Indeed, I discovered that his widow received a not unreasonable pension, which should have been quite sufficient to allow her to afford servants and the usual luxuries of a ladies' life; if she could not, it was essentially on account of the expense of keeping her sister at Holloway.

The last letter in the folder was dated March 1899 and contained a fact that gave me a painful shock. In that month, another person assumed full responsibility for the payments of Lydia's fees, indefinitely or until further notice – and that person was no other than Lord George Warburton! This information consigned more than one of my different theories about why Sebastian might possibly have been murdered to the rubbish bin.

Whatever had been the reason for Sebastian's death, it was not to prevent Lord Warburton finding out about Lydia's existence – nor did that existence appear to have provided any incentive for breaking off his coming marriage. It was sorely disappointing. Yet inexplicably, even as the motives I had sketched out in my mind thus melted away, my intimate conviction that Sebastian's death was not suicide but murder grew stronger.

I put the papers back, locked the desk, hurried to the bedroom, dropped the key back into the hatbox, piled it perfectly symmetrically atop the wardrobe, put back the chair, closed the bedroom door, rushed out of the flat, locked it, hastily scooped up boots, wrap and umbrella and rushed down the stairs to the main entrance with them all bundled in my arms, to find a trembling Ephraim standing in the cold, pale with anxiety. His interest in the crimes of others appeared to have evaporated; he thought only of rushing off to erase his own as soon as possible, and he literally pawed the ground with impatience as I buttoned my boots, and heaved an immense sigh of relief as I handed him the key and some money to put inside Mrs Munn's bag and gave him careful instructions on how to reach her home, located in the poorest section of Bermondsey. Off he went at a run, and I walked away by myself, deep in thought.

Lydia Krieger had existed; she still existed, and now I knew exactly where she was.

Lord Warburton knew it as well.

But what of Sebastian?

He had seen the same papers that I had, and he must have understood that the person named there was his aunt, if not actually his real mother. He had rushed away from the flat after reading them – where else but directly to Holloway? He must have seen her there. And what had happened? Had he somehow received an unbearable shock to his nervous system? Had he, rather, blundered unforgivably into the middle of a secret that was not really his? Or was his death due to reasons quite apart from his discovery of Lydia's existence and her refuge? To a hidden jealousy, for example, burgeoning within the heart of a friend?

If he had not killed himself, then what was I to make of the suicide note? I recalled its words.

Darling Claire,

How can I say this to you? I've found out something about myself – I can't go on with it any more. I'm sorry. I'm so sorry. Cursed inheritance – it's too dangerous to take such risks. Please try to understand.

Not for the first time, I was struck by the lack of signature. But now I suddenly understood it differently.

Was this not merely the beginning of a letter? A letter breaking off an engagement, not a life?

CHAPTER EIGHTEEN

*In which Vanessa does not accomplish the object of her
visit but something quite different instead*

Holloway Sanatorium was pointed out to me by the porter
as soon as I emerged from the Virginia Water railway station.
Vast and impressive with its multiple wings and gables,
surmounted by a great square tower, it was as grand and
imposing as any castle, and a monument to the founders'
intentions of bringing the treatment of mental illness to the
middle classes and applying the most progressive methods
to the patients, with the firm intention of effecting actual
cures and sending them back to the bosom of their families.
In principle, it was not intended as a place to permanently
harbour mad patients, but the case of Lydia Krieger was
obviously an exception of some kind.

The sanatorium was visible at a short distance from
the station, and I set forth to walk to it in a great state of

suppressed excitement. The grounds stretched, rolling, pleasant and richly wooded, all about the enormous building, bestowing upon the entire property the agreeable pastoral atmosphere that people generally expect from their country estates. A large and forbidding iron railing, however, surrounded the entire property, leaving the visitor no possible ingress – and the patients no exit – except for the tried and true method of the well-guarded main gate.

I followed the road leading to this very place and, as I approached, a surly-faced porter emerged from a small shed placed just within, and proceeded to unlock and swing open the gates to let me in. He did not allow me to go towards the building, however, but detained me while he rang for a person to come. I had to wait idly for several long minutes before a white-capped figure appeared at a distance, approaching with hasty steps. Only when she had nearly reached us did the porter consent to allow me to advance a few steps on my own and join her on the path, never removing his suspicious eyes from me until she had, by means of enquiring as to my name and purpose there, taken over from him the role of officially designated escort and guardian to the intruder.

When I explained that I had come as a visitor to one of the patients, she immediately extracted a large watch from her pocket and made a show of examining the time, but said nothing, as I had taken the precaution of informing myself that proper visiting hours were from two to four – unlike Sebastian, who must have come rushing straight here from London directly he had discovered the letters concerning Lydia, but who would certainly have arrived too late in the afternoon to be admitted before the following day. He must have been beside himself with impatience, and I could well imagine that he did not feel like returning home to face his mother before he had plumbed the depths of the situation. He had probably found himself a room at an inn in Virginia Water on the night of December 30th.

The nurse did not ask me any further questions, but led me into an impressive entrance hall with a vaulted ceiling supported by arched wooden beams worthy of some of the loveliest of our Cambridge colleges, and from there into a spacious office at the side. Here, another nurse, significantly older, severer and invested with greater authority than the one at my side, received me from behind an immense oaken desk.

After mulling over a hundred possibilities, I had decided to ask in the simplest manner to be allowed to visit one of the patients, a Miss Lydia Krieger.

The woman's face took on a look of surprise and momentary doubt, then cleared to resume her previous rather impassive expression.

'Miss Krieger; you wish to visit Miss Krieger,' she repeated, raising her eyebrows slightly. 'Let me see. I am not sure that will be possible. Please excuse me for a moment. I must check in her file.' She rose, went into a room behind, and came back bearing a thin file in her hand, into whose contents I should have dearly liked to have a glimpse. However, as she turned over the pages, I perceived from upside down that they were letters, no doubt exactly those whose answers I had already read at Mrs Cavendish's flat. The patient's medical history could not possibly fit into such a small file; it must be kept in a different place.

The nurse extracted the very last document and read it over carefully. Then she said, 'No, it is as I thought. Miss Krieger is not allowed to receive visits. I am very sorry that you have come all this way for nothing.'

Her voice held a tone of simple finality that aroused a sense of immediate furious frustration inside me. I turned my tongue around seven times in my mouth while collecting my spirits.

'Surely it is not so,' I replied as soon as I felt able to speak in a level tone. 'A friend of mine visited her less than one month ago, and encouraged me to do so.'

She looked up a little sharply.

'What friend would that have been?'

'A Mr Cavendish. Mr Sebastian Cavendish,' I replied, risking my all.

'Quite. I see. Let me explain. The fact is that precisely following the visit of that gentleman, we received a letter from Miss Krieger's guardians explicitly forbidding her to be disturbed by any further visits. It appears that Mr Cavendish's visit caused a serious problem which is not to be allowed to recur.'

'A problem for Miss Krieger herself?' I said, playing

innocent and hoping to extract some information.

'I do not know. I know nothing about it except that we received this letter.'

'But I am certain that the visit caused no harm to Miss Krieger, quite the contrary,' I persisted, 'and I do not see why she should be the one to suffer for the problems of another, of which she may not even be aware.'

'It is not in my hands,' she replied coldly, beginning (as well she might) to be annoyed. 'I am very sorry I cannot help you,' she added, and rang a bell, probably to summon someone to escort me out. I quickly staved off the moment of absolute failure by insisting upon speaking to Miss Krieger's physician.

'Dr Richards is excessively busy, as are all the physicians here, with over six hundred patients,' she replied. 'He cannot be disturbed for a mere question of visits. Besides, there is no more to be said. The letter is quite explicit.'

'Surely,' I said, 'even from guardians as severe as these, there cannot be any letter explicitly forbidding the physician to receive a visit.'

She pressed her lips together, and when the young nurse who had met me earlier near the gate knocked gently and opened the door, she said,

'Run to Dr Richards' room, Sister Theresa, and tell him that there is a visitor for Miss Krieger here, who wishes if possible to speak to him.'

She gestured with her hand to a pretty brocade chair against the wall, and I sat down and waited. At length

Sister Theresa returned and said that Dr Richards was with a patient, that he could spare a few moments in a quarter of an hour, and would I please save time by waiting in his ante-room? I followed her up many stairs and down many halls, and we passed a vast number of people bustling in every direction; patients, some in white robes and others normally dressed, doctors, nurses, young girls pushing carts laden with cups and dishes or medical equipment, and groups of well-dressed people who were possibly visitors like myself. As we went, I tried to pump the young nurse discreetly, but I met with no success at all, not least because, in her anxiety not to waste a single second of the doctor's precious time, she was hurrying me along at a pace nearly worthy of a footrace. This species of nurse is clearly trained to a high degree of functionality and discretion.

She finally stopped, opened a door without knocking, and inserted me, like a letter in the postbox, into a beautifully decorated room that had little or no relation to how I would have imagined a mental doctor's waiting room to appear. Here she left me alone, to hurry on to other duties.

An inner door of this room was closed, but certainly led to the room or office where the doctor received his patients; indeed I could make out the muffled sound of his voice, alternating with a woman's tones. I tried to make out some of his words, but could not, yet their tone evoked a spirit of reasoning. After many minutes, the door opened, and the white-clad doctor ushered a plain woman with a sickly, indifferent expression on her face quickly out of the waiting room and into the hall, where a nurse – yet another one – was waiting to accompany her to some other place. I could not help noticing a long red scratch on the woman's cheek as she passed. Dr Richards then closed the door to the hall, came towards me and said in a quick, businesslike manner, 'You are the visitor who came to see Miss Krieger? How may I help you? I do not have much time, I'm afraid.'

Alas, before he even spoke these words, I perceived in him the very type of doctor (and, let me add, of man) that I most dislike. Too refined to look openly self-important, he nonetheless had the air of a man who is in command and knows it. Here was a person imbued with a sense of his power; not a constructive sense, I felt, but an unfortunate, unhealthy sense, fed and nourished daily by the knowledge of his actual, perfectly real power over all those around him – helpless patients and respectful, obedient and scuttling nurses. Here was a man whose professional word was law, whose personal decisions bore the weight of law in the truest sense, for were he called to a court of law for any reason, either to aid in a judge's decision or to defend his own medical doings, his expert words would no doubt be held to be unassailable and his expert opinion trusted implicitly. Such people raise my hackles; I feel an instinctive abhorrence for them, and am sometimes driven, I confess it, to flout their power for the pure pleasure of being able to do so.

But this did not seem to be a moment when such a course of action was advisable. Speaking respectfully, I explained my great wish to visit Miss Krieger, adding a totally untruthful tale about having been begged to do so by a dear friend of mine, now deceased, who had seen her quite lately and was aware that the visit had done her the greatest good.

The nurse downstairs may or may not have been ignorant of the entire story surrounding Sebastian's visit; her discretion made it impossible for me to guess. But the quick glance in Dr Richards' sharp blue eyes told me that he knew exactly what had occurred, and certainly much more about it than I did.

'Surely you were told downstairs that Miss Krieger is to receive no visits?' he said coldly, and snapped his lips shut. If possible, my dislike of the man increased by a notch.

'I was,' I said, 'but I wished to enquire further, to learn why this was suddenly the case, and to make sure that it was truly for Miss Krieger's benefit. For it appears to me possible that the family's request to bar her from visits was made for a very different reason, and that it is equally essential, if not more so, to consider her own well-being. As her doctor, you must surely agree.'

It was a losing battle.

'As her doctor, I am quite able to judge for myself of the best manner of ensuring my patients' well-being,' he said. 'Visits are not useful to Miss Krieger. She is a patient whose peace of mind is fragile and must be preserved at all costs.'

'I quite understand,' I replied smoothly. 'Holloway Sanatorium is reputed, of course, for curing its patients and releasing them into their normal lives. I presume your care for her well-being is oriented towards such a cure?'

'Naturally,' he replied, his tone yielding nothing to mine. 'Miss Krieger's case is, however, particularly complex, and it will take an amount of time which cannot be determined at present.'

'Twenty-five years seems quite long already, does it not?' I murmured.

'It is long, too long. However, the methods of psychological treatment of one or two decades ago were not what they are now, and I may hope to succeed where my predecessors failed.'

I felt convinced that he was lying; that he had been tacitly or openly charged with the task of keeping Miss Krieger a prisoner for the rest of her life – for no really adequate reason, I was sure – and that he knew it, just as his predecessors had known it.

'I am delighted to think that you believe you have a chance of bringing Miss Krieger to make a normal use of writing,' I chanced, having no idea whether some earnest doctor along the way – or simply the passage of time – had actually improved Lydia's condition years ago. 'In that case, she could certainly leave the premises at once, could she not? For I am informed that she has no other psychological problems.'

The doctor's face stiffened.

'That is the assessment of an amateur,' he stated. 'A psychological problem is never confined to one narrow domain, although it may appear so to a layman. In any case, I am not at liberty to discuss my patients' medical conditions. I beg that you will not trouble yourself about Miss Krieger's well-being. You have seen our building, met our nurses. Look out of this window and you will see our gardens. You can judge for yourself whether the patients here are adequately cared for.'

He pointed out of the window as he spoke, and I followed his glance eagerly, for the window was not set in the ante-room where we were, but on the wall of his inner office, facing the door. The doctor had left this communicating door wide open when he ushered the patient out, and I had been dying to have a glance inside, but it was out of the question to let my eyes pry about indiscreetly, when his own were fixed so sharply upon my very face. Pretending to admire the grounds (which were indeed lovely), I took one or two steps forward and scanned what I could of his office. I immediately spotted the fact that behind his desk stood a set of large oaken filing cabinets with drawers, each of which was labelled with a card bearing a letter of the alphabet. A delightful idea suddenly entered my head, having the immediate effect of causing all of my spirit of rebellion to creep modestly back into the place in which it lives when it is invisible. Bowing my head submissively, I said that I would leave now. I added hopefully that I could find my own way out, but the doctor was not to be manipulated. 'That is against our rules here,' he said shortly, and rang a bell. I had perforce to wait until Sister Theresa appeared with a firm step to guide me directly to the exit, down the path, and inexorably out of the grounds.

It was an emergency!

If she were to once put me out of the gate and see it locked behind me, my last chance of learning anything about Lydia Krieger would be definitively lost. I simply could not allow that to happen! Could I dash away suddenly? No, that was impossible. What about fainting? As convincingly as possible, I made a sudden show of terrible weakness, and clutching the nurse's arm, begged to be allowed to sit down somewhere and have a cup of tea before I should have to shoulder the burden of my disappointment and return home.

Sister Theresa looked annoyed, but she must have been used to women with vapours and did not appear suspicious. Leading me to a small empty sitting room, she rang a bell which brought a little housemaid running in. I smiled inwardly at the sight of her. This was the kind of girl I knew and liked; a rosy country girl with a smile lurking behind her dimpled cheeks. If only I could arrange to spend a few moments with her alone!

'Bring tea for this lady, Polly, and be quick, please,' said Sister Theresa. The girl disappeared and I waited silently, fanning myself gently with a handkerchief and wishing that Sister Theresa would leave, but suspecting I would have no such luck. Various plans revolved in my mind, and then, to my delight, the girl returned with the tea and said,

'There's a visitor just come, Sister Theresa, and you're wanted to show him in.'

Sister Theresa rose. 'I must return to my duties,' she said to me, then drew young Polly aside and delivered to her a murmured lecture, which I easily guessed to be a strict injunction not to leave my side, and to escort me to the main gate just as soon as I should be pleased to shake off my indisposition.

Sister Theresa left and Polly stayed. Conversation flowed at once with ease and cheer, and within two minutes I had led the conversation around to the topic of Lydia Krieger. I was excited to learn that Polly knew who she was, although with six hundred patients and she nothing but a housemaid, she didn't have much actual contact with most of them. At first her comments were but simple, essentially summarised by the repetition of the words 'poor dear lady'. She told me that Miss Krieger was known to most of the staff because she had been at Holloway forever, longer than almost any other patient except the famous Mr Turner who sometimes thought he was Napoleon and sometimes Disraeli, and had already been pronounced cured and released twelve times.

But Miss Krieger had never been released, I persisted, bringing the conversation back in the direction that interested me.

'No, poor dear lady. She never gets any better, nor any worse.'

'Is she actually ill?'

'Not as you can see. A sweet quiet lady and beautiful, too. Tall. She likes to read, to sew, to walk in the garden. She likes animals, too; the patients cannot have animals here, but some of the visitors come with a little dog or such. I've seen her holding and petting them. She never has those crises like what the others do, some of them, or believe they're something else than what they really are. We get all kinds here. But Miss Krieger seems no different from you and me. Just dreamy, like, but then, there's not much for her to do here.'

A new image of Lydia Krieger arose in my mind, far more vivid than the previous ghostly shadows: the medieval Lady of the Unicorn. Seated in her garden of tapestry flowers, surrounded by dogs and rabbits and an earnest-looking lion, her gentle hand resting on a tame unicorn who smiles at her adoringly. That otherworldly beauty, quiet elegance, infinite gentleness. And with that vision, the very last shred of possibility that Sebastian had discovered something so dreadful he had wanted to end his life faded away. He had come here to see the woman who was his aunt – perhaps, very possibly, his mother – and he had found the Lady of the Unicorn.

'Do you know why they've forbidden me to visit her?' I asked.

'Have they really?' she said with great sympathy. 'That's not kind.'

'It seems that her family sent a letter forbidding visitors after a visit that she had last month, where

276

something bad happened. A young man came to visit her, and then he died.'

'Oh, of course! I remember that! We were all talking about it last month. That was the young man who killed himself, wasn't it? Sister Matilda who sits at the front desk saw his name in the paper and realised that she'd written that very name down in the visitor's book herself; it was still open to the same page, even. He killed himself on the very day that he was here, didn't he? We all heard about how the young man came here for a visit and then went and killed himself in London. But I didn't know he had come to see Miss Krieger. Sister Matilda didn't tell us that. She's very close; I think she wouldn't have even told anyone about what she saw in the paper if it hadn't been such a coincidence. But as she wasn't alone when she saw the name, she naturally cried out something right then when she recognised it, and it got around. Poor young man, I do wonder why he did it. Some people are madder outside than the ones in here, don't you think?'

'Did you see him when he came?'

'Not I, ma'am, but the ones who did said he was lovely.'

I leant forward, enjoying myself, but worried lest Sister Theresa should find a spare moment to come back and check upon our whereabouts, and lowered my voice to a conspiratorial whisper.

'Polly, can you tell me anything about Miss Krieger's writing?'

Her eyes grew round.

'We're not allowed to talk about the patients, ma'am,' she said.

I smiled kindly.

'There's no harm in talking with me,' I said. 'In fact, you could help me. You see, I'm trying to find out why the poor young man who came here went and killed himself. I'm trying to understand the reason.'

'Surely it had nothing to do with his visit here, did it?' she said.

'Well, I think that it did. Because if not, why would her family suddenly write to the sanatorium forbidding her to receive any more visitors?'

'Why, I don't know. It's strange. Miss Krieger never had any other visitors anyway. That was the only one. That's why it caused such a to-do. She never had any other. That's what they all say, at least.'

'Do you know if Miss Krieger spoke about the visit after it happened?'

'No, I wouldn't know that, I don't talk to the patients myself,' she replied. 'She might have done, to her doctor, but then again she might not. She doesn't say much as a rule. There's not much to say, really, in here, it's so shut away. If I didn't get out to see my family on my half-days, I sometimes think I'd go all strange myself.'

'What do the doctors do here, to cure the patients?' I asked. 'Do you know anything about that?'

'They've all kinds of machines,' she said. 'They have the patients spinning round or taking cold baths; ever so many things. A French doctor came here once and he put some of the patients into funny trances, so they'd do anything he said. But with Miss Krieger, they say the doctor only gets her to write. She's not allowed to write any other time, you see. We've been told to keep papers and pens away from her, and she mayn't go into the writing room. She may only write for Dr Richards. But she doesn't need the cold baths and other things, because she's always calm.'

The idea that had sprung up in my mind in the doctor's waiting-room was fast becoming an absolute determination. Time was short and no elaborate planning would be possible. But simplicity is often the best way, in any case. The vastness of the building and its long empty corridors could be turned to my advantage.

'Polly,' I said, rising and gathering my things, 'I need to find out why Miss Krieger's visitor killed himself, and I know it has something to do with what she writes. I want you to help me.'

'Oh, ma'am, I can't,' she said, turning pale. 'It's as much as my place is worth. Why, if I don't take you straight down to the gatehouse in a minute, I'll be in trouble already.'

'I won't ask you to anything forbidden,' I promised. 'In fact, I'm asking you almost nothing at all. Do take me to the gatehouse. Let's go there now.' I rose, and something passed from my purse to my hand, and from my hand to Polly's. She uttered a little cry and it disappeared into her apron pocket.

'When the porter opens the gate to let me out, you

turn back to go up the path,' I said. 'Then you trip and fall down and cry out. He'll come to you and help you get up. Cry out that it hurts and get him to look at your knee, so he doesn't look at me for a few moments. That's all I want you to do. Don't even think about me after that. Don't pay attention to anything. Just go back to the house, and go about your duties.'

She looked at me with great curiosity.

'Oh – I think I can do that!' she said. 'But are you not going to go out at all?'

'You don't need to know anything about that,' I replied firmly.

'It'll be the porter's fault, not mine, if they do find you back inside,' she said, and burst into a merry laugh. Out we went, along the corridors into the grand main foyer, out the front door, and straight down the path to the gatehouse, Polly wearing a great air of doing her duty. The porter stood up and unlocked the gate, pulling it inwards to let me out. I took a step to the side, and Polly turned away. I held my breath. A shriek from behind me made the porter whirl around, and in the flash of a second, I was hiding in the thick shrubbery next to the gate, peering through the prickly leaves to see how he raised Polly from the ground as she bent over, and clutching her knee and howling, 'Oh, it's broken, it's broken; oh please look at it, do; oh, is it bleeding?' like a five-year-old child. If he was a little surprised by my total disappearance during the short time it took him to pull her upright and utter something between a consolation and a remonstrance, he did not show it, but contented himself with locking the gate as she followed him, limping, whimpering realistically and demanding attention.

At length he sent her off, and she went back up the path, still hobbling, and disappeared into the building. I had in the meantime taken advantage of the racket to slip through the shrubbery as far away from the gate as possible, and had by now reached a place where I thought the rustling caused by my movements would not be noticeable. It seemed that I could continue to creep behind the shrubbery around the entire perimeter of the sanatorium's enormous grounds, which, apart from the bushes along the railings, were green and quite empty even of trees. I continued my thorny trajectory for what seemed an immense distance, until finally the porter's cabin was out of sight. Then I came out, brushed leaves and twigs from my clothing, and crossed the lawn with what I hoped was a confident step.

I was naturally worried about detection, but not excessively so, for several other people were dotted about the grounds; doctors and nurses, and even a number of normally dressed people quite like myself, going back and forth from the outlying buildings for reasons of their own. They did not appear to be patients, and I soon realised that the patients were not free to wander about the full extent of the grounds, but were confined to a particular, rather large and quite lovely garden of their own, set behind the building and to one side, and surrounded with its own set of iron railings. Here was a much thicker concentration of nurses, together with a number of people, some of whom appeared normal enough, but others who disported themselves strangely, uttered peculiar noises, or were covered in rugs and pushed about in wheeled chairs. There were even a few visitors who actually stood outside the railings, conversing with patients on the inside; an excellent arrangement allowing patients to receive visits while taking the air, and while protecting the more sensitive visitors from sights or sounds that might alarm them when experienced at close quarters.

I joined these people and stood looking in. The weather was unusually bright, but extremely cold, and it was not surprising that of the six hundred patients in the sanatorium, there were no more than forty or fifty in the garden at that particular moment, most of them walking about quite briskly. My heart beat; Polly had said that Lydia Krieger enjoyed walking in the garden. In the strictly regulated life of the sanatorium, this particular moment must correspond to the hour for visits and garden walks and it was perhaps the only chance during the day at which patients were allowed outside. She might well be there.

After some moments, my eyes located a figure that I thought might be Lydia. There was no way to be certain, but the gentle demeanour, the dreamy expression, the greying hair of the rather lovely woman I saw, wearing an elegant fur stole and hat, denoted the right age and style, and it seemed to me that I could detect a faint family resemblance to Tanis Cavendish. Resemblances are infinitely subtle, but my instinct told me that this could well be Lydia Krieger, and my heart beat faster as I tried to imagine a way to attract her attention. Sebastian had come here just a month ago, and he had seen Lydia, just as I believed I was seeing her now. And he had spoken to her – and perhaps she had written for him, as I would wish her to write for me, and some secret had been thence revealed. And Sebastian had died, and Lydia remained a prisoner, and no one but she now knew exactly what had taken place here on that day.

My determination to understand grew and intensified, and plans rushed through my head. But she was at too much of a distance for me to call out to her, and I was afraid of drawing attention to myself; there was nothing to do but wait and hope that she would draw nearer in her circulation. I observed her carefully, I tried to catch her eye, I readied myself – and then suddenly, I saw a young nurse hurry from the building into the garden, straight up to the very woman I was watching so closely, and speak to her urgently, taking her arm to lead her inside. The woman replied, making a gesture indicating the garden and the sky, as though she would wish to remain there, but the young nurse was adamant and drew her indoors as fast as she could, casting a hasty glance about the garden as she did so.

My disappointment was keen, but not as strong as the sudden piercing sensation of fear. What could be the meaning of the little scene I had just witnessed, other than that the alarm had somehow been raised, and the staff informed that I was still within their gates and probably determined to force a meeting with Lydia Krieger? The porter must have been surprised not to see me walking away down the road after the little scene with Polly, suspected that I hadn't left at all, and decided to alert someone. And not knowing where I might be hiding, the hospital had been very quick to spirit Lydia out of the way of a possible encounter. It might seem like a rather grand reaction to such a little thing, but Lydia's previous visit had ended with a suicide, and I could imagine how desirous they might be of avoiding any repetition of such a tragedy.

I left the garden at once, and circled the building back towards the front entrance with as tranquil and confident an air as I could muster. From what I had seen, the giant foyer with its towering arched ceiling contained no official person in the role of watchdog; this was not necessary, as visitors were accompanied up to the house from the gate, and led immediately to their proper destination. My best hope, then, was to behave as normally as possible and thus remain unnoticed. With a firm, unhesitant gesture, I pushed open the great entrance door, went in, crossed the foyer and tried to take the same path along which I had been led so speedily less than an hour before.

On I went, through a veritable maze of corridors, trying to recognise this or that landmark, occasionally returning the way I had come to search for a more familiar scene. I crossed a few busy employees, carrying domestic items or leading patients, but they ignored me and I ignored them, and kept moving along rather quickly as though I had a specific task to accomplish – which, indeed, I did.

Thanks to my observation of the route we had taken previously, I did eventually manage to arrive at a door I recognised as being the suite attributed to Dr Richards. There was no one in the hall, and, as slowly and silently as possible, I turned the knob and gave the gentlest possible push at the door, not to open it even by the smallest crack, but simply to test whether or not it was locked. Finding that it yielded, I released the knob, moved a little way down the hall to the top of a staircase, and concealed myself behind the heavy drapes that hung in front of all the corridor windows.

Ideally, what I wanted was a moment in which I could be certain that Dr Richards was alone inside. If he should be out of the office, I feared he would probably lock the door, and if a patient or someone else were inside with him, my plan would certainly fail. I waited and observed and watched until my legs were full of pins-and-needles.

Now and then, someone passed down the corridor in one direction or the other. Through a crack in the curtains I saw people being escorted away, and knew that visiting hours had come to an end. A little later, a nurse arrived with a patient who continually dragged her fingers through her hair, pulling and deforming the neat bun which the nurse pinned back for her repeatedly with perfunctory remonstrances of 'Now, dear'. These two stopped at the door of the doctor's ante-room, and the nurse opened it, went in, and knocked gently on the inner door. A murmured word, a moment's wait, and the doctor ushered a gentleman patient out into the nurse's capable hands and led the woman with her hair now half-falling down one side of her face into his inner room. He closed the door and the nurse went away with the gentleman, who was mumbling in a ceaseless monotone. I waited for twenty minutes or half an hour.

At the end of this time, my hopes were raised by the sight of a tea-trolley being wheeled along the corridor: the long rows of white cups with little dishes next to each containing scones were probably for the patients, but surely the doctors were also soon to be served. And indeed, the nurse returned, the lady with her hair now completely down around her face and shoulders came out and went away with her, and a minute later a little maid – not Polly, unfortunately, but some other similar little village Molly or Sally – arrived carrying a beautifully decked tea tray laden with much nicer things than what the patients were having. Having delivered this, she departed, and I knew that the doctor was alone, and that my moment was at hand.

I gave myself three minutes just to let the good doctor get properly relaxed, then set up a sudden and tremendous cry of 'Dr Richards! Oh, please! Oh, Dr Richards, come quickly! Please!' I was gratified to see him come rushing out of his office, hasten down the hall in the direction of my voice, and hurry down the steps near the top of which I was concealed.

I almost flew down the hall in the direction of his

rooms; within a mere three or four seconds I was standing inside his private office, which was filled with the pleasant aroma of buttered toast. Another second and I was pulling open the drawer marked 'K' that my eyes had already accurately located at my earlier visit. Five seconds later my trembling fingers found and snatched out the file marked 'Krieger', and I clapped the drawer shut. I could not hurry away now without risking crossing the doctor's path as he returned, but the risk of discovery would be too great if I remained in the room; the ante-room was the least dangerous place, and I was there in the flash of an instant, clutching my prize, lying at full length behind the settee, and trying not to breathe.

There were calls and voices from outside, and the doctor returned, flushed and displeased to judge by his breathing, and stalked into his room to finish his tea. Alas, he did not quite close the door of his private office, thereby foiling my plans for immediate escape. I remained perfectly still, and occupied myself in hoping that this obstacle might lead to some interesting event, such as a visit from Lydia Krieger. But nothing so exciting occurred, and the next person to enter was no other than little Molly-Sally, on her way to collect the tea tray. With great good manners, she balanced it on one arm while pulling the doctor's door shut behind her, and then left, also closing the door to the hall. Instantly I was on my feet and following her, hoping that the doctor would attribute the double sound of the door, if he could hear it at all, to the struggle of the young girl with a heavy tray.

I had no choice but to follow her straight out – there was no time to check whether anyone else was standing in the hall right then, but as a matter of fact the coast was clear – and off I went down the stairs, along the corridors and right out the front door, happily carrying my heavy prize concealed beneath my shawl.

Now came the difficulty of getting out of the grounds. I was afraid that the porter might recognise me from earlier, especially if he had noticed my disappearance (or rather, my failure to have properly disappeared) and raised the alarm. It was awkward, and I could not think of anything better to do than to insert myself into a group of four or five working women, probably daily assistants from the village hired to aid with the cooking, cleaning or caring for patients, by the simple expedient of asking them if they could be so kind as to show me the way to the train station. I made sure to engage them in conversation so as to look as much as possible like part of their group, and in return they were very friendly. We all exited together as easily as possible; indeed, it was quite dark outside by this time, being after five o'clock, and the porter didn't notice a thing. I allowed myself the luxury of a tremendous sigh of relief accompanied by some nervous giggles, hurried to the train station, purchased a ticket, and leapt upon the first train to London with a feeling of unspeakable triumph. I may not have been able to talk to Lydia, but I believed I had seen her – and I had obtained a tremendously important set of documents, and played a trick on the obnoxious doctor to boot!

I settled back into my seat, extracted the thick folder of documents from the folds of my shawl, and began to examine the contents. I read, and I read, and I read.

But if I had expected a revelation – and I realised now that clearly I had – I was destined to be sorely disappointed.

According to her medical records, Lydia had been pilled and syruped, hypnotised and lectured, subjected to innumerable constraints, told to speak while writing and write while speaking, to write with her left hand, to write copying what the doctor wrote, to write with her hand guided by the doctor and a multitude of even more peculiar, irrelevant and unfortunate experiments, all of which had met with total failure and left her condition quite unchanged. As time passed, the doctor's notes became briefer, his experiments rarer, and, above all, the expression of his inability to comprehend her meaning moved over the years from the description 'indicative of internal logic incommunicable to outside world' in the early stages to 'incomprehensible' and even 'ranting' towards the end.

By an unfortunate psychological mechanism which I could not rationally explain to myself, my contempt for Dr Richards' failure was not in the least diminished by the fact that, had I been shown the many dozens of pages covered in Lydia Krieger's characteristic flowing handwriting under any ordinary circumstances, I might well have been capable of using the very same words to describe their contents myself. I read them through, and read them through again, then shook my head.

Their contents were utterly beyond me. Dr Bernstein had believed that a repressed secret was forcing its way forth between the lines, but I could not perceive any trace of such a thing. Her writings strongly resembled the samples I had read in Dr Bernstein's book: they expressed a kind of religious obsession with neurotic repetitiveness, and I could see nothing more. No strange incoherencies marred their natural flow. I shuffled them all back into the stolen file, and sat back, thinking.

If there was any sense at all to be made of this nonsense, any clue to the mystery of Lydia's secret and Sebastian's death, there was only one person in the world who could help me find it. And by asking for his help, I would also be granting him his heart's desire.

When the train pulled into London, I immediately went and sent an urgent telegram to Dr Bernstein at his Basel home. I had really had enough of trains, and would have been delighted to hear that I was never to see another one, but it was not to be. Twenty-four hours later I was spending yet another night trundled and jumbled in yet another sleeping-car, on my way to yet another destination, in the search for the elusive truth.

CHAPTER NINETEEN

*In which a discovery takes place
at a most astonishing moment*

The doctor rose, struck a match, and lit another candle, then pushed the brass candlestick closer to the papers that lay scattered over his desk. I sat near him in his study, my eyes heavy, but any idea of sleep was out of the question, for the doctor was buzzing about like a frantic bee. Shock, anger, joy, indignation, fury, and a feverish desire to understand crowded together to occupy all of his possibilities of expression, so that the poor man felt the need to slap his head, utter sighs and groans, take dancing steps about the room, pronounce imprecations and evolve yet another new theory, all at the same time. We had been there for hours, and the manservant who had brought us tea and then prepared a light dinner had long since gone to bed, but Dr Bernstein's state would not admit of his stopping for a moment. It was a Sunday, and he had had no patients, and our work and discussion had been going on for hours, interrupted only by meals over which he asked me ever more questions, and reminisced with increasing openness about the past.

Alerted by my telegram – in which, in order to be certain of his immediate reaction, I had included the words 'Lydia Krieger found' – the doctor had come to fetch me at the Basel railway station, and the sight of the emotion painted upon his bearded face as he recognised me erased any impulse I might normally have had to respect the social conventions by preceding the moment of revelation with lengthy formal greetings. Instead, I lifted up the heavy file that I had been clutching almost without stopping for the last forty-eight hours, and plunked it straight into his arms with a feeling of relief at thus transferring an insoluble problem to one more competent than myself. He opened it, glanced at the first pages, and then looked at me. We had not yet exchanged a single word, and for several moments, he seemed unable to pronounce one. When he finally did, it was simply: 'Come.'

Luncheon, to say the least, was a tense affair. His eyes burning, the doctor questioned me in detail, breaking off abruptly every time his manservant entered to bring or remove the dishes. I told him all I knew and all I had done, and had the pleasure of seeing him smile for the first time as I somewhat blushingly explained about the unusual use I had made of Dr Richards' settee. I hid nothing from him, at least not a single fact or incident. I kept to myself only certain suspicions. It was his turn to question me for the present. My own time for questioning would come, and I should know to seize the opportunity when it was ripe.

The meal over, we settled into the doctor's study, coffee was brought in, and we remained undisturbed. The doctor took out the file and spread the papers over the desk.

Being a physician, Dr Bernstein began his examination of the contents with the document I had considered last; the medical report. Of this, there was only one entry of significant interest, which was the very first one, established by a certain Dr Enderson on the day of Lydia's arrival at Holloway. The moment I had read it, I had felt a tingling down my spine, for it confirmed at least one of my suspicions.

April 18, 1875

Lydia Krieger, 29 years of age, born August 1, 1846, in good physical health, primiparous.

Mr and Mrs Edward Cavendish have brought Miss Lydia Krieger, sister of the second-named, for examination in view of confinement and treatment for mental illness.

I first spoke with Mr and Mrs Cavendish in the

absence of the patient. Mrs Cavendish recounts that her sister has displayed increasingly abnormal psychological behaviour, in particular for anything concerned with the act of writing, since the age of 13 or 14 years. Miss Krieger was sent for treatment to a private clinic in Switzerland at the age of 24. Miss Krieger is now aged 29. Miss Krieger left the clinic one year ago for her annual summer holiday in England, and did not return. Mr Cavendish told me that the reason for her remaining in England was that she was found to be with child. Miss Krieger either would not say or was unaware of how this situation had come about. Mrs Cavendish moved with her to the countryside for six months, remaining with her until the birth of the child. When her sister was entirely recovered, she returned with her to London, leaving the child in the care of a local woman. Mrs Cavendish states that her sister's mental condition has become even more fragile than it was previous to the birth, and, given what has happened, she believes it would be unwise to allow her to continue to roam freely within society, when any unscrupulous person might take advantage of her mental disability.

I then saw Miss Lydia Krieger. The initial cursory examination of the patient confirmed Mrs Cavendish's observations of pronounced mental abnormality and fragility. Mr and Mrs Cavendish refuse to communicate any information concerning the Swiss clinic where Miss Krieger received treatment. They claim that the reason is that 'they wish Miss Krieger's whereabouts to remain entirely unknown to the circle of friends she had formed there, for reasons that should be obvious', even at the price of excluding all possibility of obtaining her previous medical records. In any case, Mrs Cavendish claims that contrarily to her original expectations, the Swiss treatment had no positive effect on her sister, that if anything she worsened under its influence, and that the records of it would be of no use to us. She categorically refused to give any further details on this matter. In fact, the couple had never had any direct communication with the Swiss clinic at all, the whole affair having been handled by a third person, who had been named as the sisters' legal guardian upon their mother's death.

Holloway Sanatorium agrees to accept Miss Lydia Krieger as a patient for a trial period of one month, during which time she will be examined and diagnosed for further treatment. At the end of the one-month period, a final decision will be made as to whether she may be profitably kept.

One sentence had leapt out at me in letters of flame: *the birth of the child*! So I was right, I had to be right: the age was the same, the resemblance was there: the child could not be anyone but Sebastian. He was, as I had guessed, and somehow in the depths of my soul even hoped, Lydia's son.

I waited for Dr Bernstein to say something about it, any remark at all, any hypothesis about what might have happened when Lydia left Basel, but he did not mention it, and his face was inscrutable. I bided my time, and he continued to read through the documents one by one, handing each one to me as he finished. I had glanced through the file on the train to London, of course, and read it all in greater detail during the long, long trip across the continent, but it was interesting to read it again together with him, for he kept up a running commentary on the purely medical aspects of the case that were outlined on each page; every minor illness, every drug and medicine that Lydia had ever received merited his scathing commentary, and on the whole the experience was an enlightening one even if he did avoid precisely the points that most interested me. The doctor was in no hurry. He did not rush through the pages as I had done; he read them one by one in detail, frowned often, stopped occasionally to look things up in certain large medical books he kept upon his shelves, and finally concluded his examination of the medical report with a fiery diatribe against institutional treatment in general, during which he actually took notes of his own words, probably in view of some future written complaint! Then, perhaps in deference to my nationality, he peered at the clock which was ticking loudly upon the mantelpiece and rang for the manservant to bring us tea and biscuits on a tray, draw the curtains, and light the lamps, for it was already growing dusky outside. Setting aside the large sheaf of Lydia's own writings for later, he now pulled towards him the thick notebook in which Dr Richards had recorded the efforts of five years of psychiatric treatment. The file did not contain the records of the efforts of the doctors who had held the position before his arrival at Holloway in the month of September of 1895. They must have been archived in some separate place; presumably they were too bulky to fit inside. After all, most patients did not spend twenty-five years receiving treatment, and the square files had been constructed of a limited thickness. Thus, Lydia's file contained nothing but the records of the four and half years during which Dr Richards attended her.

During the first few weeks, Dr Richards' comments upon the writing samples that emerged from Lydia's pen expressed strenuous efforts at comprehension, accompanied by somewhat forced analyses. As Dr Bernstein read them, he grunted, shook his head, slapped his forehead in deep irritation and occasionally uttered smothered imprecations. I had experienced some of the same reactions upon reading them, although I did not have the professional qualifications that he did. But Dr Richards' approach struck me as unconvincing, unlikely, and, in fact, altogether unbelievable. This feeling was strengthened, I admit, by my secret rationalistic suspicion that Lydia's madness was simply too mad to be meaningful, and no analysis could possibly make sense of it. With all my heart I desired Dr Bernstein to prove me wrong, to discover something, to convince me, yet I was conscious of a pinch of fear that the evening might end in disappointment, either because he might find nothing, or worse, because he might enter into some slippery psychological terrain upon which I could not follow him, interpreting weird occult meanings into Lydia's words that I could not perceive myself at all.

Dr Richards' overbearing personality shone through his writings, exasperating me even though I knew that he was simply and conscientiously doing his professional job. '*The previous doctors have made a mess of the case*' was the very first phrase he had consigned to the notebook devoted to the study of his recalcitrant patient.

No modern methods have been applied, only clumsy efforts at persuasion and moderate coercion, which, as might be expected, have had no effect whatsoever. It was necessary for me to proceed to a new and complete interview with the family, which is at present reduced only to the sister, now a widow. Modern psychoanalytical theory indicates repressed trauma from early childhood, which may or may not be linked to the act of writing. The patient's history of childhood communicated by the sister does not indicate the latter, but although she shared the patient's childhood, the difference in age indicates that she may not have been conscious or even born at the time of the original trauma. This is a clear possibility in view of the fact that the children were adopted together, indicating that if the second child was a baby at that time, the older one had already reached the age of two, an age at which the great impressionability and consciousness of the child does not match its ability to express itself, leading, as recent theories reveal, to frequent cases of traumatic repression. Neither the patient nor her sister has any memories of or knowledge of anything concerning the time previous to their adoption.

On the other hand, they were not told that they were adopted until the mother revealed it to them on her deathbed, when the sisters were aged fourteen and twelve respectively. She told them that they should be aware of the fact, so that they would not be surprised if they learnt it later from some unexpected source, such as an old family acquaintance who had witnessed the adoption. Both the patient and her sister claim that they were far more shocked by the death of their adoptive mother, which left them orphans for a second time (their adoptive father having died ten years earlier when the children were aged four and two), than by this revelation. Certainly the patient's irregular behaviour dates from this time. It is possible in the case of the patient that the combination of the two events, losing her single remaining parent and learning of her adoption, produced the impulse to compulsive behaviour.

In order to determine the truth, a cure of this patient must be effected, which can only be done by causing the memory of the trauma to emerge. Previous doctors have been incapable of perceiving the original cause and thus of providing adapted treatment.

'He does seem to have some idea of why Lydia began to write so strangely,' I said, after reading this page together with the doctor. We were both leaning over his broad oak desk covered with a layer of dark green leather, and the page laid open upon it was bathed in the mellow circle of light from the lamp. A very faint but not disagreeable odour of cigar smoke clung to the doctor's jacket. Together, we read through Dr Richards' efforts with Lydia over the following weeks and months, which consisted largely in applications of recently developed methods of dream-analysis and free association.

'He is missing the main point,' exclaimed the doctor. 'All these suppositions are well and good, but he cannot hope to find the answer through attempts at direct analysis such as these!' He turned another page, then half-covered it with his hand. Then he glanced at me, and took his hand away.

'Hum,' he mumbled, 'please recall that a doctor's job involves a certain necessary intimacy.' I smiled and nodded gently. I had already read the entire text and seen everything embarrassing that there might be to see, as, in fact, he might have known had he taken a moment to think about it. But there seemed no point in saying so; his delicacy was kindly meant.

By two months after the beginning of his treatment, Dr Richards was displaying frustration with the case, leading him to explore the domains that Dr Bernstein feared might embarrass me. But he needn't have worried; if anything, I found all the commentaries disappointingly tame.

The patient resists all attempts to unearth the original source of trauma, opposing a consistent attitude of dreamy absent-mindedness to my questions. Her responses are indicative of a deeper resistance than the respect for appearance and manners that has certainly been inculcated into her. No matter how I phrase them, she deflects my questions about sexuality with vague and general remarks. She will not react to any hints and shows no will whatsoever to investigate her deeper self, or, in fact, to be cured of her affliction at all. She will not rise to the bait even if asked whether she does not wish to leave this place and to live outside like other people. She has been here for twenty years now, and any desire to return to the real world has been lost, perhaps replaced by the nameless and unspoken fear of freedom well known in long-term patients and prisoners. She opposes all insistence, even provocation, with a fatalistic sigh.

On we read together, through the months and years of efforts on the part of the doctor to understand the origin of Lydia's problem, and to influence or modify the static condition of the problem itself.

December 4, 1895

I asked Miss Krieger if she remembered the very beginnings of her condition. She replied that she did remember more or less, but that it had been gradual, not sudden. I asked her to describe these gradual beginnings, and she told me that it had begun at the age of fourteen, after the death of her mother. Until that time, she had been schooled by governesses, and had not experienced any difficulties. She recalls that after her mother died, she occasionally felt a strong desire to write down certain words. Encouraged by friends who were involved in spiritualism, she associated these with the desire of her mother to send her messages from beyond. She had no precise memory of exactly what those first words might have been. At that time, the inner pressure to write down words became increasingly strong, but it took a year before it actually began to interfere severely with her attempts to write other texts. At that point it became necessary for her to keep a second paper near her when writing anything, which she used to note down the irrelevant words that pressed into her mind. Over the course of a second year, she gradually lost the ability to write words of her own choice. She did not recall this development as being particularly unpleasant, and had no sense of being mentally ill. She described it as a person who slowly begins to limp while walking, due to some developing defect of the leg. At first it seems like nothing, and then little by little one accepts the situation without making a fuss about it. For many months, she continued to believe that she was receiving messages from her defunct mother, but her sister shed doubt upon this idea. This situation continued until the two sisters reached the ages of twenty-two and twenty-four. At that time, the patient's sister married, and the couple came to the decision, to which the patient did not object, to send her to a clinic in Switzerland specialising in psychiatric treatment of trance and automatic writing. The patient spent four years in Switzerland, returning home only during the summer holidays. Details and records from this clinic have not been provided for use in the present treatment; neither the patient nor her sister consent to speak of it or even to identify it. It is very possible that the treatments she received there provoked a new trauma. I reserve the possibility of discovering more about this at a later stage, if investigation of the original source of trauma does not yield results.

I peeked at Dr Bernstein out of the corner of my eye as we read this passage. After all, it was his clinic and his treatment that were being referred to here in such cavalier terms! He twitched nervously; indeed, I noticed that his forehead was glistening and he was clearly in the grip of a strong emotion. But once again he said nothing about what interested me so particularly.

December 18, 1895

I asked the patient if she understood that other people were able to write down anything that they were able to think in their heads. She replied that she understood this. I asked her if she understood that a person might, at will, take a piece of paper and write a note, for example thanking someone for a gift. We discussed at some length the words 'Thank you for your kind gift' and the awkwardness and difficulty caused by the fact of being unable to make such communications by writing. The patient stated that in her youth she had overcome such difficulties by the expedient of dictation, then by the use of the telegraph, and later occasionally even the telephone. She denied that her disability had ever placed her in a position of being unable to behave normally in social situations, or compelled her to be rude. Indeed, she seemed shocked at the suggestion. I asked if it had not made her uncomfortable to be always dependent on her friends and family. She replied that such was the lot of women in our society, and that perhaps, were they granted a general freedom from the yoke of such forced dependence, the psychological effect induced by this freedom would have had some effect upon her own condition. We then entered into a discussion of social mores which convinced me that she is no fool and has a penetrating understanding of the forces and necessities that govern the order of society. Whilst she may deplore, she does not protest, being of a character more attuned to resignation than to rebellion.

December 31, 1895

Today, I decided to perform a thought experiment with the patient's collaboration. First, she was to watch me writing a short thank-you note, simultaneously concentrating on the movements of my arm and hand, and on the words appearing on the page, which she was to read out as they appeared. I concentrated upon the notion of thanks, feeling that expressions of simple courtesy and polite gratefulness were very natural to her, a condition reinforced by careful upbringing and a sense of duty.

Having ascertained that she was able to perform this action with the utmost normality, I set her to a more difficult task, asking her to imagine someone she knew well, her sister, for example, in the process *of writing a similar note. Now she was to visualise the situation in detail, imagining each gesture, seeing the pen dipping into the ink and tracing the words. She was then to read out the words just as her imagination caused them to be traced one by one upon the imaginary paper. She was to follow all gestures of arm, hand and pen, just as she had done with me, but entirely in her imagination. This exercise was exactly as successful as the previous one. There could be no distinction between the patient's performance and that of a perfectly ordinary person. Finally, I asked her to apply the same concentration to envisioning a picture of herself writing the same now-familiar note. I asked her to envision the scene in detail and to describe to me everything that she saw. She appeared to undertake the exercise willingly enough, and described herself moving towards the writing-table, sitting down, drawing the paper in front of her and taking the pen in her hand. She then stopped her description. I encouraged her to continue. She told me that no sooner was the pen in her hand in her imagination, than the thoughts in her brain began to be taken over by the words which seemingly poured into it from an outside source, and she felt the stirrings of the irresistible compulsion to write them down in an automatic manner, even though there was no actual pen in her hand. As she pronounced the word 'outside', she unconsciously pointed her finger towards heaven. She explained that because she felt slightly distanced from the situation of writing due to its being in her imagination and not real, she felt able to slide in and out of the state of trance at will, exactly as though she were opening and shutting her ears to the flow of words. Letting her imagination show her the picture of herself putting pen to paper immediately activated the flow of words, whereas focusing her eyes upon real objects in the room, in particular her own empty hands, brought her back to reality. I asked if she could envision herself writing and pronounce, rather than write, the words that flowed into her mind. She said that this would be possible and indeed she had been aware of the possibility for many years, but that she avoided engaging in the exercise, from a fear of thereby opening a door to the entrance of the trance-words into other aspects of her life than that associated purely with writing. I explained to her that I thought it possible that if the trance-words could be made to intrude into other aspects of ordinary life, then ordinary life could also be induced to arise in moments of trance, and perhaps mingling them would be a positive catalyst for change. She resisted my suggestion, asserting that she was convinced that trance-words would enter her ordinary life but not the contrary, as the one had always seemed to be within her power and the other not. I very much wished to make the experiment, for I believe that if there is to be any hope of a treatment, some change must be provoked in a situation which has remained static for thirty years, even by somewhat violent means. But the patient refused absolutely, claiming that she has always been aware of the risk of a complete slide into madness, and held it at bay by maintaining a certain mental discipline.*

I recalled as we read this passage that the following one was of particular significance, and kept an eye firmly trained upon the good doctor as he read.

January 7, 1896

Today I decided to make an attempt to break through the patient's resistance by confronting her directly on one sensitive point that I have chosen to avoid completely until this point: the birth of her child. While obviously unconnected with the original trauma, the source of her troubles, I have reached a stage where I believe that any means must be used to break down the wall she opposes to any penetration into her inner mental life. I reflected at length before coming to this decision and choosing a strategy, and finally decided to ask her point-blank what she could remember of the birth itself.

As I had expected, she was sincerely shocked by the question, and refused to discuss it in the most absolute terms. Alternating between attitudes of brutality and gentleness, a system that often produces excellent results, I admitted that her attitude was quite understandable, and amended my question to asking whether she actually possessed specific memories of the event itself, without requiring any description. She replied that she did not, as she had been plied with chloroform by the attending physician, and repeated that in any case she would not speak about this. Reverting to the direct approach, I asked her whether she did not wish to know what her child had become. She replied that she did, but that destiny had decided otherwise. I asked if she was even aware now of the child's age, phrasing the question in a slightly provocative tone, as though to question whether the fact of her own motherhood held any importance for her. She replied quietly that he had just passed his twenty-first birthday, but that it was quite useless my asking her any further information upon the subject, for none had been vouchsafed her and therefore she had none to provide.

I took this moment to explain to the patient that by the very nature of repression, unconnected pieces of repressed knowledge become associated with each other in the unconscious mind, and that by digging forth one such piece of which she had at least some conscious knowledge, I hoped to unearth the other, which was the initial cause of her malady. I said that it might be a painful procedure, *analogous in some ways to the extraction of bad teeth, but was unavoidable if a cure was to be effected. She replied that the project seemed reasonable, but that she had no knowledge on the subject of her child to share with me, repressed or otherwise. I responded that this was certainly untrue, for if nothing else, she must be aware of the identity of the father.*

She would not discuss this subject. I developed a thesis upon the notions of social conceptions of morals and honour, and the necessity of rejecting such a system of values in the context of a psychological analysis. She replied that she disagreed, considering that dignity was more important than health. I objected very strongly to this, claiming that a medical operation deprived no one of dignity, and using the example of a purely physical operation to remove something like a tumour located in an intimate place. Would she say that the patient undergoing such an operation had lost his dignity? Was he not, on the contrary, being helped to regain that dignity which illness had partially removed from him? She replied that the doctor's calling was a noble one, but that the loss of dignity was something which must be felt differently by each individual and that it could be that there were some who would rather die than undergo the operation, and she could not fault them if such were their feelings. As for herself, she would not continue with any discussion on the subject of her past. It was impossible for her to imagine discussing these things with a stranger or with anyone at all apart from God, who alone was and would ever be witness to her memories.

From this time on, it became clear that the doctor lost interest in his patient – if it would not be better said that the patient lost interest in her doctor. The doctor's conclusion after the failure of his efforts was expressed as follows:

This patient is unfortunately handicapped, in view of any possible treatment, by a sexual repression entirely supported by her social and moral conditioning, which prevents any access to her inner world. The prognosis under these conditions is not hopeful. The patient's experience with motherhood has not served to increase her conscious self-awareness, but rather, having been so abruptly and perhaps ill-advisedly interrupted, has sealed her even more tightly from any possibility of normal self-expression.

It was the end of any attempt on the doctor's part to perform anything like an analysis. Lydia's treatments now evolved into regular sessions of rather rudimentary physical and medical experiments, training activities, guided movements, sedatives, even a session of hypnosis performed, as little Polly had told me, by a visiting French doctor who specialised in that area of treatment. All these methods and more were applied in the attempt to modify her writing activity directly, without any further examination into its deeper cause, nor for that matter any success whatsoever. The sessions became increasingly rare – no more than one a month in the last year or two – and the doctor's entries increasingly perfunctory. We were able to read through the later ones far more quickly than the first. The very last consultation marked in the book, as I pointed out to Dr Bernstein, had taken place on the day following Sebastian's visit to Holloway, and followed the previous one by a mere ten days. Clearly the unusual event had caused a spark of interest in the doctor, but he had fallen too far into Lydia's disfavour to be able to obtain anything important from her now, no matter how striking the stimulus.

January 1, 1900

I called the patient in for an unscheduled visit today, after learning that yesterday she received an unexpected visit, her first in the twenty-five years that she has spent within the walls of this institution. Although I was not informed of this visit until after it had occurred, and therefore had no chance to see the visitor with my own eyes, the description of the visitor provided me by the accompanying nurse, as a young man of about twenty-five bearing a strong physical resemblance to the patient, convinces me that this person can have been no other than the child she is known to have borne in 1875, about whom she has had no knowledge or information from the time of his birth. If I had been aware that there was any possibility whatsoever of such a visit, I would have left instructions for the visitor to see me before leaving, for much information on the patient's state of mind might have been had in this way. Furthermore, I was informed by the nurse that at the termination of visiting hours, the young man left carrying a sheaf of papers in his hand which she did not recall him holding upon his arrival, and I conclude from this that the patient wished to demonstrate to her visitor the reason for which she has spent half her life under psychological treatment, and provided him with several pages of her automatic writing. In general the patient is forbidden access to paper and pencil, but it is to be presumed that if she told him of her abnormality, the visitor procured them for her in order to witness it for himself.

I could not possibly have foreseen this event, especially as the patient's sister had made quite clear that she herself had no intention of visiting at any time, and had mentioned no other possible visitors at all. As for the patient herself, she refused to respond to my probing queries, giving only her usual bland remark that she did not wish to speak of these things. In spite of her stubborn silence, however, it was quite clear that she was very much moved by the unexpected troubling of the peaceful course of her life. She appeared unusually disturbed, and her hand trembled as she allowed herself to be placed at the table for her customary writing. For this session, I allowed her to write in complete freedom without any form of interference, for I wished to see if the emotions produced by yesterday's visit would have any tangible effect on her writing. In this, though, I was disappointed, for the sample appears identical in spirit to those that I have obtained from her over the past five years.

'It is a pity that the doctor managed to so completely lose Lydia's confidence,' I observed mournfully when Dr Bernstein had finished reading this final entry. 'If only she had told him all about Sebastian's visit, and he had written it all down here, we would finally know what it was that Sebastian learnt that day.'

'No, I do not think that we would,' replied the doctor. 'You see, even if we may safely assume that Sebastian learnt for sure on that day that Lydia Krieger was his true mother, you who are seeking the cause of his death must seek deeper than this. What matters here, what Sebastian must have discovered, is the hidden secret, the one that Lydia herself could not express in any other way than through her writing. And this Dr Richards was not capable of understanding that even after studying Lydia for so long.'

'So you really believe there is such a secret,' I said, and in spite of my doubts, I prayed that he was right, for otherwise my investigation was at a dead end. 'You really believe that her writings actually mean something.'

'Of course,' he said. 'Even that fool of a doctor realised that, with all his talk of repression and trauma, but he did not understand *where* to look for it! Lydia is not mad – her writings are not the products of an insane mind. There is no nonsense in automatic writing; it is like another language, invented by the writer to simultaneously hide things and yet speak them. You know this – you have read my book, and you saw Hélène Smith at work! That imbecile doctor never looked in the right place for what he sought. He should have been examining the writings themselves, not her thoughts and actions while producing them. *These* writings!' And he slapped his hand down upon the thick sheaf of papers that we had not yet begun to look over together. Lydia's own productions.

By now the evening was already well advanced, and the doctor, seeming unusually agitated, ran his fingers through his short grey beard several times, took up the pile and put it down again, rose nervously, strode about the room, and finally suggested that we have supper before starting work upon them, as it was likely to take a considerable amount of time. I was more than willing, so we left them on the desk and went into the small dining room, to partake of a light meal consisting of mushroom soup, followed by a cheese omelette, all prepared by the admirable manservant. During this repast, we avoided the subject of Lydia Krieger by common consent; instead, the doctor entertained me with a sketch of the development in methods of psychoanalytical treatment since the ideas of Sigmund Freud had begun to be adopted all over Europe. It was fascinating, but I could not bring myself to believe in it all. My own dreams being often quite nonsensical, I found it difficult to convince myself that they represented anything more than a great collection of visions, observations, hopes and fears, all ephemerally tied together in a random hodgepodge of kaleidoscopic images. Freud's theory of the interpretation of dreams, published in a book which had appeared but last November and which the doctor could not resist fetching and thrusting under my nose in the middle of the omelette, struck me as most inapplicable to myself. Goodness me, if some of the nocturnal messes in my head really represent desires, whatever am I to think?

After dinner, we returned to the study, the manservant brought coffee and was given his well-deserved dismissal for the night, and the doctor, who did not seem to know weariness, eagerly snatched up the first page of Lydia's writings, radiating a tense and silent expectation which I observed with mixed feelings. Fascination at seeing the man at work, flushed with the conviction of his beliefs and irrepressible hope that complete understanding was finally at hand were tempered by doubts and fears. Quelling all expression of these conflicting emotions, I joined the doctor at his desk and we began to read.

The writings in the file began from the time of Dr

Richards' arrival at Holloway; her earlier work must have been archived somewhere along with the medical observations of the preceding psychiatrists. Dr Richards had taken up his post at Holloway in September of 1895, and the first sample dated from that month. There were at least a hundred of them collected through the years, the last one dating from the day following Sebastian's visit to Holloway. They were piled in inverse order, with the latest one on top, and quite naturally, just as I had, Dr Bernstein began to read them as they appeared, from the last one to the first. In a style reminiscent of Sebastian's suicide note, Lydia's large, flowing handwriting dominated the space on the paper, covering an entire page with just a few sentences.

In the final sample, from the day after she saw Sebastian, Lydia had written:

The Father, the Son and the Holy Ghost. The Father, the Son and the Holy Ghost, redeem our sins and our transgressions. The transgressors of long ago give birth to the sinners of today, the transgressions of long ago give birth to the sins of today. The Son will redeem the transgressors, the Son will redeem the sinners. On the Day of Judgement the truth will emerge and the sinner and the Son will be reunited. Unnatural no longer, sinful but natural, pure love, sin redeemed, abomination redeemed by lesser sin and lesser sin redeemed by the Son, all truth will emerge and shine on the Day of Judgement.

On December 20th, she had written:

Child of the Father, look to the Father, look to Heaven for salvation, there is no evil but abomination, there is no abomination but denial of the Father, there is no denial but the unnatural. Unnatural is the ripping of the veil, when the child of God rips the veil of God then is Evil done, all natural sin is not evil for man does not decide, all comes from God, yet Evil exists, but then how could he do this? How could he do this?

Back we travelled through the months and years of Lydia's incarceration, and though I could make out nothing more than a prophetic ring to her outpourings, I could not but be impressed by the power of the inner, unconscious force that had compelled her to continue producing them so unchangingly for so long, resisting all efforts and all pressures.

April 18, 1899:

Birth from sin, birth from abomination, pain of the abomination, joy of the birth, right and wrong, good and evil, mingled in a birth of joy and abomination. On the day of judgement will emerge the truth. Suffer the little children to come unto me. Children of God born of sin and abomination, children of the Father, it is his will though the fabric of the universe was rent as the veil of the Temple was rent, from top to bottom.

January 7, 1899:

The meaning is hidden it is God's will, it is God's will for all is God's will, but the unnatural is Evil and how can Evil be God's will? All that exists is God's will and Abomination exists and so it is God's will but it is God's will that abomination should exist, then how could he do this? The world is full of sinners, sin is natural and God will forgive. There is no sin, there is no right and wrong for all can be forgiven. Sin is not evil, evil is not sin, all comes from God and the heavens above and the earth below glow with beauty and God's gift to us is this beauty and so he cannot be angry with our sin. But abomination is not sin: is abomination evil sent by the Father to his Child? Should not the Father love his Child and does he not, for we are surrounded by beauty. But then how?

July 15, 1898:

God sees below with the eye that sees all and the acts of his children are all visible to Him. All are equal, the acts of the children of God, all are equal in the eye of God because they are sent by Him. Sin is not evil in the eye of God because sin is natural and natural is the harmony of the universe sent by God to his child. What looks like sin may be Good and what looks like Good may be evil for we have not the eye of God. The truth will emerge on the day of Judgement and then and only then

may we know that all is right in the eye of God
for all comes from Him. The truth cannot now be
known because the sinners are aware of their sin
and not aware that in Heaven sin is no sin and all
sin is forgiven and right and wrong are not. Only
Abomination is not forgiven.

Dr Bernstein read each passage slowly several times, sometimes murmuring the words aloud, and examining them with a detailed thoughtfulness that seemed to take forever. By the time we reached the bottom of the pile, I was possessed by alternating feelings of dreadful boredom and acute despair, with little room left for optimism. I felt more than ever as though I could easily write such stuff myself, given a quiet hour and a sufficient heap of paper, and were Dr Bernstein to seek a deeper meaning within it, he should be wasting his time. It was with a sense of relief that I saw that we had reached the very last page, which was really the earliest one, from the day of Lydia's first encounter with Dr Richards.

September 11, 1895:
Madness in the red sky, mad red storm in the
swirling sky, madness of abomination and evil
in the mad spinning red clouds, clouds of our
confusion and our sin. The eye of the storm is the
eye of God, centre of all things, seer of all things,
the mad confusion of the wild red churning sky,
tumult of sin we are blind here below. All that

comes from God is given by the Father to his child, but the mad storms hide the Truth from us, that will emerge only on the day of Judgement.

I pushed the papers aside, and leant back for a moment's repose, but Dr Bernstein was far from finished. He looked through them all again, concentrating with fevered intensity, driven by a will to understand which could only be explained by a more powerful passion than the purely intellectual desire to know. He bent his eyes close to the pages, he read and re-read the same sentences again and again as though they did not occur in a hundred other places, he murmured words aloud – he even wrote things down. Some of the passages he read out to me, and doing my best to encourage him, I sought inside myself some observations of my own, so as to stimulate at least some kind of a discussion.

Dr Bernstein had only one clear intention in his mind: the search for a coherent, deeper meaning. He rambled on, speaking half to me and half to himself, suddenly holding forth in spurts as an idea struck him, then falling silent. He spoke of historical references, he tried anagrams of certain words and phrases, he tried substituting certain words in a systematic way for others. He took thick books from his shelves and read out to me strange and astonishing accounts of long-past cases of automatic writing and prophetic seizures. I watched him at work, sometimes joyfully influenced by his certainty, at others feeling merely dull and increasingly tired.

Sometimes I tried to gently oppose a little simple logic to some of his wilder ideas. Hours passed; it was the middle of the night now, and I was quite exhausted, but I dared not interrupt the flow of his inspired research. Once, I pronounced the name of Dr Richards, only to find myself violently interrupted, in a tone whose indignation seemed proportional to the doctor's own feelings of frustration.

'Do not mention his name to me any more! The doctor was a fool – he utterly missed the point! He did not *read* what she wrote! He asked stupid questions, he probed vulgarly and stupidly – but he did not *read*!'

He strode about the room, clutching a paper in his hands, his eyes like glowing coals, reading out snatches, repeating them aloud and under his breath, changing the order of the words as Lydia herself frequently did.

'The truth will emerge on the day of Judgement!'

'All truth will emerge and shine on the day of Judgement!'

'The Truth, that will emerge only on the day of Judgement!'

Periodically he relit the lamp and also one or two candles, whose flicker added an element of peculiar mystery to the whole venture. Midnight passed, one o'clock, two o'clock, then three. Eventually the doctor fell silent, staring moodily at the papers and books piled and scattered over his desk, and I found myself drifting into sleep. To prevent myself from nodding, I rose and wandered over to the window, pushed aside the heavy curtain and leant my forehead against the icy cold glass, peering out into the night, across which light snowflakes were spreading their soft curtain of fairy dust through the glowing light of . . .

Dozens of lanterns, held in a hundred utterly immobile white-gloved hands!

A voiceless Inquisition? A silent troop of ghosts come to fetch me to the land of mystery into whose secrets I was trying so hard to penetrate?

I jumped backwards, pale with shock and disbelief, closed my eyes for a moment, then carefully advanced and peered once again out of the foggy pane. No, it was not a vision. The unearthly sight was there as before, soundless under the falling snow, hoods, hats and wigs grouped in a frozen pantomime.

'Dr Bernstein!' I managed to articulate. 'What on earth is happening in the street?'

He came to the window, glanced out and smiled. Now I saw that under shocks of yellow and red woolly hair were the most grotesque masks I had ever seen; mad weird distorted faces, some with giant noses, others with fixed wide open mouths or gigantic teeth spilling over the painted lips. All were poised in positions of activity as though caught in a moment of petrified time: some held drumsticks aloft, others fifes and flutes, but of music, motion or sound there was none. On the pavements on either side, a few people in ordinary dress, also clutching lanterns and bundled to the nose in woollen wraps and scarves, stood watching them. The utter silence and immobility of so many people, the monstrous masks illuminated from below by the shafts of eerie light emanating from the many lanterns, came together to form a terrifying and magical vision.

'Why, tonight is Fasnacht – the beginning of the carnival,' said the doctor. 'I had forgotten. Take your coat, and let us go down into the street.'

I wrapped myself up solidly against the cold, imbued with a strong feeling of unreality. The doctor led me down the stairs and outside. Standing with other spectators on the pavement, we now became not just observers, but a very part of the uncanny scene. I stood still, staring about me, having no idea what to expect. I had never seen or heard of any carnival consisting of freakish masks standing utterly still in the pitch darkness in the deepest part of the night.

Then the cathedral bells began to toll, and struck four.

As though on an instantaneous cue, the masked figures came alive together and began to play music, strange, ancient, gay little marching tunes, while stepping forward at a regular pace. We followed them up the street and around the corner; at each crossroads we saw other groups in ever more outlandish and wild dress, proceeding up and down the cobbled streets, some, like ours, with fife and drum, others with blaring of trumpets, still others with violins. The masks were enormous, twice the size of a normal head; a group of twenty shocking Mozart-faces with mouths open in fixed toothy grins, bird-heads with bodies covered in multi-coloured feathers, stiff golden faced Napoleons in clown suits with giant buttons and tri-cornered hats, and the weirdest figures of all, with grins stretching from one eye to the other, mops of blue or yellow hair, noses reaching up to their foreheads, teeth nearly down to their chins, and a general air of insane glee.

I asked no questions, for the whole appearance of the carnival was itself a conundrum of cosmic dimensions, and I did not want to spoil my profound intuition that it was all somehow closely connected with the object of our research by the acquisition of any dry factual information. I continued to look about me, trying to absorb impressions, to observe only, and not to think. A shower of tiny paper confetti rained over our heads and shoulders, drenching us both in bits of red, whilst crazy laughter echoed behind and around us.

'What do I want? What am I seeking here?' I asked myself, as we wandered on through the icy cold amongst the crazy masks and falling snowflakes. 'Something here is trying to speak to me. There is a message for me somewhere in all this. There is something that I have to realise, or to do.' And all at once, I knew what it was; something very simple, something that I should have sought already, inside myself, but that I had not sought because I was inhibited. In such surroundings, inhibition seemed to belong to another world, a world of normality that was shut into the tight walls of the warm, protected houses, shut away from the wild streets that were the scene of wild freedom from normal behaviour.

I myself was free now, and the fact that had slipped through my mind without leaving a trace strong enough to rise to the surface came easily to my tongue. A group of harlequins in white satin with giant black buttons, playing a wistful and yearning tune on tiny flutes, passed us and disappeared around a corner, and I found myself with the doctor, momentarily isolated in a little island of quiet. I could hear another group approaching from a distance.

'I think Lydia conceived her child whilst she was living in Basel,' I said, wondering incongruously why I had not seen this before, why I had allowed my mind to assume that it was while under her sister's uncaring protection that Lydia had been led astray. 'She first came to Holloway in April 1875, and the child was already born. In early January, she said that he had just passed his birthday.'

The doctor did not reply, and I went on.

'The child was Sebastian. I am certain of it, and so was Dr Richards. Lydia's sister had been married for five years already when Lydia's baby was born, and she must have feared, or perhaps even known for certain, that she herself would never bear a child, so she adopted her sister's. He must have been a beautiful baby.'

Still no response.

'Lydia must have been already expecting her child when she left Basel in June for her holiday that summer.'

Nothing. But in my new, wild state, I did not feel inclined to let the matter rest. If Lydia had fallen pregnant while living in the doctor's house, then chances were that he knew or could guess who the father was. A vague vision of Herr Ratner floated through my mind. He had been a younger man then, and a friend of the doctor's.

'Did you know anything about it?' I asked relentlessly.

'I must have been blind,' he replied finally, with an effort. 'No, I did not know. I am a doctor, yet I did not see.'

'It was very early days, of course,' I said.

'But I should have guessed! I should never have let her go! I should have told the family that she was unwell and could not travel. I should have kept her near me forever!' He was not looking at me, but into space, into the darkness, or perhaps simply into the past.

'If you think back now,' I said, 'can you guess who fathered the child? I have been wondering – is it not possible that while he was in Zürich Sebastian guessed the identity of his true father as well as that of his mother?'

'No. That is impossible,' he replied, and now his eyes came to rest on mine with defiant certainty.

'How can you be sure? The father could have been there, at the concert, and at the party that evening. He could have noticed Sebastian's resemblance to Lydia just as you did. He could have realised the truth, and told Sebastian about it.'

'You are not guessing right,' said the doctor into the feathery snowflakes that floated between our faces. 'Yes, the father of Lydia's child was there that evening, and he saw what you say that he saw. But he was not certain of what it meant. He could not be certain, for he had never known of the existence of a child, and could not quite convince himself of something so momentous, not when it might be nothing but an error, and when the young man himself seemed so perfectly convinced of having his own quite different parents. His mind was in a turmoil, and in the end he did not utter a single word on the subject of paternity.'

'But now he knows?' I asked carefully, feeling my way into the intricacies of this discourse.

'Yes. Now he knows for certain. Sebastian was his child.'

'He told you?' Like the flame of the candles in the lanterns, the truth flickered in my mind.

'Have you not understood?' he responded, and turning, he moved out of the square, away from the direction from which the newest group of masked revellers was now nearly upon us.

'It was you?'

'It was I.'

Without quite knowing this, somehow I must have known it, for I was not really surprised. The doctor began to speak, rebelliously, quickly, loudly into the darkness, flinging the weight of his guilt at me as though I should be able to catch it and take some of its burden from him.

'Yes, it was I. Yes, I betrayed the marriage bond and I betrayed the doctor's oath: a double infidelity. That is exactly what I did. In moral terms, there could hardly be a more heinous sin. But it was a sin of love such as is beyond expression and beyond morality. Her family took her away from me. They spirited her away and I could not find her although I searched for months and years. My letters remained unanswered, her guardian died, I could not find her trace! I lost her suddenly and without knowing why. And the passion I felt for her has continued petrified, unchanged and undiminished in my heart since that day. It was that passion that made me speak, the evening I saw Sebastian. I did not speak of my love, of course – I did not say much, yet I said too much, for what I told him drove him to the search for Lydia that ended with his death! I did not understand then that it was the death of my own son. That knowledge only came to me from you.' He had been shouting almost convulsively, but the last words came out in a whisper, and I understood with a kind of shock why he had remained silent, pressing his lips together, about precisely the points on which I most wanted his opinion, those concerning Lydia's motherhood, and what it was that he had come to understand over the course of the evening that had driven him into such a frenzy.

I did not know what to say to one who has discovered the existence of his child only after that child is dead. But the doctor clutched my arm, and I realised that there was someone even more important to him than the son whom, after all, he had never known.

'Thanks to you, though, I have found the treasure that I lost. Our son died because he found her, but I shall not die, because I am stronger than my enemies, who are *her* enemies. Twenty-five years too late, I will find her and free her, and, if she will, I will marry her.'

'What enemies? Who are they?' I said in confusion, staring in surprise at his transformed face.

'Her words tell the story of what happened,' he said. 'Now I see it plainly! It is all in the words themselves, just as I told you! Do you not remember what she wrote on the day after Sebastian came? *The Father, the Son and the Holy Ghost*?'

'Yes, I remember that,' I said.

'The Son! Do you not see?'

'Yes.' I paused. 'The Son', indeed; she had written that word directly after Sebastian's visit. But her writings were all full of religious phrases. What was the doctor so certain that he saw? Was there really a meaning to it all?

'I described that,' he exclaimed, and now he was walking quickly, almost running towards his home, dragging me along by the sleeve. 'In my book, I told how the words of a secret shared with Lydia would emerge in an unrecognisable context the next time she wrote!'

'Yes, I remember,' I said, hurrying and slipping on the slushy cobbles. 'But was that really the first time that she ever used the word "Son"?'

'You tell me. Do you remember any other instances through all the pages that we read?'

I tried to recall another, but failed.

'There are none!' he exclaimed in confirmation. 'Look again, and you will see that she never used the word "Son" before that day. It is the words, the words we must consider! We must find out which are the true ones. Come, hurry, hurry! We have work to do!'

CHAPTER TWENTY

The dawn was leaking palely through the window by the time we had finished the task upon which Dr Bernstein insisted: counting the number of times each word and phrase appeared in the hundred samples of Lydia's writing, and setting them down one by one in order of frequency. But all desire to sleep had fled. So clear, so unexpected and so diabolical were the conclusions necessarily provoked by the list finally tabulated and thrust under my nose by the trembling hand of the overexcited doctor, that I pushed it away with a spontaneous cry.

'Impossible!'

Yet I took it back and stared at it, horrified and mesmerised. It read:

Unnatural
Love
Birth
Abomination
Father
Child
How could he do this?
Evil
Sin
On the day of judgement the truth will emerge.

CHAPTER TWENTY-ONE

'But what does it mean?' I said at length, sitting down weakly. I felt the perspiration break out on my brow and my legs weaken beneath me. I did not understand, but the feeling of the presence of evil was so strong and so convincing that there was no need to know the identities of transgressor and victim to sense the truth at the heart of the list of words.

'Such words never came from Lydia herself,' the doctor was saying. 'These are undoubtedly words and fragments of sentences that were told to her in secret.'

'You think so? They were words that she heard? You do not think these reflect some experience of her own?'

'Incest? For that is what is being described here; there is no doubt about it. No, this was not Lydia's own story. The birth of a child was involved in the story echoed here, and when Lydia came to me she was innocent and without sexual experience. That is certain.'

'But she did have a child before writing these,' I said, blushing in the darkness at the awkwardness of thus referring to the doctor's transgression.

'Yes, but during the years she spent with me, she wrote the same things, repeatedly. I recognise them all. If only I had understood it then!'

Tears of emotion stood in his eyes. Between the shame of the horror revealed by Lydia's words and that associated with the doctor's illicit relationship with his patient, the conversation was fraught with awkwardness and difficulty, but as I have often noted, there is nothing better in such circumstances than to keep as calm as possible, to breathe deeply, and to say what needs to be said. I did so, and felt the wrestling match taking place in my mind between doubt and certainty diminish in intensity and disappear, the former yielding definitively to the latter. In my heart, I knew now that contrarily to what I had believed, the list of words in front of me did carry a meaningful message. My eyes were opened, and I could see it clearly, even if I did not fully understand. I had been blind, stupid and stubborn, that was all. A rather large all.

'Think,' the doctor was continuing. 'Lydia's father died when she was four. The psychological scars left by incest are strong even when repressed, but she was entirely free of them. Lydia did not suffer an incestuous relationship, but all the signs point to her having heard talk about someone who did.'

'But why would the talk she overheard not simply have brought the fact to her consciousness?'

'Either because she was sworn to secrecy, or because she did not understand what she heard. I suspect the latter reason is the right one, for surely she would have chosen to reveal the secret in confidence to a doctor, rather than suffer endless years of incarceration in order to keep it. And then, she did not have the knowledge to understand such things; she had been brought up very protected. I think it far more probable that she did not understand the words she heard, yet she sensed that something was deeply wrong. Remember that I knew Lydia very well. I am certain that she had no conscious memory of these words at any time, and no awareness that the words emerging in her writing had either the meaning or the origin that I see in them now.'

'But how could she have heard and remembered words unconsciously but not consciously?'

'It would be possible if, for instance, she was extremely young. A very small child, unable to understand anything other than the seriousness of what she was hearing. Small children often have strong memories of which they are unaware, which can emerge unexpectedly many years later.'

'But she only began the spontaneous writing at

fourteen,' I said. 'Why would she have carried the words inside her silently for all those years, and then suddenly begun expressing them?'

'Do you remember what event triggered the beginning of her writing?'

'It started when her mother died. Is that it?'

'Yes. It seems rather as if, at that point, Lydia lost the only person with whom she could share her trouble, even if she was conscious of neither the trouble nor of sharing it.'

'So you believe the words were spoken by her mother?'

'I believe so. I think it is possible that the mother held the child close to her for comfort in her pain, and expressed her feelings of horror and despair, perhaps simply murmuring broken words, feeling secure in the knowledge that the child was much too small to understand. The words survived in the unconscious memory of the child, together with the child's sense that the words corresponded to a dreadful secret that must be repressed at all costs. As long as the mother lived, the unconscious mind of the child would not have to bear the full burden of the secret. But after her death, the weight of bearing it alone must have produced a strong urge to discover another way to both keep the secret and share it, all without any of this ever reaching the conscious mind.'

'But what *was* the secret? Lydia's mother was a married woman, and Lydia and Tanis were adopted children. What experience of incest could she have been alluding to? Do you think it was something from the mother's own childhood?'

'It might have been that,' he said. 'But time and changes in life tend to soothe and relieve ancient pains if they are consciously expressed, as Lydia's mother appeared to have been doing. It seems to me more likely that she was describing something which was causing her great pain at the time she spoke of it.'

I thought over all that I had heard of Joseph Krieger and his family, and remembered the words of Prosper Sainton.

'There was a daughter who died . . .'

'A daughter? Whose daughter?'

'A daughter of Joseph Krieger and his wife, who died before Lydia and Tanis were adopted.'

'Died? How did she die?'

'I don't know. I don't even know exactly when she died. But wait – there is something.' I tried to recall exactly what I had read in the old diaries of the French violin professor. I cast my mind back . . . I could see myself sitting in Professor Wessely's office . . . I could almost see the notebook in my hands. 'Her name was Xanthe. A friend of the Kriegers wrote about her in the winter of 1848. He had met Mrs Krieger somewhere, and she had mentioned this girl who had died, who had been sent to the country for her health, and who had died there. And then later I found out that Mrs Krieger refused to be buried at Highgate, where her husband had purchased a family tomb. She asked to

338

be buried with her daughter instead.'

'In the country. The girl was sent to the country for her health,' the doctor repeated attentively. 'It is a phrase which so often indicates pregnancy. Does it not?'

'Well,' I said. 'I suppose it sometimes does. But I was imagining that Xanthe was a child. Prosper Sainton wrote . . . well, I guess he wrote nothing indicating whether she had died recently, or many years before they spoke, or how old she was when she died. But Mrs Krieger cried, and said she wished she had children to take care of, and Sainton wrote that she was too old to have any more.'

'So, she may have been in her late forties or even fifty or more at that time. This would indicate that the girl who died may not have been so very little.'

'Yes.'

'She might have been fourteen, fifteen, sixteen, and still been referred to as a child who died.'

I digested this idea.

'So you think that Xanthe Krieger might have died in childbirth?'

'Childbirth itself, perhaps, or else the consequences of giving birth at too young an age. Twice. Is it not possible?'

'Oh, my God. Yes, it is. And the little girls—'

'The little adopted girls—'

'From the countryside—'

'Were Xanthe's children. Fathered by her father.'

'Oh, my God.'

'Years of incest. Under the mother's eyes.'

'Perhaps she did not understand at first.'

'But she must have realised when the first child came. She must have tried desperately to put a stop to it.'

'Maybe she believed that she had.'

'But then, a second child came.'

'When Xanthe died, the mother must have seen her husband as a murderer.'

'Yet at the same time, the horror of it all would finally cease . . .'

'And she would have insisted on adopting the babies.'

'And he could not refuse.'

'And then he died himself, and the whole thing was buried in a grave of total silence.'

'How did he die?'

Until this point, my remarks and the doctor's had fused together as if produced by a single mind. But this last question of his started me.

'I don't know. Why do you ask?'

'Don't you see?'

'No! What do you mean? Can you believe—'

'Yes. He would not have been able to stop. The *pulsion* of paedophilia and incest is a disease.'

'You think – he turned his attention to Lydia?'

'I think it is certain that he did, or began to.'

'Horrible, for his wife!'

'And then he suddenly died.'

'He suddenly died,' I repeated as his meaning sank in. 'I see what you mean. She couldn't bear it any more.'

'What would you have done?'

'I think – I think I would have taken the children and gone off somewhere, far away.'

'But she was not the same type of woman as you are. She was probably a dependent, submissive character, who had been made more so by the domination of such a husband. It would be easier for such a person to take control within her domestic sphere than to flee. And then, she was motivated by something more than merely saving the remaining children. There may have been a desire for revenge.'

'Revenge?'

'For the sacrifice of the daughter by the father.'

We spoke simultaneously.

'Agamemnon.'

'Clytemnestra.'

CHAPTER TWENTY-TWO

Is the capacity to murder a character trait? Or are we all potential murderers within?

No – some faced with the choice of life or death will choose life at all costs, others will choose death. Not all can kill.

Like the capacity to go on a stage and enthrall a crowd, the capacity for murder belongs to only some.

Can it be inherited?

I must ask Carl.

Joseph Krieger died suddenly. Perhaps he was ill. Perhaps he committed suicide. But perhaps not.

He created havoc beyond compare in the heart of his family; he had caused horror and the death of his daughter, and suddenly he stood before a fresh temptation, another child, a little one, a fragile one, the very fruit of his horrendous sin, whose life was in his hand to crush and destroy.

If he were capable of feeling remorse or shame, such a temptation itself could be a motive for suicide. It could, indeed. Yet nothing in the picture of him that had put itself together in my mind from all the pieces I had collected from different sources indicated any sign of a capacity for those emotions.

If Mrs Krieger had put an end to her husband's life, and abandoned him in death to his lonely tomb, I could not but feel that it was a deserved judgement for his crimes. But that was not the only question. I also had to ask myself whether Tanis Cavendish had played a similar role in the death of her adopted son.

It was not the first time that this thought had assailed me. I had thought of her once before, on perceiving as a possible motive the necessity of preventing it being brought to Lord Warburton's attention that she had a mad sister interned at Holloway. But my theory had collapsed completely when I discovered that the person who paid the monthly fees for Lydia's hospitalisation was no other than Lord Warburton himself. The whole cycle of realisation, suspicion and disproval had occurred within a space of less than two hours; I had simply felt like a fool, and not spent any further time on the hypothesis.

Now, unable to find rest even in the rhythmic rumble

and chug of the sleeping-car that was carrying me back across France, I could think of nothing else. My theory was alive again, for even if Lord Warburton knew about Lydia, it was clearly out of the question that he could ever be allowed to learn of the events the doctor and I had just realised – the dreadful truth of the parentage of his prospective wife.

Sebastian had understood it all; of that I felt certain. For nearly half a century, Lydia had kept her secret from everyone, including herself. But he had understood what even she had not. He had been imbued with the family atmosphere; he had carried inside himself all the family inheritance of ideas and attitudes; he had been familiar with all the expressions, the tensions, the nuances of mood and the subjects of reserve of the woman who had raised him. Seeing her reactions over the years to the natural questions of a child concerning births, parents, his own origins and hers, he must have gleaned, if not exactly an inkling of the truth, at least something of the sensitive atmosphere surrounding all the words that we had discovered in Lydia's writings. Perhaps for him, conditioned by living with her as he was, those same words had leapt off the page as they could not have done for anyone else.

Anyone else but Tanis. A mere baby at the time of the facts, she could not even have conserved the unconscious memories that her sister had retained. Yet she had grown up with Lydia, and with Mrs Krieger, the woman who loved her but was not really her mother, who had lost her only child to the evil of the man that she called her husband, and who never planted any other than yellow flowers on his grave; *yellow – Xanthe*, the meaning of the dead child's name in Greek – as an eternal reminder of his crime. Mrs Krieger, who had brought up the children of that crime by herself, who had visited the grave with them each year, and who had let them see where her grief truly lay – and where it did not. Impossible to guess what Tanis actually, consciously knew. But whatever it was, something of it had been silently transmitted to the boy she had brought up.

He must have had a thousand bits of fragmented knowledge that could have come together as he spoke with Lydia and read what she wrote, forming a sudden, coherent and terrible whole. Now, finally, the mystery of his possessing his grandfather's famed genius found its natural, if dreadful, explanation. Now he could finally comprehend the meaning of the reticence and seeming indifference of the father who had raised him, but who was, in fact, not his true father; a reticence that extended even beyond death to his very legacy. It must have all made sense to Sebastian on that day.

Why had Lydia been sent to Holloway, to be shut away there forever? She was sweet and gentle; she could easily have lived outside. To be sure, she would not have been the only case in our severe times of a woman sent off to a madhouse on account of an illegitimate birth, but these poor creatures do not generally remain there, forgotten and unvisited, for twenty-five years! There are charitable institutions that concentrate upon the rehabilitation of such unfortunate creatures, and insist upon their release, even seeking gainful employment for them once it is deemed that they have been brought back to a sense of moral responsibility. No, this was something else; this was to be an eternity of enforced silence. Tanis knew something, and she knew that Lydia knew something. But Tanis could control herself and Lydia could not; her writings poured forth unrestrainedly, filled with revelations that, if visible to Tanis, could become visible to anyone sufficiently probing; anyone, for example, who might fall in love with Lydia, and learn to understand her.

No wonder Tanis Cavendish wanted her sister to disappear forever. Between the trances and the pregnancy, she probably had no difficulty convincing her husband that Lydia was quite mad and better shut away. The rigid mentality of society under our dear Queen, in regard to all moral questions, would have made this normal, even seemly, twenty-five years ago, although now we may hope that times are slowly beginning to change widespread attitudes towards such things. But Sebastian must have had understood all this.

And what had happened then?

He had seen Lydia, he had read what she wrote, he had understood more than he had ever expected to, and he had returned home on that fateful 31st of December. So much was certain. No one knew the exact time of his arrival at the flat. Mrs Cavendish claimed that she had already left for the centennial ball; Lord Warburton had confirmed her punctual appearance there, and neither the police nor anyone else had seen any reason to doubt her words. Finding the house empty, then, Sebastian had decided to swallow poison, write to Claire and retire to bed to die alone?

Ludicrous! Absurd! Quite out of the question.

And if Mrs Cavendish had not yet left the house when Sebastian had arrived straight from the train from Virginia Water? If she had been waiting for him, in order to go to the ball together as planned? Then there would have been a violent confrontation; of this I could not have the slightest doubt, for the two would have been at terrible cross-purposes. Sebastian would have bitterly reproached her for her lies and her deeds, and demanded, perhaps even with threats of immediate revelation, the instant release of the woman he had just discovered to be his true mother.

Mrs Cavendish would have remained cool. A long explanation, perhaps, filled with gentle reminders of the necessity of keeping up appearances. A promise to discuss everything in detail, to make amends. And a nice cup of coffee laced with arsenic for an emotionally ravaged boy who would fling himself on his bed in rage and confusion, unable to face the idea of going to a party.

Sebastian was no longer her son; he had never been her son, in truth, but now that both mother and son were aware of that fact all pretence was abolished. Mrs

Cavendish would have put on her hat and left the house, promising no doubt to talk everything over in the morning, but actually concerned above all to prevent Sebastian's knowledge from ever reaching Lord Warburton's ears. And what would Sebastian have done, alone at home, before the poison drove him into the agony of death?

He would have written to his beloved; to the one person in the world with whom he shared everything. He would have told her that he felt sullied within by the knowledge of his terrifying heritage of lies, cruelty, incest and murder. He feared, perhaps, that such an inheritance lay at the root of the wild forces he sometimes felt within himself – 'the devil within', as Rose had described it. He would have cried out in despair that such a person could not marry, could not engender yet more children to carry on the curse! Rose had told me that he was extroverted and generous. He would never have meant Claire to suffer for the rest of her life without understanding why he was doing what he was doing, and what it all meant.

> *Darling Claire,*
>
> *How can I say this to you? I've found out something about myself – I can't go on with it any more. I'm sorry. I'm so sorry. Cursed inheritance – it's too dangerous to take such risks. Please try to understand.*

This was not a suicide note, but a confession; an outpouring into another, gentle heart of the horror and disgust that now filled his own; an attempt to purify himself by releasing her from the loathsome attachment.

What would have happened had he lived? She loved him; she would not have accepted release, and perhaps he would have married her anyway. And then what? Perhaps her quiet normality would have tamed him with time, or perhaps he would have ended a slave to his own inherited power, dominating and subjugating the world around him as his grandfather had, carrying on the family burden of evil, and transmitting it onwards to yet another generation.

In any case, that curse was ended now.

CHAPTER TWENTY-THREE

'So this is also London,' said Carl, looking about him. 'Another London. Nothing like the one I have visited with such pleasure so many times. Here is another world altogether.'

We were sitting together in a hansom cab, looking for all the world like a couple, and the ambiguity of the situation worked strangely upon my nerves. Hansom cabs will accommodate two, but only in conditions of the most suggestive intimacy, especially when it is very cold, so that even withdrawn deeply under the sheltering hood and with the wooden slats firmly closed over one's legs, the warmth of the other occupant forms an irresistible attraction. Carl Correns had been paying the most assiduous attention to me since our first meeting, and the fascinating information he had given to me about the true nature of inheritance, combined with his ardent interest in my detective activities, had led me little by little during the course of a dozen or more pleasant rambles, teas and visits to confide all the difficulties of the case to him, and to discuss, analyse and theorise over them with him at length and in great detail. It was a pleasant change to have so supportive an ear and an arm, without the reserve and even the hint of unspoken disapproval that discouraged me from discussing these things with my husband, however much I knew that I could count on him one hundred per cent in the final pinch. The fact was that although Arthur would always stand by me and had done so significantly more than once, I knew that in his heart of hearts he was repelled by the signs of human cruelty and tragedy that invariably emerged during my investigations, and that he preferred insofar as possible to know nothing about them, taking refuge instead in an abstract world of numbers and equations.

But Carl was a professor of biology, not of mathematics, and the vagaries of the life force had an entirely different meaning for him. Just as the use of a mathematical law to explain the unfathomable mystery of inheritance had fascinated him so that he devoted years of his life to resurrecting and re-proving Mendel's forgotten theory, so was he fascinated by the application of logic and reasoning to the mystery of human behaviour. Each time I saw him, he asked for news of my progress and my discoveries. His youthful face behind the generous blonde beard was radiant with fervour and excitement as we talked, and although we both kept up a polite pretence that this enthusiasm was purely inspired by the stimulation of detection, it eventually became clear to me that it was my presence quite as much as my work which caused his blue eyes to shine with such intensity.

Absorbed by all that I was discovering, I had pushed this observation to the back of my mind for weeks, cheerfully taking things at their face value, letting myself be warmed by Carl's ardent interest, so different from Arthur's quietness, and avoiding asking myself questions. But now something had changed, for I needed more than a willing ear; suddenly, now, I found myself in a situation where I was in need of actual masculine assistance in the plan I had outlined in my mind. A plan whose goal was to surprise the revelation of a truth that I feared might otherwise be entirely and definitively unprovable.

There was Arthur, and there was Carl, and I stood between the alternatives thus presented and contemplated them both. Arthur, stable and loving and dependable, but hating it all; Carl, an unknown quantity, exciting and eager and more than willing.

I chose to ask Carl, not knowing exactly what I was choosing when I did so, not knowing exactly where it was all going to lead. I asked him to help me discover the truth, and within myself I was aware that I was referring not only to the truth about Sebastian's death, but to another truth as well, which desperately called for clarification from within the depths of ambiguity: a truth about the state of my own heart.

Thus it was that I sat in a hansom cab for the first time in my life with a man who was not my husband, pressed together in a proximity so intimate, in spite of the heavy winter coats and wraps, that I found myself quivering with a mixture of nameless feelings, not least of which was acute embarrassment. Carl reminded me of a medieval knight; they chose and served their fair ladies with strong arms and absolute devotion, quite regardless of whether or not the ladies in question were married. It did not appear to have been a question of any importance in the Middle Ages, and, as far as Carl's mentality was concerned, it did not seem to have increased in relevance since then. But I myself felt torn a hundred ways, between inclination, desire, interest, and the beginnings of what might be a new love, compared to a deeply established and tender one.

There was no use troubling myself over this knotty problem at present. I put my feelings to one side, and decided to concentrate on my plan, or, to be precise, on its first part, which consisted of a visit to Mrs Munn. Thus we drove through the miserable streets of Bermondsey, a splendid steak-and-ale pie of the most generous dimensions reposing in a large box that Carl held upon his knee. The hour was close to supper time, darkness was falling rapidly, and the poverty and misery of the streets through which we drove seemed diminished by the crystal purity of the frosty air, and by the near-absence of ragged passers-by, all but the most courageous of whom had been driven indoors by the cold.

Mrs Munn and her husband lived in the little curve of Jacob Street, separated from the Thames by the Bermondsey Wall, but quite near enough to suffer from all of the unhealthy vapours emitted by that river, what with the filth from sewage and the waste from the leather tanning factories in the area. Having been there on his bag-returning mission, Ephraim had been able to describe the place to me very precisely. I was rather ashamed of that incident, it must be admitted, and determined, perhaps a tad immorally, to make no mention of it whatsoever (let alone provide a much-deserved apology), but I really preferred Mrs Munn to continue perceiving me as a benevolent and beneficial presence in her life. We came out of the cab, Carl paid the driver, and I led him – sniffing the air and looking about him in all directions as though to absorb to the full this new experience of an unknown London – straight to Mrs Munn's door, and knocked firmly.

She opened it, as I had been certain that she would. A woman like Mrs Munn, with an invalid husband at home, is not likely to be gadding about at suppertime on a dark winter evening. She was amazed to see me, and even more so Carl who, with his Teutonic elegance and beautiful hat, looked quite incredibly out of place in the dirty street, but she invited us quickly inside, probably as much in order to close the door as soon as possible and keep out the freezing draught as from some rusty and little-used sense of hospitality. Still, though, she did not seem displeased to see me, and it was almost with a smile that she called out to her husband that good gracious me, here was company, here was a visit, she didn't know why.

The fire burned low and the single room was chilly; only a few lumps of coal remained in the scuttle next to the hearth. The only other light was given by a lamp that stood on the table, shedding a small pool of clarity outside which everything else was in semi-darkness. Half the room was taken up by a tumbled bed in which sat a dishevelled man, peering at us with a mixture of curiosity and hopelessness. The only other pieces of furniture were a few wooden chairs, one of them of a particularly solid construction, with a square backrest and a footrest also.

The sight of the pie, which I took from Carl and presented to Mrs Munn at once, caused a stir of excitement. Placing it in a large dish, she set it to heat in front of the fire while I rather awkwardly introduced Carl, not knowing at all exactly how to describe him or explain what he was doing there with me. But Mrs Munn did not seem unhappy to have a strong, able man in the house, and immediately requested the guest to help her install her husband in his special chair. This job, which must have been quite an effort for Mrs Munn to accomplish by herself, was the work of a moment between the two of them together, her expertise aided by Carl's strength, and Mr Munn was settled at the table with pillows behind him, a rug around him, and the light upon him. There were more introductions and explanations, and the poor man's manifest pleasure in the unexpected change to his evening routine warmed the atmosphere.

'Pleased to meet you,' he said, shaking hands all around. 'Betty told me all about the talk she had with you,' he added to me.

'I told Bill everything you said,' she put in, setting some plates and glasses upon the table.

'It seems you want to know more about why the young man took poison, over there where Betty works,' went on Bill, speaking alternately with his wife in the kind of seamless duo which denotes endless years of closeness, and smiling up at her as she dished up the four rather tired potatoes and the drop of gravy that she had been preparing for their dinner. She now provided each of us with one of these, handed a knife to her husband, and set the pie in front of him to be cut.

'I have much more to tell you,' I said. 'I have come on purpose to tell you everything I know, and to ask for your help with a plan that I have, if you agree with me.' And as we ate, I embarked on a complete explanation of the entire story, including all my hypotheses and suppositions, and the details of the tangled and cruel past of the Krieger family.

'That poor young girl, with such a father, and dying like that,' said Mrs Munn, when I had completed the tale. Her tone held all the simplicity of a background which recognises suffering as an intrinsic part of human life, and does not turn its face away and utter sanctimonious nothings from behind its fan when it encounters it face-to-face, as so many of the ladies I frequent would feel the need to do; not necessarily from a feeling of superiority, although it often appears that way, but from a sense of shame at the very existence of certain phenomena that will not allow them to look them directly in the eye.

'Yes, the first and worst victim of the whole story was the eldest daughter, Xanthe,' I said. 'I do not see how there can be any forgiveness in this world or the next for that kind of sin. I should like to discover her grave, and visit it someday.'

'One girl died, one girl locked away, and now a young man dead,' said Mr Munn thoughtfully. 'It doesn't stop, does it?'

'No,' I said. 'It doesn't stop. It cannot be a question of chance. It is all related; it must be.'

'He was a handsome, lively lad, Master Cavendish,' said Mrs Munn. 'Not one to poison himself. That's what I thought.'

'But you think he didn't poison himself at all, don't you?' said Mr Munn, looking at me astutely. 'You think he was poisoned because he found all this out and someone didn't want it known. Isn't that it?'

'I don't know what I actually believe,' I quickly qualified my thoughts. 'Let me say that I suspect it. I think that it might be the case, and I am determined to find out. If Sebastian's death was murder, I do not want it to remain hidden and secret forever as the other crimes did.'

'But who would have done such a terrible thing?' said Mrs Munn, looking as though she knew exactly what I was about to say.

'The obvious candidate is Mrs Cavendish,' I replied firmly. 'She is the one who had most to lose from the facts becoming known to her future husband or to society in general, and she may very well have still been in the house when Sebastian returned home. If he left Holloway after the end of visiting hours there, he might have arrived home as early as six or seven o'clock. She says that she had already left for Lord Warburton's, and she certainly did arrive there, but their paths still could have crossed, perhaps even for just a few minutes.'

'But her own son!' cried Mrs Munn.

'He wasn't really, you know. Her sister was really his mother, and on that day they both knew it.'

'Still, though, it was she who raised him.'

'But you told me yourself that their relations with each other were pleasant but never close.'

'It's not so much whether it's likely she did it,' intervened Mr Munn, 'but whether it's more likely that she did it or that he did it. Someone did it. The poison was given. That's certain. And there doesn't seem to have been any reason for him to do it himself. You were surprised enough about it when it happened, Betty, weren't you? So if it's between him and her, then why not her?'

'Or someone else, a third person who came to the flat that evening,' I said. 'The fact is, we don't know, and it will be virtually impossible to prove anything at all unless we take some kind of radical step.'

The firelight flickered over the miserable room with its bed in the corner in which the invalid spent his days, the shaky wardrobe and the table that now looked rather dismal with the plates containing nothing but a few crumbs. But the two faces before me, wrinkled, gnarled with the thousand strains and stresses of a life of illness, hard work and poverty, were nevertheless alight with human feeling and the effort of imagination. Carl hovered over us all without speaking, but listening intently to every word.

'Go on,' said Mr Munn, 'tell us what you think happened. And what you want to do.'

'This is my idea,' I said. 'I believe that Sebastian returned from Holloway very angry, found that his mother was still in the flat, and confronted her with what he had discovered. He couldn't blame her for the dreadfulness of all that had happened in the past, of course, nor even for having kept it all from him. But I think he could not bear to discover that his real mother had been imprisoned in a madhouse all these years; especially not now that he had seen her, and knew that she was really not mad at all. Holloway is a luxurious and superior place, but it is nevertheless an asylum for insane people, and for the patients it is not much more than a prison. Sebastian must have seen in Lydia what anyone would see: a beautiful, gentle, sweet person, a victim who might arouse anyone's chivalrous sympathy – and on top of that he found a mother, and realised that twenty-five years of life had been stolen from her, and twenty-five years of a true mother's love from him. Anyone can understand that he must have been livid.'

'Yes, that's right. He'd have been furious,' agreed Mrs Munn. 'When he was angry, he was very angry; hot anger, not cold anger like his mum. Anything could have happened if she was still at home when he came back. But you'll never get her to admit it even if she was. She had already left, so she says and so she'll always say. There was no one to see or hear.'

'Well,' I said quietly, 'but perhaps there was someone. Perhaps *you* were there, Mrs Munn. Perhaps you came back for something you had forgotten, and when you reached the door, you heard the two of them quarrelling, and listened for a while, not wishing to walk into the middle of a scene.'

She looked at me with surprise and a shadow of fear reflected in her face. 'I wasn't, though,' she said tensely. 'Worse luck.'

'Hush!' said Mr Munn. 'The lady's saying something – I think I see.'

'This idea is a little risky,' I said, 'but here it is, for what it's worth. I think that if you were to write a letter to Mrs Cavendish saying that you knew she was at home when her son returned, that you came back the way I said, and you heard what they were saying, she could not but react. What I am suggesting is that you do something to provoke her to react very quickly and strongly. If we once see exactly how she responds to such a letter, then, I think, we will know the truth.'

'Why, she'd just deny it all,' said Mrs Munn.

'We mustn't leave her that possibility, if what I suspect

is indeed true. I suggest that you write her a letter in which you say you heard her and her son together and you know that she lied to the police. Tell her that you stayed and listened, and that you heard all they said – but don't say what you heard. Tell her that she must bring you some money by tomorrow night. Give her the letter tomorrow evening when you leave the house, and suggest that she meet you at midnight in some lonely place near here.'

'That's too dangerous. I won't have that,' said Mr Munn. 'That's blackmail; it's illegal for one thing, and too risky for another. Why, someone who kills once may kill again! What could poor Betty do in some lonely place if Mrs Cavendish decides to murder her?'

'I will be the one to go and meet Mrs Cavendish, not Mrs Munn,' I said. 'I do not think my plan is really dangerous for either of you. If she is innocent, she will know that Mrs Munn must be lying, and she will say so. Think of it from her point of view. If she never saw Sebastian that night, then she will know that there was nothing to hear, and so she will know that Mrs Munn cannot really know any secrets.'

'But the law is severe against blackmailers,' objected Mr Munn. 'If she really didn't do it, we might find ourselves hauled up before the magistrate.'

'Not to mention out of a job,' added Mrs Munn. 'Couldn't you write her the letter yourself?'

'It wouldn't be believable coming from me,' I said. 'I am a complete stranger. I was acquainted with neither

Sebastian nor her on the day he died; why would I have been coming to their door? She would take me for a professional blackmailer horning in on a case from the newspapers, call my bluff and deny everything. I might succeed in blackmailing her by threatening to tell her secrets to Lord Warburton, but I would never have any chance of obtaining a confession. Your situation is different. For you to have returned there for something you forgot after having left the house would be quite believable, and you would be a witness to a lie concerning the actual murder.'

'But I didn't even go to the flat on that day,' she objected. 'It was a Sunday.'

'Oh, so it was. Oh dear. Couldn't you say you left something there on the Saturday, and had to come back for it?'

'When I was going back in to work the very next morning?' she said.

'You could say it was to take some food, knowing that she and her son would both be out,' intervened her husband suddenly. 'The Lord knows it wouldn't have been a crime, and we need it sorely. If it wasn't for the food that used to come from the house there, we'd have starved years ago. Since the boy died it's been terrible. Betty's whole salary practically goes just for the rent, and she's got to have a coat and skirt to go to work in.'

'So you think I should do it?' said Mrs Munn, turning to her husband. 'If she's done nothing, I'll lose my job without a reference. I'd have had to find another place

362

anyway, when she gets married, but that's to be in another six months, and she'd have given me a good letter at least.'

'I will help you find another job,' I said, 'and write you a reference myself. Would you not be happier working in a larger family? I have a lot of friends. I am sure we can find something. If you were going to be looking for a job anyway, then we might as well start right now, don't you think?'

She looked at me gratefully, and I determined to help her find work by every means in my power, not hesitating to resort to a lie or two if necessary. With all my London acquaintances, I felt reasonably certain of success.

'There's still the problem of her taking Betty to the police over the blackmail,' said Mr Munn.

'She would never do that,' said Mrs Munn. 'She wouldn't want the publicity. She'd call my bluff and put a stop to it.'

'I believe you are right,' I said. 'Still, if that happens, I am quite prepared to declare that I wrote your letter myself, and that you had nothing to do with it. I do have a certain talent for forgery,' I added modestly, 'and I am not too much afraid of the police; I have several friends at Scotland Yard. What matters to me above all is what she says when she confronts me, expecting to see you. You must lend me a bonnet, so that from a distance she is not aware of the change. I am counting on being able to tell from her reaction whether she is innocent or not. As I said, if she is, she will not hesitate to deny everything,

363

knowing that she is in the right, and that it is quite impossible that either you or I can know anything really significant. If she said that to my face, in that situation, I would believe her. But on the other hand, if she really did see Sebastian that night, then we must write your letter so that she thinks that you know it for a fact, and denial would be useless. The letter will be a little delicate to write, but we can do it together. Shall we begin now?'

I had prepared writing-paper and pen in my handbag, just in case, but she had some at home already, of an inferior but very authentic-looking quality. In an inversion of the natural procedure, we used mine to write a rough draft, with much discussion over each line and phrase, arriving finally at the following result.

Dear Mrs Cavendish,

I am very much in need of money and I am sure you would be willing to help me out if you could. The fact is that last December 31st I came to your flat in the early evening. I thought that you and Master Cavendish would have left for the ball already and that I would be able to get something to eat from your larder. I know this is a dishonest thing to do but it was the night when everyone was celebrating the New Century and we did not even have a sausage with our mash. Master Cavendish was in the habit of giving me a gift of money each New Year, and flowers also, but he had been away and had not had the chance. Anything I took, I would have put back.

Anyway, I was in front of your door and before I could go in I heard that you and he were both inside the flat and you were talking very clearly. I could overhear most of what you were saying, especially the young master who spoke up very loud when he was vexed. I know you told police that you had already gone away from the flat when he came home.

I am telling you this because I am in need of money very badly for my husband who is an invalid and can't work. I don't wish to cause any trouble to anyone. It's best to keep this secret but I am in very much of a hurry, so I am asking you to come to meet me at the south tower of Tower Bridge tonight at midnight and bring one hundred pounds and a written reference for me to look for another job.

Yours sincerely,
Elizabeth Munn

I then dictated it to Mrs Munn for her to write it out on her own paper in her own writing. I preferred this method to her copying it, for I wished to preserve any particularities of spelling that might help the letter appear absolutely convincing.

'You must give her this, or leave it at the house tomorrow after work,' I told her again. 'Just in case of any worry at all, I think it would be best if you spent the evening somewhere else, with some neighbours or friends near here.'

'If I really thought he had taken the poison himself, I wouldn't be doing this,' said Mrs Munn, folding the letter and sealing it. 'I think it would be an evil thing to do. But after all you've told us, I don't believe that any more: I believe you. Your explanation makes more sense. It's as simple as that. I think she must have given him the poison, and I don't want to work for a murderess any more. I shall go there tomorrow, but it will feel strange. I wish I didn't have to.'

'Let us not judge before we know the facts,' I said. 'When you leave work tomorrow, Carl and I will be waiting for you outside, and we will accompany you home to make sure you arrive here safely, and help bring you and Mr Munn to some other place. The rest is up to us.'

'You will come and see us, and tell us what happened?'

'Of course we will, as soon as we possibly can. Leave everything to me. Thank you for trusting me,' I added, shaking Mr Munn's hand and that of his wife, and taking the rusty bonnet she offered for my disguise.

'I do trust you,' said Mrs Munn. 'It's important to right a wrong.'

CHAPTER TWENTY-FOUR

Through the darkness of the winter night we walked, and I was not leaning on Carl's arm so heavily uniquely for the pleasure; the pavement was slushy and slippery and both of us stumbled from time to time in the darkness. I felt the tension in his arm and his body, but also the strength, and it lent me confidence and courage.

Well before the appointed time, we were walking up the road leading onto the splendid Tower Bridge, one of the most recent engineering marvels of London. There was no discontinuity between road and bridge, and we found ourselves looking down over the thick wrought metal parapet into the chill black water below, under the stars in the black sky above, whose expanse was crossed above our heads by the giant double band of the bridge's upper level.

When we came to the south tower, Carl entered and concealed himself by the stairs inside. I, feeling strangely unlike myself in Mrs Munn's bonnet but filled with a sense of alertness and clarity that dominated my fear, stood under the archway in the icy chill of the winter air, holding my dim little lantern, and waited. As the minutes ticked past, I reflected on what I was doing, and recalled all the evidence that had led me to my final conclusions. A hundred times I asked myself if Mrs Cavendish might be perfectly innocent of the death of the young man that she had raised as her own child. In a sense, it was easier, and more desirable, to believe so. If she did not come, or came but denied everything in the letter, I knew that my conviction of her guilt would seriously waver.

If, on the other hand, my guesses corresponded to reality, she would not, she simply could not doubt that what the letter claimed was the plain truth. She would not deny it because she *could* not deny it. It would not just be a question of her word against Mrs Munn's in front of police, or even in the public arena. If Mrs Munn also knew the secrets of the past, she could reveal them, and they could be verified, and Mrs Munn's word would be proven to be the true one. In that case, she would have to react swiftly: in fact now.

There was nothing to do but wait in the cold and silence. Invisible within the tower, Carl was an abstract; I knew he was there, yet could not feel his presence in my heart. I knew that his ardent feelings were straining towards me like fingers of desire, but they could not touch me in that bitter darkness. No one passed at all, the bridge was silent and empty, and I stood shivering in the night air, waiting, waiting, waiting. I heard Big Ben strike a quarter to midnight, and then, after what seemed like an hour, midnight. The chimes were so deep and strong that they shivered the air, and other chimes answered them from bell-towers near and far across all London. So loud and manifold were the echoes that I nearly missed the smaller, nearer sound of quiet footsteps approaching, yes, undoubtedly approaching along the bridge.

It was Mrs Cavendish. Tall and handsome, her upright bearing did not betray for a moment the slightest hint of disquiet, nor for that matter of anger, fear, or any other visible emotion. She had seen my bonnet glimmering in the ray of light from my lantern before I had noticed her, and was walking directly towards me with all the quiet authority of her character. I braced myself.

'Oh!'

Even one so versed in self-mastery as Mrs Cavendish could not restrain the surprise and confusion of seeing an unfamiliar face in the place of the well-known one she had expected. The surprise had the effect I had wanted; she hesitated for a moment, her own strategy, whatever it might have been, momentarily thrown off course. Perhaps she thought, for a moment, that I was there by chance and had nothing to do with the letter she had received. I held up my lantern, she looked at me straight in the face, and her expression changed.

'I recognise you,' she said. 'I saw you backstage after Sebastian's memorial concert, with the musicians. And you were at the little boy's scholarship ceremony as well. Have you been following me? Who are you? What are you doing here?'

'I am here,' I said with as much quiet poise as I could muster, but wishing that she was not quite so much taller, 'because of the letter you received from Mrs Munn.'

'What do you know about that letter?' she said sharply.

'Everything,' I replied calmly, 'since Mrs Munn wrote it together with me. I know that you lied to the police when you said that you had already left for Lord Warburton's party when Sebastian came home on the night that he died. You were still there when he arrived, and he confronted you with everything that he had discovered that day: the identity of his true mother, where she was, who put her there and why, and the truth about your own mother who was also your sister; all the infamy from the past and all the lies from the present. I know everything about it.'

She stared straight at me, her eyes unnaturally large. I stared back, knowing that if she now said that my words were false, *must* be false, for she had never seen Sebastian on that day, I would believe her. I looked straight back at her, giving her the chance.

But instead, she said, 'What business is it of yours?'

'Murder is everyone's business,' I replied.

'Murder!' she snarled with sudden antipathy. 'What do you know about murder? That was no murder – it was suicide!'

I hesitated, startled, then pulled myself together. She had been there, or at least she was not denying it. She had been there with him.

'It was not suicide – you killed him!' I burst out. 'When the police know that you lied about not being there that night, they will realise that as well as I do. And when they know the reasons for your quarrel – when Lord Warburton knows – when everyone knows – do you think they will not ask you who made the cup of coffee that Sebastian drank that night?'

My words were hard, yet once again they contained a challenge as well as an accusation. If she had not done it, let her defend herself! Her eyes were locked into mine and mine gave her another chance, and yet another. *Say it – say that he took the poison after you left, and I will believe you. Tell me that he was destroyed by your words, by your acts, but not by your hand; that you destroyed him unintentionally; that your heart is filled with regret and despair, and I will believe you.*

But it did not happen that way. Instead, my words freed Tanis Cavendish of the need to lie, for her lie had served only the single purpose of silence, and mine indicated that that precious silence was to be necessarily and inexorably shattered and lost for ever.

'It was suicide,' she said passionately. 'I tell you that

it was, for Sebastian could very well have chosen to live! I gave him the chance, and he took it and flung it to the winds. I told him what I would do to satisfy his miserable romantic fantasies about his victimised long-lost mother. I would have had her taken from Holloway if the place shocked the poor dear boy so badly. I would have set her up in some house somewhere where she would have been well looked after. What did I care, as long as she was kept where she couldn't cause any more harm than she had already done! That selfish vixen, set from a child on destroying everything I was trying to make of my life, hell-bent on pouring out on paper things that should be hidden from every decent God-fearing person until they are erased from human memory! She wouldn't stop! She wouldn't stop! She wouldn't let them cure her – she liked playing with them, toying, showing her sick little secret, and enjoying the feeling that they still couldn't guess what it was. "Oh, what have I written?" she would say in that mincing voice of hers. Was she really too stupid to read her own words, or was she just pretending? I knew what she was writing – knew it from the very beginning. Who did she think she was fooling with all those half-hidden mixed-up fathers and children and abominations? I saw my father reaching for her, touching her; I may have been only two years old but the memory is burnt into my brain, how he reached for her and pulled her onto him and she screamed and struggled and my mother screamed and struggled and my father railed and hit and swore and then my mother put the white powder into his drink and he died. I saw it all but I could grow up and never speak a word, not to Lydia or to anyone else, not a single word in my entire life, because that was the only way to make it go away and everything become right! Oh, how I hated Lydia, that blabbermouth Lydia, trying to wreck everything with her sick little games, filth leaking from her pen while she went singing about the house like an angel. Oh, how I hated music, and talent – that damned, hateful talent that would not shut its devil's mouth but must yowl, yowl my secret out in music from generation to generation!'

She paused for breath, and I reached out my hand and grasped hers, for however horrible her deed, the pain in her words and the horror she described was beyond any that my life had given me to witness before. But she ripped it out of mine with enmity.

'For the first few years of my marriage, I thought I had won,' she said, her jaw strained with the effort of controlling her white-hot anger sufficiently to speak. 'The doctor couldn't cure Lydia, but he was such a dunce that he seemed to have no idea what she was ranting about either, and anyway, she was far away. After four years I hadn't conceived a child and the doctors said I never would, and I knew it was for the best: no more fruit from the rotten tree. Then I thought I'd mended the cracks once and for all and locked away the wrong and could go on living in the sunshine of the right and the good. It was the only time I ever knew happiness. All could have been well, all was well. And then what had to happen? Lydia, the angel Lydia, comes home from Basel pregnant – like a common whore, a mad whore, back she comes to London and it all starts again; the shame and the disgust and the loathsomeness and the filth of it all, everything I thought I had finally escaped. Thank God that Edward agreed with me about what was best to be done with her. He didn't understand, of course; he saw nothing of her perverse tricks, he simply thought she was loose and quite mad, and I was glad that he did, and grateful to him because even though I was her sister, he never thought that I might also be mad. I rue the day that we decided to adopt her brat. I wish he had died at birth, and his mother with him! I should have known that nothing good could come of our stock. I fell for those blue eyes, that open little face of his that looked so good and so healthy, and I let myself be dragged into giving our family's rotten blood one more chance – more fool me! Nature had stopped the trail of horror with me. Why did I force it back into existence again? Idiot that I was – twenty-five years of seeing him grow up into *her* – hearing him play the violin like *him* – the devil's fingerprints all over the boy no matter what I tried to do!

'Through all the years I kept on working to make everything right and decent and true and straight. I never gave up, not for one moment. My dear husband died and I was going to marry again – a man of honour, a man of standing, a man who knew about my sister's state and accepted the situation with tolerance and generosity and compassion. Everything was under control – and then it all has to start again, like a nightmare, with that idiot Sebastian digging up these things that he was never meant to know, and trying to smash all my life to pieces again! I always knew he would do it sooner or later, child of sin and monstrosity that he was, even if I was the only person to know it! He came back that night and demanded that his dear sweet mother come to live with us; yes, with us, nothing less than that, knowing that everything was certain to come out in the end if that madwoman started her writing tricks in public, with all the craze there is these days about automatic writing and trances and such rubbish. I spit on it all, and all the filth it pretends to hide, and the people rushing to peek at the filth just as they rush to the public dissections of the naked corpses in the hospitals, pretending it's all for the sake of scientific knowledge – the prurient liars!

'I tried to reason with him, but he wouldn't listen to reason; oh no, he wouldn't listen to reason. He was going to talk to Lord Warburton. Everything was my fault; his mother was sweet Rapunzel and I was the evil witch that had locked her away in a tower and stolen her child away from her! Little could he understand that evil is what I've struggled to fight off all my life while it's dogged my steps and stood whispering over my shoulder that I'd never be rid of it as long as a drop of my father's blood still ran on the face of the earth! Fool, idiot, imbecile that he was, thinking that I'd let him run about with his heart on his sleeve, gasping out my secrets to the world at large! Oh, I was right to do what I did;

it's no use your standing there with your narrow little morals thinking how good you are and how bad I am. I know that he'd have let everything out. Why, when I came home that night, I found the letter he'd written to that silly fool of a Claire, telling her he couldn't marry her because he'd discovered incest in his background – *incest*. Yes, he wrote down the very word that I spent fifty years refusing ever to hear, think or speak; and madness, too; madness and incest, all so terrible, and dear, darling Claire would understand, of course, that he couldn't marry her now because he felt tainted, the poor dear, and one never knew what dreadful things one might pass on to one's children and he couldn't take the risk. Such a load of rubbish it all was, nothing to do with whether they should go on with their silly marriage or not – all he really wanted was to *tell, tell, tell* – all anyone has ever wanted to do is *tell, tell, tell* – no one knows how to keep a secret, not even the ones you'd think would most want it kept! Filth! Corruption and filth and defilement! Pursuing me everywhere while I struggle to keep clean from it, and you come here accusing me with your nasty little mind and probably thinking how wonderful and how righteous you are, when you understand nothing about it, nothing at all! How dare you!'

Her hands shot out with a speed that took me by surprise and with tremendous strength she dragged me towards the wrought iron railing at the edge of the bridge. I felt her trying to lift me and push me over. The barrier was very thick and hard to grasp and not particularly high. I clung to the railings with my arms, not finding a purchase for my fingers, afraid to let go of it to struggle with her, and screamed for Carl. If he had not been there, I could have screamed myself blue without being heard by a soul on that miserable night, but, thank God, he had been watching everything from the shadows of the tower, and the moment I cried out, he leapt forward and, seizing me by the arm, pulled me strongly towards him and enfolded me tightly. He might have done better to snatch at Mrs Cavendish instead of me, for seeing that her victim was lost to her grasp, she disappeared with such suddenness that at first we could not comprehend where she had gone. But a moment later, when the beating of our own hearts slowed down, we heard the faint echo of her feet running upwards – yes, undoubtedly, she was running up the tower stairs and the sound of her steps echoed down to us through the night.

Carl let go of me and ran into the tower. I followed him, up one flight, two, three, four – the staircase went round and round in a crazy square that seemed never to end, and my chest was burning; Carl was ahead of me, but Mrs Cavendish was already at the top and out onto the narrow walkway, high above the water, under the stars. We heard a jagged scream, muffled by the thick stone walls, and I did not hear, but imagined I heard, the faint sound of a splash far below. Panic overwhelmed me. I clamped my hands over my ears, but I heard my own voice from within myself, crying in uncontrollable horror. Carl came down and wrapped me in his arms, then opened his coat and wrapped it around me as well, pressing me to his chest. We remained so for long minutes. Then I looked up at him.

Carl had offered me love and admiration and his help and protection at this critical moment. But life makes our decisions for us, for his arms as he held me did not have the power to still the shuddering inside me, and I longed for something else: for another pair – for someone who alone could help me reason away the dreadfulness of it all, by showing me that every other alternative to what had just happened would have been worse. Carl was at my side, but I knew now that he meant nothing to me. I looked up at him and saw the face of a kind stranger.

'I need Arthur,' I heard myself say.

His blue eyes were filled with understanding and resignation.

'Of course,' he said. 'Come. I think we must first go to the police. There are things that must be done.' He laid my head against his chest and patted Mrs Munn's bonnet gently. 'Do not worry. I will not leave your side until you are safe at home in Cambridge where you belong.'

HISTORICAL FACTS AND PERSONAGES

The fame of geneticist Gregor Mendel (1822–1884), reclusive monk and scientific genius, is so widespread today that it is difficult to imagine that the importance of his work was entirely unrecognised, and the work itself ignored and forgotten for several years after his death.

Like Darwin and other scientists, Mendel compared the effects of cross and self-fertilisation on plants whose characteristics were simple and easily identified and compared. But the difference is that Mendel was able to explain his observations via the theory of alleles and the theory of probability. His seminal paper dates from 1865; Darwin certainly knew nothing of it, since he made no mention of it in *The Effects of Cross and Self-Fertilisation in the Vegetable Kingdom*, published in 1876, in which he gives detailed results of very similar experiments to Mendel's, without, however, deducing the theoretical model explaining them.

Carl Franz Joseph Erich Correns (1864–1933) learnt of Mendel's work through a botanist friend of his parents who had been acquainted with them. The ideas contained there fascinated him enough to set him to try to reproduce them, as soon as he found himself with a university position that offered him the freedom to organise his own experiments. It took him eight years of work to confirm Mendel's results, and he published his findings in 1900, championing their originator and giving the name of *Mendel's laws* to the probability theory governing heredity. Strangely enough two other scientists, Hugo de Vries and Erich von Tschermak-Seysenegg, published similar rediscoveries of Mendel's work in that very same year (de Vries without citing Mendel's work, causing something of a conflict between him and Carl Correns). It seems that at the turn of the century, the time was finally ripe for Mendel's discoveries to emerge and be generally understood. Coming as it did contemporaneously with Freud's discoveries in psychology, this was the beginning of the application of Mendel's theory to explain the inheritance of human traits, both physical and mental (insofar as many mental traits are also of physical origin), culminating in the work of the Human Genome Project.

As for the story of the medium Hélène Smith, it is entirely historical down to the last syllable of her Martian language. Quite famous at the end of the nineteenth century, when automatic speech and writing were highly fashionable, Mlle Smith's visions gave rise to a number of written analyses. The most important of these was the book *Des Indes à la Planète Mars (From India to the Planet Mars)* by the Swiss professor Theodore Flournoy, which was the main source of information on this subject.

In what concerns the musical aspect of the book, it should be noted that the professors of the Royal Academy who appear there, Prosper Sainton, Alexander MacKenzie, Alessandro Pezze and Hans Wessely, were all real people, as was the young student Wolfe Wolfinsohn, who (although in reality he was about a decade younger than in the story) indeed went on as predicted to become an extraordinary chamber musician, first violin of the legendary Stradivarius quartet. The description of the difficulties facing women cellists at the time is also historically accurate; there was, however, a small number of enterprising young women who did manage to overcome all obstacles to reach the pinnacle of international success. One of the first of these, if not the very first, was May Mukle, a student of Alessandro Pezze. The Wolfe Wolfinsohn String Quartet Prize and the May Mukle Prize for cello students are both still awarded yearly at the Royal Academy of Music.

ALSO BY CATHERINE SHAW

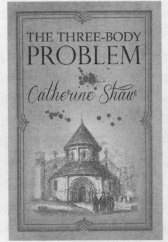